We Are Not Yours

Alex Morton

Arts & Letters Publishing—Madison, WI
ISBN: 978-1-969853-00-5
eBook ISBN: 978-1-969853-01-2
Library of Congress Control Number: 2026930878
Title: *We Are Not Yours*
Author: Alex Morton
Digital distribution | 2026
Paperback | 2026

This is a work of fiction. The characters, names, incidents, places, and dialogue are products of the author's imagination, and are not to be construed as real.

Published in the United States by Arts and Letters Publishing
(A Love-LovePublishing imprint)

DEDICATION

We Are Not Yours was edited, re-edited and edited again by Mina Tsalis Morton. Her ideas helped give form and depth to this book. Providing support and patience beyond measure, was our family: Andrew, Nikki, Ariel, Anise, Max, Jasmine, Martin, Jeremy, and Julia.

Spider Robinson provided validation, encouragement and great help along the way. Seymour Hamilton gave writer-to-writer support and was a willing audience for my morning warmup epistles.

Wendy DeGilio, brave companion of the road and first reader, was always ready to cheer me on.

While I was writing this book, old-style Greek Rembetika and island music played from recordings or reached me directly from bands at village parties while I scribbled notes in the dark and the dancers laughed to see me. In my ear were the ancient and traditional instruments, the baglama, lyra and the oud, the whining violin and the bouzouki. I inhaled them as I wrote.

We Are Not Yours was inspired by the life and spirit of Mikis Theodorakis. I first heard his music back in the days of the junta, when it was illegal in Greece to even hum one of his tunes. Popi Moraites took us into her house, locked the doors and played records that could have had us all jailed. Thank you Popi!

I will always be grateful to Anna Contes Maguire, who taught me how to see art. She could stare at a painting, tilt her head slightly, point at it and say, "you know", and it would always be clear exactly what she meant.

A special word for Erica Hughes and her crew at Arts and Letters for their patience, guidance and belief in this book.

I'd also like to thank Dr. Aladdin Elsecheta for my life, without which this book would not have been possible.

And, of course, Cousin Nick Tsalis.

Before we start, I want to ask you something. Without the struggle, what is there anyway? Some moments of contentment and the occasional cup of coffee?

INTRODUCTION

There is a refrain of an old Greek pop song that my wife's uncle sang as he tended his gardens and olives on the island of Ikaria. He'd sing just that one line, but it was strong and sweet enough that I've always remembered it.

What I didn't know at the time was that a couple of villages above Uncle Anthony's house, far more powerful music was being written that was stirring and giving courage to a nation under a government that was choking its people. My wife and I were young and basking in paradise, while just up the mountain, Mikis Theodorakis was in exile, writing and smuggling out songs to a nation in distress.

The world knew Theodorakis through the music he wrote for the film, Zorba the Greek, but in Greece he was the rebel composer, the radical whose songs gave the people courage and enraged the government to the point that they outlawed his music and shipped him off to exile on the island of Ikaria. We'd only managed to hear his songs because a relative had taken us into her house, and shut the windows, shutters and doors before playing the recordings she kept hidden. So, we knew his music. But no one told us he was our neighbor.

In the following years, we returned to Ikaria many times ... long after the plague of that government came to an end and democracy returned. It doesn't really matter about the politics of it because, ultimately, it wasn't politics that won. It was the spirit of the people, regardless of the banners they flew.

Late, one night, in a tiny café in a seaside village, with my wife whispering translations, I overheard the conversation of some very old men sitting at one of three tables under the stars. They were fishermen and were talking of the days when Theodorakis was exiled to Ikaria and how they helped "the bird" "fly away" to nearby islands to give secret concerts.

That night, with the Milky Way overhead, the air filled with the scent of souvlaki, wild oregano and wine, and the sound of the old men laughing at their own bravery, I knew I was going to write this book. It would be about "the bird." I couldn't write about the man, Theodorakis, because I didn't really know him since he'd only been my unmet neighbor.

But I knew the bird. I knew it in village parties on the island where Dionysius lived, and in the sound of ancient instruments in the warm Greek night. I knew that bird in the intermingling of the lyra, the baglama and the violin that lifted everyone to dance, from tiny children to ninety-year old yayas and even the local priest.

We Are Not Yours is about one particular Greek bird, the Perdiki. It is a type of partridge that runs along the ground, and is hunted by men with rifles. But my Perdiki is different. Sometimes, he can fly.

CHAPTER I

The Old Man and Spiro

As close in time as fifty years ago it was dangerous to openly criticize the government and the conversation in the cafes was carried out in hushed tones and oblique references. Even non the tiny island of Mythos, so far from Athens that it was nearly in Turkey, the government of the military junta stretched its arms and choked off speech so tightly that it could only come out as a gasping sound.

Now, the junta was long gone and the wild young men and crazy wind were fifty years older and it was no longer necessary to speak of anything in whispers, not even in the slow-paced little villages where only words travelled quickly. Now, it was 2009 and Greece was racked by a faltering economy and although you could talk of it aloud, nobody on the island did. In Athens, there were mass demonstrations against the government's inability to heal the broken economy. Tear gas and Molotov cocktails shook the city, but on Mythos, they just wanted to drink coffee and be left alone.

There were six tables in front of the café where I sat, and another half dozen or so inside, which was about all old Katina could handle by herself. Her menu was simple; salad, souvlakia, and potatoes, along with wine, ouzo, beer and Greek coffee.

I'd eaten at Katina's cafe most days since arriving on the island. It was cheap and close to the old family house where I lived in the tiny village where my father was born. Katina had not yet come for my order when one of the old men from the next table leaned over to introduce himself. He held on after we shook hands, looking me over with bulging, dark, watery eyes that were overhung and surrounded by eyebrows that curled white and black and were as wiry and untrimmed as the old olive trees in the neglected terraces above the village.

My instinct was to draw away, to retreat, and I knew he could sense that, but he hung onto my hand so tightly there was no chance of escape.

"Who are you?" he asked. His face moved closer to mine. "Wait, don't bother to answer. I already know. I know all of your history. Glaros Spiro," he said, giving my family name first as is customary in Greece. "Isn't that you?"

When I agreed that he had correctly identified me, he finally released my hand, turned his chair, pushed it up to my table, and reached back for the remains of his drink. The man was very old, but his hands were steady, despite the nearly-exposed veins and brown liver spots. His nose was wrinkled as if it had once been bulbous and had now grown thin with time. He raised his glass, stared into the liquid in its bottom, and then drank without taking his eyes from mine.

"My family is from this island and I want to know about them," I said. "They're all gone, except me. I'm it."

"What do you know about what happened on this island?" he asked.

"Not much."

"And in the years after?"

"Even less."

"But you know something, *neh*?"

"Only a few pieces," I mumbled. "Not enough."

"You need everything, then," the old man said. "For that I need another drink. And so do you." He signalled to Katina to bring more wine and another glass. Before she could turn away, he told her to bring some food as well. Wearily, she turned back into the café to fetch our order.

The wine arrived in a dented, metal carafe, carried on a tray held at waist level by Katina's tired hands. The tray also held a dish of olives, four sticks of souvlaki and a salad that was mostly chunks of tomato and cucumber. Slowly, Katina set each item on the table, then immediately turned and headed back toward the kitchen as quickly as she could hobble, lest we ask for anything else.

The old man watched her shuffle away, with a sad expression on his face. "I remember her when she was young," he said, wistfully. "What a shame."

"Was she very beautiful?"

"No, that's just it. She was always ugly, the poor thing."

He laughed and coughed a few times before continuing. "I should tell you, though, that she's a very good woman. I've known her for many years. She used to drive a taxi." He stared thoughtfully in her direction before continuing.

"*Lipon*, listen, I am going to tell you a story that is true. True enough, anyway." He stared at me sharply. "And though you don't yet know it, you will need to tell me your story. Then we can fit it all together."

He waited for my response, until I finally nodded my head. I wanted to hear his story but hoped to escape having to reveal my own.

"I don't know all of the details," he began, giving me another deep stare before letting his face settle back into a smile. "But the little facts are not what it is about, anyway. You will notice that the politics occasionally turn upside down in my story, but remember this is only a story and politics could never turn upside down in the real world, *neh*?" His laugh turned into a hacking cough and then back into a deep laugh again.

"The rest of the world sits beneath our island. Think of the way a telescope works. When we look at you from the right end of the telescope, our end, you look so huge that we avoid you. And you? You look back through the other end of the telescope and we look tiny to you. Insignificant. Not worth any attention. So, you don't bother with us. And therefor we win. Now eat some of this food. It's good, but even if it were bad, it would still be better for you than the food anywhere else in the world. When I tell you enough, you will agree."

The old man reached for a stick of souvlaki. "This is not bad." He held the plate up to me. "You should try one while it's still hot." When he saw me take a stickful of meat and put it on my plate instead of eating, he shook his head and continued his story.

"The most important people have always come to Mythos," he continued. "And they do great things while they are here. They teach us everything they think we want to know. Back in the time when our enemies were our own countrymen, twelve thousand important people were sent to our island by the government. These were educated Greeks who did not care to goose step along with the government. They were made to live with us in our houses, maybe as punishment.

We had no electricity in the villages, no running water, and after the world war and our own civil war, not much food. But we shared what we had, and taught them to avoid scorpions, snakes, and the enemies among us.

"These exiles were all leftists and they told us of a new world to come, a world in which people would share and work together. They told us of it as we worked with the other villagers to repair the steps on the paths through the mountains, at the communal oven where we baked our bread and at our village parties where we all danced together, children, adults, old folks and even priests.

"One of the most important of the strangers to come to Mythos was the musician they called Perdiki. But he didn't come with the others, and they never did manage to keep him in a cage for long. He was here twice you know. The first time was during the civil war. You've heard of the Greek Civil War? When we finished fighting the Italians and the Germans, when we were exhausted and bleeding, our partisans came down from the mountains where the air had apparently turned them all into communists. The new Greek government objected, or maybe it was the Americans who shook their heads 'no.' They decided that the partisans, who had fought for Greece against the Italians and the Germans, were now the enemy. You figure it out." He stopped, and coughed deeply.

"The hell with that part of it. Have some of this wine to kill the taste of all this political talk. Let me tell you, instead, about Perdiki, the famous composer. He came to Mythos twice. Both times as a prisoner. People now pay American dollars to stay in our hotels, and they tell us this is paradise. But back then, the government sent people here to punish them.

"The first time, Perdiki was exiled to Mythos during the Greek Civil War in 1947. He was a prisoner along with twelve thousand others, each one smarter and more educated than the next. They were the intellectuals, the artists, the doctors, lawyers, professors and writers. They were exiled here to keep their intelligence from interfering with what the government perceived as the natural order of things. So, they were sent to Mythos as punishment. Imagine, this island as punishment? But what the government didn't realize is that ours is the island where wine was first discovered. We understand vintage, grapes, where things grow best, and planting. We did it deliberately, but the government did it entirely by accident. They planted the communists on our island, and they took root. We became communists. Eventually, though, we realized we were already communists, and so nothing much changed in our lives. All political nonsense, now, though," the old man sighed. "Enough politics. Let me tell you the story of the second time Perdiki was fortunate enough to be exiled to paradise."

CHAPTER 2

Perdiki
The Moonless Night

It was a battle to get the boat to the island. The wind of the summer storm walloped the little ship into near disaster each time it drew close to the shore on the North end of Mythos. It was a cyclonic wind, whistling and whirling and corkscrewing its way down through the island's mountain ravines until it was spinning in circles by the time it reached the sea and hit the poor old rusty *Dedalus* on her fat nose. The sudden shifting winds and accompanying freak sea never let on where it would catch the tubby old boat next. The sea crashed over one side of the bow, and then the other, causing the small ship to suddenly veer twenty degrees off course, one way and then the other. The *Dedalus* would eventually get through, but not without a struggle. The prickly sea and wind that had protected the island from the tyrannies of pirates and priests for centuries weren't about to make it easy for a rusty, old ship in the anonymous night.

In the midst of it, the musician sat on a wooden bench that was bolted to the deck a meter back from the rail, trying to write with a hand that was manacled and attached by a chain to the flaking, metal armrest. But it was nearly impossible as the boat rose and dropped from wave to wave, with the wind occasionally whacking the hull on its high beam to send it nearly spinning like a prize fighter after a wicked right.

With his left hand holding the small, black, speckled notebook, his right fought to keep the pen on the paper, while the sea and the weight of the swinging chain did their best to yank it away. Perdiki's feet pushed against the deck to keep his body jammed against the armrest of the bench while he tried to write. There was no one to watch his struggles. He was alone on deck at two in the morning. Up above, on

6

the bridge, someone was at the helm, but the crewman in the wheelhouse was as interested in him as the waves beating against the hull.

Perdiki could feel the force of the island trying to keep the boat away, just as years before he'd felt its opposite holding him to its side, like magnets lined up and locked to each other. But, now, he was at the other pole, and the boat he was travelling on was being pushed away, repelled, that was the word, he thought, looking up from his notebook.

Although the wind and sea were fighting where they met and the old ship was being thrown from side to side, it was a summer storm so that despite the turbulence on the surface, the sky was clear and unaffected. Perdiki could make out a few lights on the island, but they were outshone by the bright stars of a moonless night, and it was hard to keep the eye from being drawn upwards to their magnificence. The constellations shone clearly, each dot projected out at him from within the depth of the unending blackness of the night. One huge swath of stars and light ran like a brushstroke across the sky. The milky way, as they called it in English. Our own galaxy, he thought, our *Galaxia*.

The island below the stars, Mythos, showed little of itself at night other than scatterings of light at various heights indicating the villages. Without a moon, the clusters of lights were the only indication of the steepness of the mountain range that ran the length of the island and divided it into two distinct sides and coasts. The shoreline, itself, could only be distinguished in the night by its solid shape against the chop and roll of the sea and the huge splashes where waves collided with boulders and threw their spume high into the air.

The musician, Perdiki, was trying to form what he saw into a song, and although he felt a rhythm through the movement of the tiny ship against the stormy night, and could almost hear the music, he couldn't *get* it because the snap of the chain against his wrist as each big wave crashed against the boat, kept tearing his thoughts away from the words, which were to him the most abstract part of a song, and the hardest to hold onto until they were on paper. The music, which had already begun to make itself known, would hum within him for hours, almost on its own, and coming from what seemed to be an eternal spring that was always bubbling up something new, almost without effort. The music would stay with him until he had time to write out the score, but the words came from a less accessible place, where he had to reach and reach until at an unexpected moment, just when he'd dropped his guard, something would suddenly arrive. He always recognized when the words hit him properly, and had to get them down on paper, immediately. A second or two of inattention, and they would be gone as quickly as they had come.

Resignedly, when the words wouldn't fight their way up from the feel of the chain pulling on his wrist, he closed the notebook, clipped the pen to it and meticulously folded it back into a waterproof envelope of sheet plastic before stuffing it under his shirt. He would try to finish his work, when and if the boat landed on Mythos. It might not be the same song, then, but it might be also be better, so what did it matter? With the concert on the island of Samos now an impossibility, he'd have lots of time to write music.

A light suddenly flashed on deck, as a door was opened. A man's voice called from the open doorway.

"Perdiki! Hey Perdiki! Mister bird man, are you still alive out there, or have you drowned?" The voice that called out had a hoarseness built up by damp nights onboard old ships and years of smoking. It started up as a low growl in the night, like an engine in the fog, then ran up in volume and pitch through each sentence as if the words were being forced out in a directed stream over the noise of the ship.

"Are you still there?" The voice called again.

"Captain," the musician answered, "I haven't saved your masters in Athens from the chore of having to kill me, if that's what you mean. If they want my blood, then it will have to stain their hands. I won't settle for less."

"You may not need to," the captain called back, "I'm supposed to deliver you to Xenos. Remember him?"

Having said too much, the captain grumbled and slammed the big iron door, and with it closed off a conversation that was his only way of showing concern for the famous man manacled to the deck like an animal. What could he do? The musician, the famous "bird of Greece," was being exiled again to Mythos and the captain's only role was to deliver him into the sadistic hands of that son-of-a-bitch, Xenos, and according to orders, that meant chained to the deck. Had it not been for the police, who were now sitting in the warm, dry main salon, drinking coffee and smoking cigarettes, he would have given Perdiki free run of the ship. But under the current government, he was no more free than the man chained to his deck.

Behind the door, the Captain's huge, Newfoundland dog, Argos, pushed against his leg, a signal that he wanted to go out on deck. "*Exo*, out," said the Captain, pushing the heavy iron door open against the wind. "Keep Perdiki company. Bastards. I wouldn't even chain you out there Argos, and you smell bad. Go, keep Perdiki company. They can't arrest *you* for talking to him."

He held the door open while the hundred-fifty-pound dog stepped carefully over the high lip of the door, gauging the roll of the deck and adjusting his body as he went, with the skill and experience of a dog raised at sea. The Newfoundland would refuse to go out on deck if the sea was too wild, knowing well the point at which his big paws would slip and he would either rebound off the rail, or worse, slide under it and into the sea. Once, as a pup, he'd gone overboard and had to be scooped up with a net from a lifeboat. It was a lesson he didn't care to repeat, especially after the way the captain and crew had treated him, swinging between solicitousness and anger for days.

Argos was about to turn back into the cabin as the motion of the deck neared the edge of his safety point, when he caught the scent of the musician out alone in the night and decided to investigate. Moving only during the lulls between waves, he traversed the deck, reached the bench, and pushed himself against the man's legs just as the ship was hit on the beam by a wind that had suddenly shifted direction, and it slewed to one side. The man clung to the dog as the boat crashed into the trough at the bottom of a wall of water, and nearly went over on its side.

Dog and man were slung from the bench by the force of the boat's awkward landing in the valley between two huge waves. The chain that linked Perdiki to the bench snapped and came apart as he and the dog were thrown across the deck, leaving the musician with his arm free and his fingers dug into the beast's black fur. Together, they struck the rail with enough force that they both lay there like the dead until Perdiki finally managed to hook an arm around the rail to ready himself for the next wave, and Argos hitched a hind leg up to brace it against one of the rail's iron supports.

While the boat climbed the next wave, a light flashed as the cabin door was again opened. The voice of the captain growled its way across the deck and over the noise of the struggling engine. "Did we get you with that one, Perdiki? Or do I have to go out there on such a night to find your corpse?"

"I told you before," called out the musician, with the small amount of strength that could be drawn from a body that felt as if it had again been tortured. "If the government wants me dead, they can't get away with just an accident. They either have to do it themselves, or forget about it."

"Is my dog out there?"

"Ah, now, I understand your real concern."

"Is Argos with you?"

"If the animal you are referring to is a big, furry monster, then, yes, Argos is with me."

"Just don't let him go overboard," called the captain, and let the heavy iron door slam without ever having looked out on deck. With the door's closing, the only light on deck was eliminated.

Lazy bastard, thought Perdiki. Too damn warm and comfortable to come out to check on me. Or too scared they'll think he's being friendly. Serves him right that I'm free. "Look at this, Argos," he said to the big dog. He raised his hands and the shackles fell off. "The whole thing came apart." He pushed his strong frame up into a sitting position, with his back to the rail, and noticed, with surprise, that he was still hanging onto the dog. When the next jolt came, as the ship tried to punch its bow toward the island, he clung to Argos and the rail. Attached to each other, they held their ground through the boat's next twists and crashes. Despite the ferocity of the storm, the captain didn't bother to check on the musician again.

When the *Dedalus* reached midway along the coast of Mythos, the wind and sea finally eased, as if the island had given up its battle and would allow the boat to leave off its cargo. The ship ghosted through a sea that was now nearly flat and with the wind gone, the summer night became mild. Perdiki could make out the few harbor lights that signalled the tiny bay at Agios Yiorgos where the ship would anchor. Within the hour, they would be loading him onto a small boat to be delivered into the arms of his new keepers.

What now? Thought Perdiki. Back in the clutches of Xenos, who always wore a black suit as if he were perpetually attending a funeral? More of the same? More beatings? The stink of the cells and then the isolation in blank rooms with no chairs, no beds, no desk, no noise except the occasional death scream in the distance? That damn bell that rang every time that Xenos struck.

He watched the coast carefully as it slipped past, searching until he spotted three familiar huge boulders that were twenty meters offshore. Without hesitation, he tucked his plastic-wrapped notebook under his shirt, slid under the rail, and kicked off to get himself as far away from the boat as possible, hitting the water after a longer drop than he'd expected. Directly behind him was another splash, as Argos, following an instinct bred into generations of Newfoundland's giant canine lifeguards, leaped into the water to save him. Within seconds, they were alone in the Aegean, a half mile offshore, with the *Dedalus* fast disappearing.

After winning a brief tussle with Argos, who insisted on trying to rescue him, the musician began to swim for shore, with the huge dog paddling beside him. Despite the circumstances, the water was warm, the sea had settled down and the swim was almost a pleasant one. Every hundred metres or so, he would rest for a few strokes, floating effortlessly on the salty Aegean as he gathered his breath. At each brief stop, Argos swam circles around him, watchful that the man wasn't in trouble.

Perdiki reached the first of the big boulders he had spotted from the ship, and considered briefly climbing on it for a few minutes rest, but quickly dismissed the thought, realizing that at any moment, his absence from the boat might be noticed, and when that happened, he needed to be out of the sea and as far from sight as possible. He stroked more quickly to avoid the temptation, thinking of the time when he had climbed aboard this very boulder with a girl. It was at the beginning of his last exile, when the guards were still slack and they let him wander the island at will. He and the girl were wrapped in each other and their clothes were drying on the boulder, when a fishing boat chugged around the bend and they had to scramble quickly into the water. The big boulder hadn't changed in the twenty-five years since he'd last seen it, but certainly the girl, Kiki, would not be as he remembered her.

There were shadows moving nervously on the rocky hill directly above the shore and he thought at first that they might belong to men searching for him, or perhaps waiting for him to reel himself in from the sea. There was no real light to deepen the shadows. They existed only by starlight in the clear, moonless night, so that his view could never become any more focused or clear. There was no sound from where the shadows moved, none that Perdiki could hear. The night was completely still, except for the light rattle of stones where the sea brushed the shore, and there were no voices in the little bay behind the boulders, where even a whisper would be heard skipping across the water.

Perdiki swam straight for the shore, hoping the shadows were other than what he feared. If his absence from the ship had been discovered, they could easily have radioed the police station, just a kilometre west of the rocky bay where he was headed. Swimming quietly beside him, the big dog, Argos, occasionally gave an anxious glance in Perdiki's direction to check that he really didn't need to be saved. Perdiki had the thought that the dog would already be barking or growling if there were anyone waiting onshore.

Nevertheless, the shadows onshore continued to move, until a small crowd of them gathered in one spot, now, ten or fifteen metres from the shoreline. As he reached water that was belly-deep, Perdiki lay very still, but Argos, after giving the musician a sniff to assure himself that he was all right, bounded out of the water straight toward the group of shadows, which scattered at his approach, their small, cloven hooves clattering on the stones, as the herd bounded away and up the cliff.

Perdiki laughed at himself, and sat upright. But there was one last shadow remaining on the beach and that one suddenly began speaking.

"The gun is old, and I'm even older, but we can both still shoot you easily enough. Wouldn't be the first time." The voice was deep and cigarette-gruff, and spoke an old-fashioned kind of island Greek, with an occasional word that came directly from Turkish, and there was a directness to the delivery that would never have passed in Athens. "What kind of man swims into my cove at night?"

Perdiki pushed himself to his feet and stumbled over the rocks for the last few meters before addressing himself to the man on the beach. "Were those your goats?"

"Sheep," the man answered with a hint of amusement to his voice. He looked toward Argos, who was now seated, regally, like a lion, staring directly at him. "What manner of beast is this?" he asked. "Does it have a name?"

"The dog is named Argos."

"And you would be … Ulysses returning home?"

"Perhaps."

"More likely a prisoner escaped from the ship that just passed."

"I prefer Ulysses."

"Come closer," the gruff voice said. "You sound familiar."

"Are you with the law?"

"Not if it can be helped. I am with this island, nothing more. But you, come closer. I think I know you."

Perdiki approached, smiling because the voice he heard was now sounding familiar, as well. "Zev, how is your daughter?" Perdiki asked of the man in the shadows.

"Kiki is married, has made me a grandfather four times over, and is well rid of you." The man laughed as he said this. "But I am glad to see you anyway."

Perdiki remembered that when Zev joked, his, sun-ravaged, bulbous nose wrinkled, but in the dim starlight, he could barely make out the shape of the man's face.

"And I am pleased to almost see you, again," countered Perdiki. "How does it go with you?"

"I am older and more stupid. Other than that, nothing changes." Zev turned at the sound of the shadowy flock of sheep clicking against the rocks as they moved back down off the cliff and onto the beach, again.

"Your dog," Zev asked the musician, "does it have a taste for lamb?"

"I don't know, yet. He has only been my dog for the past hour."

"This breed, they grow quickly, *neh*?"

"He jumped ship with me."

"A fellow musician?"

"Too soon to know."

"*Lipon*. We must go quickly. Please instruct your dog."

"Argos."

"Yes, of course, Argos. Tell Argos that I will give him a bone when we get to the mountains. He is not to take his own from one of these sheep."

"I will discuss the matter with him."

"And, by the Virgin Mary, keep him quiet."

"I have not yet heard him make a sound."

As they quipped at each other, the two men carefully negotiated the scattered rock of the shore, then followed the base of the cliff, bypassing the obvious path upward, until they came to a large, jagged rock that overhung the beach by a meter. They carefully climbed the cliff beside it, until they were atop the overhang. From there, they followed a trail that zigzagged up the cliff amongst the rocks in such a way that they were concealed from sight both above and below for most of the climb. At the very last steep pitch, when the big dog's claws had trouble gripping the smooth rock, the men had to push Argos up and over the lip of the cliff.

Perdiki lay on a boulder overlooking the sea, breathless and exhilarated, while Zev restlessly scanned the unpaved road that lay across their path, fifty meters ahead. The land they would cross to reach the road was a pasture for the shadowy sheep Perdiki had seen when he first pulled himself from the sea. The shaggy animals were now slowly starting to return to their pasture, having found their own paths back up the cliff.

"This is luck, these animals returning," said the old man. "We will become sheep for a while and as our flock drifts over toward the road we can make a quick run across. From there we can get to the mountains without being seen."

He regarded Argos. "This dog already looks like a big black sheep, but can he act like one?"

Without waiting for an answer, Zev hunched over and moved ahead through the shadows of rocks and trees, until he was in the midst of a group of the woolly creatures who were moving in the direction of the road.

There were no lights, only shadow and deeper shadow to distinguish landmarks and animals as two men and a dog meandered along with the sheep. Several times they were forced to stop for minutes they couldn't spare, while the sheep sniffed at the sparse vegetation and wandered wherever there was grazing to be found. The dog, whose black fur made it the most invisible of the group, trailed behind Perdiki, content to follow him in circles if it so happened. His was the only back that didn't ache from crouching over.

When they were within a few meters of the road, Zev tapped Perdiki on the shoulder and signalled that they should slip across, one at a time. With a slight push, he started the musician off.

Perdiki felt himself becoming caught up in the adventure of the night, as if he were in a heroic song or a movie. It was a dangerous attitude because the consequences were real and he knew them too well. Years ago, the police had tied him to a chair and broken his leg in a village not far from where he now crossed the road. Broken his leg because he was Perdiki, not for anything in particular that he'd done. There was no admission to be gained by torturing him. They always knew that they could hear everything he had to say in his music.

On the other side of the rutted, dirt road, the trees offered shelter as the two men and the dog huddled together, waiting and listening. Perdiki tried to keep his focus on the present, peering into the darkness for any sign of pursuit or entrapment.

He was suddenly startled when the olive tree beside him rattled as Zev brushed past.

"This way," Zev whispered, then checked himself and pressed a hand against Perdiki's arm, to restrain him.

"That … can you hear it?"

"A truck," the musician whispered, hearing a low rumbling in the distance. "Probably police."

"Quickly," Zev said. "Keep low, and run behind me as fast as you can, until I stop."

"Then what?"

"Then, my friend, we will be either safe or dead. Life is sometimes easy that way. *Lipon*. Let's go."

At first the land was nearly flat, with only the occasional, low, crumbling stone wall to step over, but then as they began to near the mountains, and the land rose upward, there were terraces filled with neatly-planted, spiky olive trees, and had walls that were often two or three meters high. Each wall had a stone stairway built into it that was nothing more than rocks jutting out as footholds. There was no standard pattern to predict where they'd appear, and unless like Zev you had the way ingrained in you from childhood, it would be easy to stumble around for hours looking for a way up to the mountains.

Argos stopped once and turned to stare back down through the terraces with his ears raised and his nose slightly in the air. The men stood beside him and waited until, after a moment, they began to hear the crackling of stones from below, and it became clear that someone else knew the way.

"Listen to me," whispered Zev, pulling at Perdiki's sleeve. "We are going back down, but by another way."

Zev led them across the breadth of first one terrace and another, working their way down slowly, occasionally descending a set of steppingstones. The dog found his own way, but always remained as close to the pair of men as possible, until at one point, he suddenly leapt up and began jumping down terrace after terrace, disturbing the night with his loud crashing. After a dozen giant leaps, he began barking ferociously, with a hundred fifty pounds of strength behind him.

Immediately, voices began shouting. "Get this dog away from me."

"Where did that animal come from?"

"Somebody shoot him."

"The commander said no shooting."

"The hell with the commander, that big beast will kill us. Shoot him, by the Virgin Mary, shoot him." Several voices could be heard at once, shouting and arguing, but no shots were fired. In the midst of the confusion, Argos slipped away and quietly made his way back up the terraces until he reached the men, who were already fifty meters further over and on the move back up the mountain.

"Good dog," the musician said softly, patting the big dog's side as he kept climbing.

"Yes," whispered Zev, "he showed us the enemy position. Very good dog, indeed. I will give him a whole one of my neighbor's sheep for himself."

"You were always generous that way."

"When you were here before, you never objected to eating my neighbor's sheep."

"I thought I was a communist then. The sheep belonged to us all."

"And now?"

"Now I am a musician in trouble for having *views*."

"Let us save the dialectic and our breath. We will be in the pine forest, soon, and after that we'll get to the stream."

"I know where you mean."

"Yes, I am sure both you and my daughter know that place." Zev turned away and quickened the pace as they reached the last of the terraces and arrived at a stretch of cactus and bramble with only one path leading through its treacherous thorns. It was dangerously exposed, but there was no other way. As they rushed along the rocky path, the smell of wild oregano was in the air, along with the sound of *zizigas*, cicadas, thousands of them buzzing in tandem.

Thorns and cactus spikes scratched at the two men while they ran with shoulders hunched-in and arms out front as if they were diving into the brush. There was no stopping to examine wounds, nor even time to think about them. The patch of cactus and thorns went on for much longer than he remembered from when he was last on the island, until finally Zev began to run out of wind, and the pace slowed.

By the time they neared the stream, the men had slowed to a walk. Argos trotted ahead and lapped up his fill, and was already resting beside the bank waiting for them when they reached it. The two men dipped their hands in the stream to drink, then sat for a brief rest in the shadow of a large boulder.

The dog, as if suddenly remembering his duty, stood up and took a position beside the musician, sniffing and searching the night.

Nothing moved except the water in the stream. Beyond it was the bare rock face of the true beginning of the mountains. There were many paths that could be taken to the old hidden villages, where, for centuries, the islanders had hidden from pirates, tax collectors, and avaricious priests from the mainland.

"We are going to a deserted village," whispered Zev. "I haven't been there in years, and probably no one else has either. It's far away from everything else and mostly just rocks now, but there is, well there was, anyway, one little house built into the mountain like a cave that should be still there. The entrance is hidden behind big boulders, so you would never see it."

"It sounds elegant."

"Oh, it is. And you will have lots of company."

"Female?"

"Scorpions, maybe female."

"Safer."

Perdiki and his old friend laughed and then warily stood looking for any signs of pursuit before setting off for the black wall of the mountain. They bore far to the left, remaining in the shadowy lee of the high cliff, until they came to a ridge that crossed back the way they had come as it rose up the mountain.

Zev shook his head. "Not this one, my friend. There is another just ahead." He slipped into the darkness along the wall, leading for another ten minutes before stopping in front of a ledge that led up the mountain. It was wide, almost a walkway.

"There is nothing up here, *kyrie* mister musician, but we will go this way, regardless. Partway up the mountain the path has collapsed and then there are only rocks above."

They followed the wide path up the mountain until they reached a point where it petered out to become a pile of rocks with no obvious way to go on.

"Now," said Zev, turning to several man-sized boulders on one side of the path. "We will climb over these little pebbles and you will see something."

"What about Argos?" Perdiki asked. "We can't leave him."

"It would save one sheep."

"It's only your neighbor's sheep. What do you care?"

Zev ignored the comment. "I will feel more comfortable once we're over this rock. You go first and when you get to the top, call your monster. I will push him up from below by his great big smelly butt, god save me. And then, I'll follow, if lifting him hasn't crippled me."

Perdiki climbed the boulder easily, but when he called for the dog, Argos took off in another direction and there was nothing to be done except reach down to give Zev a hand up for the last couple of feet, and hope the dog would somehow find a way up by himself. By the time they were picking their way down the far side of the boulder, Argos was waiting, below, for them.

"How did he do that?"

Zev laughed. "Dogs always find their own way, *neh*? It's their nature. There is no such thing as a lost dog. Sometimes they wander away and find somebody more interesting than their master, but they're never lost."

They scrambled over several other large rocks and each time, Argos picked his own way through, often arriving on the other side of a boulder ahead of the men. The sky was beginning to lighten when they reached a narrow path that zigzagged along the mountain, from ledge to ledge.

"Quickly, now," Zev urged. "Once it's light we can be seen from below if anyone's looking. And don't forget I need to come back down again."

"Be careful when you do. They will be watching everywhere, looking for me."

"What have you done, this time, Perdiki, written a bad song?"

"Worse. I gave a free concert."

"And you offended everybody?"

"Some seemed to like the music."

"But not the police."

"They have no taste."

"You don't need taste if you have power, my friend. And if you don't have power, then it doesn't matter."

The trail was a good one, allowing them to keep a fast pace and although Zev was breathing hard, he never stopped, never slowed down on this stretch, until they'd crested the rocky face, and were looking down into a narrow valley, with a few struggling, twisted trees and some scrub.

"Here we are," said Zev, panting from the climb and barely able to get out the words. "The village of Agios Nikolas."

The "village" was no more than ten meters long by four or five meters deep and consisted of a few piles of rocks, where once there had been houses. Perdiki followed Zev to a spot where rock was piled against the mountainside. To one side, was a green patch of vegetation that might once have been a garden.

"Let's see what is hiding behind this lovely façade," Zev said. "I think it should be your new mountain villa." The craggy rocks tore at the musician's hands as he and Zev pushed them aside, uncovering a low wooden door, no more than five feet high.

A hard push against the door forced it open, accompanied by the screech of old, rusty hinges. As the door swung back, a musty dead-rat smell was released from inside. Zev used his dimmed flashlight to reveal a cave whose walls had been roughly squared, and at one time plastered. Against one wall was a table thick with old, green paint, and a pair of café chairs with the wicker gone and replaced by roughly-shaped boards. Along another wall was a low, sleeping-bench, with a mattress that rats and mice had chewed into clumps. The back wall held a long counter, made of flat slate with piled stone supports. At its center was a stone sink, and above it a grooved stone spout set into the rock wall poured an endless stream of water.

"You even have running water," said Zev, "but you do not have stopping water. There is no way to turn this off."

From a stack of chipped old dishes and cutlery on one side of the sink, Perdiki selected the largest bowl, rinsed it, filled it with water, and set it on the floor for Argos. Then he turned to Zev. "Is there any way I can get some food?"

"Not until the late afternoon," Zev said sadly. "Now, I must leave immediately, or I might be seen. Someone will bring dinner for you and the dog before it is dark again. And take this flashlight, I can get down without it."

"Zev. For all these years I have had no contact with you, and now you do all this. How can I express my appreciation?"

"For putting you in a hole in the ground, far from humanity? Think nothing of it. Nothing. It is what we do only for the finest of our musicians." With that, Zev departed, calling back softly over his shoulder as he walked quickly down the path, "Write me a song one day. Old Zev, the mountain goat. It could be a very short song if I don't get home before light."

Perdiki sat on a boulder beside the entrance to his new home, trying to follow Zev's sounds, but there were none as the sly old man slipped off into the fading night. Already, there were lighter places on the landscape and prominent features were beginning to show. If he looked over the boulders that sheltered the cave-house from view, he could see the beginnings of the horizon showing over the sea, and the last stars were fast disappearing. It was too far from any of the other villages for him to hear the morning sounds he knew so well from the days when he'd lived on the island. As the sun hesitated to break out from the horizon, there'd be the earliest of roosters, the first of the coughers and hackers out for a cigarette and a breath of morning air, and the clunk of goat bells moving along the paths.

Perdiki wanted coffee to greet the dawn, but had to content himself with a cup of the earthy water that ran continuously into the sink in his little grotto. It was unlike what came out of the pipes in Athens. The water in Athens always tasted to him like blood after the police found a butcher, who was a leader of the underground, floating in the reservoir with one of his own knives stuck through him.

The fresh water was a fitting breakfast for Perdiki's first morning of freedom since they'd picked him up in the alley behind the flat at 1071 Anastasias.

CHAPTER 3

The Old Man and Spiro

Katina was trying to avoid the old man's signalling for her attention. There was a pile of souvlaki sizzling on the charcoal grill at the back of her little café, salads to be prepared, and her brother at the back door with a box of tomatoes he was supposed to have brought in the afternoon. Another thing to be done and the old man to be served who'd been talking half the night with his companion and the two of them drinking wine almost as quickly as she could fetch it.

The old man slapped his hand on the table in exasperation. "She sees me," he said. "Like when you see the truth and you don't want to face it. Or worse when you're not willing to face the inevitable." He drank the last drops from his glass. "To be honest, though, the inevitable is often worth avoiding, but only the truth can help forestall it." He banged his hand on the table again. "Damnit, we need some more wine. Has that woman no pity?"

CHAPTER 4

Perdiki

Perdiki sat on a boulder outside the cave-house thinking about Athens when he'd last been there, when he couldn't see the city from the back of the closed freight truck, and it reached him as a whiff of chicken cooking in olive oil, the shouting arguments at every street corner, and the changes of light filtering through the cracks as the truck bounced from broad avenue to narrow street and back again.

Athens may have been under military control, but the stores kept selling to everyone, regardless of which side they were on, and tourists crowded the streets, oblivious to the political dynamic. While Perdiki rode in the backs of trucks in terror for his life, travellers from all over the world pushed through the crowded market of Plaka and filled the tavernas at night with their laughter.

The truck suddenly swung sharply to the right, continued for a few meters and bounced to a stop. Grabbing his pack, Perdiki swung open the door, jumped out, and quietly closed the door behind him. The truck immediately took off down the alley as the musician slipped into the back door of the small apartment building where he'd been living with Athena for several months.

"I'm lost to you if I'm known," she told Perdiki. "Eventually they will see you in the street or someone will talk. You think none of the neighbors hear you and Stratos playing all night? What if one of them doesn't like it? You think they won't call the police? Then they will follow you and find me."

"They will not find me," Perdiki said firmly.

"You're wrong. The one thing for certain is that they will find you, Perdiki-mou, that much I know." Athena brushed back her straight dark hair from a face that rarely smiled and filled with dark shadows when she spoke of the future. "You are too public and you seem to think that the police don't know that you sneak around the city at night to play at small clubs and record in the studio."

Athena's hands were in constant motion when she wasn't holding a paintbrush, or working in clay. Now, they sculpted tragedy in the air.

"I have to work," she said. "My show is opening in New York, and I'm not ready." Her hands conveyed the depth of emotion that even her complex face couldn't express. "Nothing is getting done. But if I'm going to waste time over you, then I need you to be here, not in jail or on the run." She pressed her fingers hard to the table until they whitened at the tips. "I don't think they will kill you. No, they can't. You're too well known, internationally. But me, I don't know. Maybe I'm not famous enough. There's a price somewhere." She stood back, suddenly unable to hold her weight to the chair and rushed out to the balcony.

The apartment on Anastasias overlooked Lycabettus Hill, whose limestone rock reached high into the air. At its peak, the church of Agios Georgios sat austerely in the twilight, while traffic fought for space in the wide street a thousand feet below. Coffee on such a balcony, the great luxury for Athenians awakening from their afternoon nap, was denied to Perdiki, who couldn't risk the exposure.

Athena, rather perversely, began taunting him to join her on the balcony, with a tone that would later become the basis for his song of political implorement, *Athena Calls*.

Finally, he stopped her. "I have to go out tonight. Don't play with me. Let's spend a few minutes together. Come inside."

"When will you leave?"

"Tonight. Soon. When it is dark enough."

"You can't. I need you here with me for a while."

"Don't, Athena. Just don't."

"Make me dinner, and I will come back inside."

"There's no time. Come and say goodbye, while we still have a few minutes left to us."

"I will," she said. Then her tone instantly changed. "We have trouble."

"What?"

"There's a car in the street that's just stopped in front of this building." She was quiet for a second. "Four of them getting out at once. They think their uniforms make them men. You have to get out of here now. Go out through the roof, where I showed you."

She ran in from the balcony, gave him a quick, deep kiss, and pushed a key into his hand as she shoved him out the door. "Don't try to contact me here, Perdiki-mou. If I can get away, I'm leaving the country. I'll be in Paris. The gallery will know where, but don't contact me unless you've left Greece."

He ran without looking back, climbing the steps three at a time until he reached the trap door at the top, which opened with the key Athena had given him. As soon as he was on the roof, he lowered the trap door slowly behind him, hearing the lock close with a satisfactory click. It wouldn't slow them down for long, but it might just be enough.

From rooftop to rooftop, the buildings were nearly all the same height, barely inches apart, with only metal railings to separate them. Perdiki vaulted over several, from one building to the next, before reaching a fire escape that was nothing more than a rickety series of ladders and metal landings and was only a little less dangerous than being caught in a blaze. It was bolted onto the building with more rust than steel, and the rungs were bent and in some cases broken clean through.

Not trusting even the more solid looking rungs, Perdiki gripped his hands around the sides of the ladder, wrapped his feet around its outside rails, and slid rather than climbed down it, until he reached the first of three rickety, metal landings. As he put his weight on the metal platform it began to pull away from the building, and he had to leap for the next ladder before the landing gave way. His hands slid along the rust of the rough rail for a couple of meters before he could get his feet in place and manage to slow his descent. By the time his slide was under control, his palms were burning and his right index finger was torn and bloody, but there was no time to examine his wounds before he reached the next platform. This one he avoided stepping on entirely, but instead maneuvered his body so that he could twist his way from one ladder to the next without putting any weight on the metal landing.

As he slid down the next section, he heard gunshots and although it was too far away to hear anything else, he imagined he could hear

Athena screaming. The dark shadows of her face played on his conscience, but there was nothing to be done but keep running.

Hovering at the top of the final ladder, he stopped to look below for any sign of the police, but except for an old car with four flat tires that looked as if it hadn't been moved in a long time, the alley was empty.

The final ladder had been chopped off a couple of meters from the ground to keep vandals from climbing it. When Perdiki reached its end, and his feet suddenly ran out of anything to wrap around, he let go and fell the last couple of meters. His ankle gave out as he landed, and he collapsed clumsily, scraping an elbow and a knee.

Limping badly on one ankle, the musician forced himself to hurry to the cover of the old car parked halfway down the alley. As he reached it, a dark figure stepped out from behind its shelter with a handgun aimed at Perdiki.

CHAPTER 5

Perdiki

The big dog snored and the sounds echoed in the cave-house. Argos's lower lip quivered and his nose fluttered with each deep breath, causing a deep thrumming tone that was soothing to the man who lay nearby and was trying to find his way back into the most peaceful sleep he'd known in months. Perdiki had gone into the house that was dug into the hill a few minutes after Zev's departure, intending to rest for a few minutes. When he passed through the doorway, he felt as if he were entering the mountain and being enfolded by the island. Inside, with the door closed, and no windows, there was little to distinguish day from night, and the minutes he'd planned to sleep turned into hours as he dozed away his exhaustion. It was only when a few rays of sun managed to eventually find their way through the cracks in the doorframe, and one of these aimed itself directly across the musician's eyes that they were finally forced open.

When Perdiki sat up, the dog awoke with a grunt. Argos stood and stretched, first forward and then back, with his tail straight out behind him, and his big black nose sniffing the air to acquaint himself with the remainder of the day.

Perdiki pulled open the door to let in some light and then hacked and spat before taking a drink from the stream of water that ran unceasingly from its source in the rock to the sink below. The desire for coffee plagued him so much that he thought he could catch the scent of it in the air coming up from one of the villages below.

Before stepping through the doorway, he peered outside for a while, searching his surroundings. A few meters in front of the entrance to his new home was a stone wall that had been constructed to hide the deserted village from below. He could walk around freely in its ruins without fear of being observed. On both sides of the village, were the remains of terraces that had once been cultivated, but now contained only overgrown, awkwardly-shaped olive trees and thick brush. In the far corner of one parcel of land, was a clump of a variety of cactus that bore, prickly, stone-filled fruit. The air carried the scent of sage and wild oregano.

Near the top of the wall, he noticed a rock that was used to plug what was obviously a spy hole. When Perdiki pulled it out and looked through, he could see where a rockfall had deposited the huge boulders that he'd had to surmount with Zev the previous evening. The hidden village where he now found himself must have been abandoned when the rock fall made the path too difficult to traverse. Over the years, the traditional piled-stone houses had become hollow after all the usable wood was stripped and carried off to be used elsewhere. There were a dozen or so hulks, dark at the doorways, and mostly roofless because beams were too valuable to leave behind. The slate from the roofs lay in neat piles behind the houses, too heavy to carry away, but left waiting as if some day they might be used again. Of all the houses in the village, only the cave house where Perdiki had slept remained intact.

Through the spy hole he could see that further down the mountainside were terraces that were free of weeds and filled with neatly groomed rows of olive trees. Mixed in with them would be figs, almonds, and apricots, but from the distance, only the olive trees were discernible. Below the terraces there was no sign of habitation because most of the houses on this part of the island were as hidden as his own roost, tucked behind and under rocks and overhangs.

The sun was setting behind the mountain at his back, and the light was still clear, but dimming. Zev had told him that when it was nearly dark someone would bring food, but that would not be for another hour and a bit. At least he wouldn't die of thirst, he thought, heading back into the cave for another cup of water. On the table inside was his notebook, still wrapped in its sheet plastic envelope. He pulled one of the two patched-together board chairs to the table and carefully unwrapped the notebook, trying to keep out the drops of water that still clung to the plastic wrapping as evidence of his recent swim to the island.

When the black speckled notebook was unwrapped and lying on the table in front of him, he could see where water had seeped in when he'd swum, and had soaked a half inch of the upper right hand corner. Fanning the notebook freed most of the pages, and the rest he unstuck by hand, pulling them carefully apart. When he was finished, he set the book standing up, resting it on its covers as legs, with the pages fanned out.

A moment after he finished, there was a noise outside, and then a young woman's voice called softly, "*Kyrie Perdiki*, Mister Perdiki, are you in there? I hope you are hungry."

The door swung open and a girl entered. He looked up from the notebook to see that she was in her early twenties, with the blond hair, blue eyes and dark skin that was more typical of Athenians than of the locals. But, it was apparent by her lack of makeup, simple shift and sandals and an air of confidence beyond her years that despite the blond hair she was an island girl.

She lifted her slender arms to hold up two large bulging cloth bags, then rushed to say everything on her mind at once, as if she would forget something if she didn't get it all out quickly enough.

"My uncle, Zev, sends these," she began, as she placed the two bulging bags on the floor beside the table, and unpacked each item. "Mostly food, a bottle of wine, some coffee and a little gas ring and a briki to cook it in. Some matches, of course. And a light too. He said to warn you to be very careful with the light, and only use it with the door closed. Your enemies have sharp eyes." She continued unpacking the cloth bags. "Here is a small sack of dog food and a big bone for your dog. My uncle says he likes that dog and wants to make him a present of one of our neighbor's sheep someday." The young girl sparkled as she said this and it was obvious the delight she took in her uncle's humor. "I'm Maria," she added as an afterthought.

She stared at Argos, who looked her in the eye and wouldn't break his gaze until she glanced down. "My uncle said he was big," she said, "but I didn't know he was this big. Is he safe?"

"From what?" he teased.

"Does he bite?"

"Only food."

"How about coffee?"

"He doesn't drink coffee."

"I mean you. Would you like me to make some coffee for you before I leave?" She didn't bother to wait for a response, for what

Greek ever turns down coffee? Placing the little gas ring on the old kitchen table, she lit it expertly, filled the briki from the ever-flowing water, and balanced it on the burner.

"Are you an angel?"

"No. Just the niece of Zev. It's a lot easier." She winked at him and laughed.

The pretty young girl stirred two spoons of pulverized coffee into the briki, added a spoon of sugar and stirred again. While the pot heated, she took a pair of tiny cups from one of her bags, and set them on the table beside the gas ring.

Maria was blue-eyed, like an Athenian, and had thick blonde hair in dense curls that were tied back in a pony tail. Her eyebrows were a darker blonde and thick as if they were black. There was the tiny dimple of a scar on her right cheekbone that highlighted the smoothness and innocence of her lightly tanned skin. Perdiki guessed her age at twenty-two or three.

The girl stared into the briki as she again spoke. "I know some of your songs."

"You know who I am?"

"Don't worry. I don't talk to anyone. My uncle taught me."

"Are you the daughter of his sister or brother?"

"My father was his brother."

"Was he killed in the war?"

"I don't know anything."

"That's how it is?"

"My uncle taught me."

The coffee boiled up in the little, torso-shaped, copper pot. As the foam neared the top of the briki, the girl lifted it from the flame, and poured half into each cup, before returning the pot to the little gas ring. When the coffee foamed up a second time, she poured the remainder into each of the cups, before turning off the gas.

Perdiki looked across the rough table at the girl. "So you know who I am. And you are?"

"You remember Kiki?"

Perdiki had an instant of unbounded emotion until she added, "Don't worry," she laughed, seeing the look on his face. "She is my aunt, not my mother. My aunt didn't start having children until long after you left, when she was married." She smiled at him and touched his arm.

"When he sent me here, my uncle thought I should know something about you."

"What did he tell you?"

"Not to let you sing to me."

"The coffee is very good," Perdiki said, ignoring her words and sipping his coffee over the lip of the small, thick, white cup.

"Will you sing to me?" she laughed, as she cut cheese and bread and put it on one of the two plates she had brought, accompanying it with some olives and figs.

"Your uncle, Zev, wouldn't like that," he said. Perdiki was eating with his fingers, too hungry to bother with a fork and not caring that his fingers became greasy from the olives and soft goat cheese.

"Maybe I am not an angel after all."

"Shh, child. Let me finish this food." As he spoke, he took a few rapid sips of coffee and then continued eating until the plate was empty and he could see its faded illustration of the Acropolis faintly visible under a web of cracks in the glaze.

Maria watched until he finished eating, and then looked sharply through the open doorway, noticing that the valley below was filling with dark shadows, and the distant mountains were beginning to blur.

"It's been much too long. I have to go home now."

"You live with your mother?"

"No. She is ... " she hesitated and turned her eyes away, " ... difficult. I live with Uncle Zev until I go to university."

"When will that be?"

"I will go when I can." She looked nervously at the nearly dark valley. "I have to leave now. This minute," she added, mostly to herself. "Be careful. Goodbye," she called softly as she left, moving swiftly, without a sound. Maria was out of sight within seconds, hidden in the rocks that protected Perdiki's aerie from the world.

It was quiet without the girl, and he felt a momentary wave of loneliness before turning his attention back to his surroundings. The air carried the scent of wild thyme and not a hint of anything else. At this time of year, there were usually cicadas buzzing ominously to disturb the silence, but not this afternoon. A small fluorescent-green lizard slid across the rocks and then there was no motion, only Perdiki's thoughts, and those he tried to keep to a minimum. He wanted only to think very small thoughts for a while.

The valley below darkened, with deep bands of shadow filling the spaces between the rocks. When a wind began to rattle the olive trees, Argos came to stand beside Perdiki, letting the breeze ruffle his black fur.

After they'd captured Perdiki in the street below Athena's apartment, word reached him in jail that she had escaped to Paris, and was spending her time painting and refusing to talk to anyone. He could imagine Athena walking on a Paris street, with dark shadows across her face, scanning the road for the images that would find their way into her work. She had the long stride that short women adopt in order to keep up with the taller world, but it was executed with such grace that she never seemed hurried.

In Paris, she would probably sit in a café, as she did in Athens, making angry faces at anyone trying to come near. There was never a sketchpad, no pencils, nothing. She let the images of the day flow at her and eventually went home to paint whatever was burned into her mind.

The first time they met, she told Perdiki that she would rather paint people than talk to them. It was backstage after his free concert. Dressed in paint-spattered jeans and an old blouse with holes in the cuff, Athena had pushed her way through the crowd to meet him and ask that he sit for her.

Everywhere there was a sense that things were closing down, that a lid would be placed on the country to muffle what the government didn't want heard or seen. Most of the people he knew were nervous all the time, and there was never any peace in their presence.

Maybe he was attracted so quickly to the artist because she had no political involvement. It was a relief to be in her presence. More than that. She had cast her eyes down when she asked him to sit for her, and after he'd agreed to pose, only then had she looked straight up at him, and he understood that she had wanted him to agree on his own, without her persuasion, because the intensity of her eyes could have moved him to anything.

"I thought you would be more fierce," she said, as she looked carefully at him, examining how he returned her gaze. "I saw photographs of you on record jackets that made you look like a hawk, but I knew those were stupid pictures, so I had no idea until this minute."

"Am I, then, still a hawk?" A group of people surrounded Perdiki, trying to get his attention, but his focus was only on Athena.

"I told you those were stupid photos."

"But, you said I am not fierce."

"Just dangerous. Very dangerous."

"Is that what you want to paint?"

"Maybe. When can you come to see me?"

"Tomorrow afternoon."

"No. That's too late. I mean tonight. What time tonight are you free from this?" She motioned at the surrounding crowd that was threatening to push her aside in their efforts to get at the famous composer.

"I need an hour or two."

"Make it less. I want to paint you as you are after this concert."

Perdiki remembered the smell of turpentine and paintings on all of the walls, and the big easel holding a large canvas that had been stretched over a circle that contained only a few tentative charcoal lines. In the middle of the room, burning beside a drafting table, was a rough looking thick candle on a waist-high wooden stand. Athena sat him next to it, on a high stool that was set in front of a white screen. He sat as she directed and watched Athena light a cigarette with a wooden taper that she touched to the candle flame.

Perdiki was trying to remember what she'd said when his attention was brought back to the present by a movement down below. It was on his side of the rock impasse, which meant that if it were anyone other than Zev or his niece, it was most likely his pursuers. He waited, watching through the spy hole and hoping for the sight of a goat or a sheep. Some white furry flash that would restore his momentary peace.

Instead, there was a clink of metal, and then another. As the minutes passed, Perdiki still couldn't see anything, but the day was so quickly darkening that it was unlikely that he would. Again, there was the sound of metal striking against metal, and then a voice, in loud conversation, found its way up the mountain, faint, but discernible.

"It's too dark now to go up there," said the voice he feared the most. It was Xenos, the man in the black suit who had been responsible for his torture, the man with the bell. "But he has no way out," Xenos said very loudly, obviously for Perdiki to overhear. "He can't get up that mountain unless he's a goat."

Perdiki's hand rested on the rock beside the spy hole, feeling its grain against his palm, the light nearly gone, the day more pleasant than he'd realized, the company of the young girl, the taste of the water that flowed endlessly in the house where he'd slept so deeply, coffee and food at last, all of it in his thoughts at once as a collage. There was nothing he could do, the next events would occur, and whatever followed, including the man in the black suit and his damn bell.

Where was the dog? Argos would keep him company until the morning and then he'd chase the dog away so that at least one of them would remain free. He gave a soft whistle, assuming that the big animal would respond, but although Argos did not immediately reveal himself, Perdiki thought he could hear the faint sound of pebbles ticking among the rocks in a slow progression along the cliff above his cave house. But the cliff seemed too steep for the big dog, so he assumed that it was a wild goat, zig zagging down the mountain. As the sounds drew nearer, he could begin to make out something moving in the shadows. Odd though that the goat didn't leap down the rocks, and displayed no more than two legs at a time.

The final drop of the sun was sudden. It fell below the top of the mountains and vanished, leaving the landscape too dark to reveal anything other than oblique shapes in the night. The two-legged goat disappeared along with the details of the steep rocky mountain he was descending.

There was no sound from below, where his would-be captors waited for the morning. Only the water eternally running into the sink in the cave-house disturbed the silence with its light splash and served as a background to Perdiki's erratic thoughts. He found that his hands were knitting, that he was obsessively rubbing his fingers together and counting his steps as he paced the width of his house, back and forth, staring up at what he couldn't see.

Tonight there was the beginning of a moon that rose on the horizon as a curved spear, stabbing its way upward into the night. It was too thin to provide much light, and the details of the mountain remained obscure. Time became a matter of non-visual features in the night. Lacking a watch, he'd no idea of the number of the hour but the impact of each passing moment on Perdiki was profound. The pain he imagined was nearly palpable, his screams already bottled up, the peacefulness of the night unable to relieve him.

Something touched his elbow, and startled Perdiki. It was followed by a gravelly whisper, that put him back at ears. "Now I know why I gave up being a communist," the voice said, "The hours are too long and the working conditions are terrible. No employer could get away with it."

"Zev. They are down below. Behind the boulders."

"Yes, I know. They caught Maria after she left here. I'm sure she told them she was just walking and did not know anything of you. If you are not here when they arrive, they might believe what she says and let her go."

The big dog, Argos, suddenly nosed his way up to Perdiki, who patted his furry side until even in the near-darkness he could see dust coming off it.

"Your beast knew I was coming. It met me on the trail a few minutes ago."

"How can we get out of here?"

"Up the mountain, the way I came. It isn't much of a trail. Maybe we can make it. I don't know. It was very difficult coming down. I don't want to think about the way up in the dark. Give me a drink of water, and then we will go. Maybe your dog needs water, too." He rubbed Argos's head. "I like him because his politics consist of who smells bad and who smells good."

Not wanting to attract attention by striking a light, Perdiki fumbled in the dark of the cave-house to find his notebook and slip it into his shirt. He filled a cup with water for Zev and a large bowl of it for the dog. Both vessels emptied quickly as they readied themselves for the night.

As he exited the house, Perdiki heard sudden voices from below, the words difficult to discern, but the tenor clearly in the range of uncontrolled anger. Zev appeared beside Perdiki and held his arm as he whispered.

"Xenos," he said, "I know that voice." He listened for a minute. "I can't quite hear what they are saying, but I think someone is telling him what he believes to be your location."

They listened to the conversation for a minute and then there was a shouted command and a voice acknowledging the order.

"*Panagiamou*, mother of god," rasped Zev. "He is going to send soldiers with torches up here right now, in the dark. Xenos believes you are trapped, but he can't wait until morning to get his hands on you. A moment longer is too much for Xenos. He wants blood now, like a vampire."

"I have none to spare. They took all the extra last time they were my hosts."

"Then we had better leave, immediately. Be sure to take anything that shows you were here." He handed Perdiki a small, burlap sack. "Put it all in this, and wrap the metal things in the towel so they don't make noise."

The musician quickly filled the small sack with the few things Maria had brought, and then helped Zev replace the rocks that had been covering the door when they'd first arrived. When Zev was satisfied that it looked undisturbed, he motioned to Perdiki to follow him up the mountain.

There was no obvious path, nor could they see much in the dim light of the tiny sliver of a moon, but Zev was able to lead the musician a hundred meters up the mountain before he had to stop to find his way. Argos, who'd been following Perdiki up to this point, pushed past the two men and without hesitation made his way around a rock overhang, dropping below it by five meters in order to clear the sharpest point.

"Do we put our lives in his big feet?" asked Perdiki.

"We have no choice," Zev whispered. "He found his way to me earlier, and I had no idea which way to go on my own. We followed the politicians, we can certainly follow your beast."

"But the politicians led me here," said Perdiki.

"Then it's for the best that we follow a dog to lead us out. Better hurry before we lose track of him."

Under the rock overhang, even the dim moonlight was blocked, and they had to make their way slowly in the dark, feeling, rather than seeing the hand and footholds. Once they were out from under it, they found Argos waiting for them.

CHAPTER 6

The Old Man and Spiro

The old man and I were the last two in the courtyard outside the café. Katina brought us one final carafe of wine and hobbled inside to clean up and make her way home. When it was finished, the old man stood to take a break in his story, giving his body a minute to sort itself out from the hours of sitting, and then we made our way through the dark down to the little harbor below the village.

It was a night of exceptional beauty. The silver moon reflected itself in the sea as a sharp sliver in the shape of an urn and it was as if we were standing on the edge of creation, where every shape is first sketched out in the sea.

There were a few runabouts, an old wooden sloop with its sails neatly bagged and several wooden, fishing boats tied stern-to, as is customary in Greece. We stopped at one of the boats near the end of the dock.

"Help me push out this board," the old man told me. "This is my cousin's boat and he won't mind if we sit here for a while."

As soon as the single, warped board that served as a gangplank was in place, the old man walked as steadily along it as if it were a wide sidewalk. "Now you," he said, and stepped off it into the cockpit. The board was wet from the night mist as well as warped so that it didn't sit solidly at either end. As I took a first step onto it the old man called out, "It's always best not to think. Just do it. I'm going below to see if there is any coffee." The board wobbled as I crossed, but I'd spent a lot of time around boats and this was nothing new to me.

"Down here," called the old man. "Wait a minute until I light this."

A match flared and revealed the old man standing beside a hanging, brass lantern. When the wick caught and he lowered the glass chimney, light filled the rough cabin of the wooden fishing boat. The old man stood in a small galley that was not much more than a nook with a couple of overhead cabinets, a tiny counter with a built-in sink and an ancient, two burner kerosene stove. He pulled open a cabinet above the stove and found a tin of coffee, another of sugar and a plastic coca cola bottle half-filled with clear liquid. He sniffed it and laughed. "I was looking for alcohol to light the stove, but this is tsipouro, Greek moonshine." He put the bottle on the counter. "We'll want this later." Searching through a cabinet under the sink he pulled out a small, tin container with a screw top. "This is alcohol, for sure."

He unscrewed a cap on the stove to check that there was kerosene in the tank, closed it back up, and pumped up the pressure with the small pump built into the stove. He poured just enough alcohol to fill the little cup that surrounded the burner, lit it into a blue flame with a match and when the alcohol was nearly gone from the cup, quickly turned the burner on to release an aerated stream of kerosene that flared up orange and wild until he adjusted it to a controlled blue flame.

The sink had a water pump which he used to fill the briki with enough water for two cups of Greek coffee. He added a couple of spoons full of coffee and sugar and set it on the burner to boil.

I sat on a hard, wooden bench across from the galley, waiting for the coffee, the tsipouro, and more of the story.

CHAPTER 7

Perdiki

The wind was up, stirring the trees in the olive grove into wild motion. It covered any of their sounds as Perdiki and Zev moved from tree to tree ignoring the lashings they took from the wind-whipped branches.

There was no conversation. The noise of the wind made it too difficult and there was nothing to say. Zev led because he knew where they were going. The big Newfoundland dog, Argos, stayed beside Perdiki, his massive, furry head held down to shield his eyes from the wind as they pushed against it.

The trees were laid out in long lines along the terraces in this part of the island. Each terrace had a wall with steps built into it that led up to the next one. Whenever they came to a set of these steps, that were really just slabs of stone jutting out from the wall, Argos would rush ahead to climb up first, then stand at the top and wait until the men were beside him.

When they reached the highest terrace, above which the land was too steep and rocky to cultivate, they stopped to rest.

"You are running with no place to go," Zev said. "No place on this island, anyway. We can get you to Samos by boat, and you can hide out there for a while, but not until I can arrange it. Now, though, I have a place for you to stay. You will have to get there on your own because I need to be at home to find out if they have released my niece." He stared intently back the way they had come. "I don't think we were followed, so you should be safe enough. Work your way around that big clump of pine trees and you'll find a trail up the mountain. Near the top is a stone hut where my cousin stays when he's working on the grapes. Right now, he's on the other side of the island for a few days so you'll be alone. It isn't as well-appointed as your last place. No running water. You'll have to pump it from the well. It will be much windier up there, so it might be cold at night but don't light the woodstove." He looked down at the dog. "Let this furry beast keep you warm." He thumped Argos on the side and the big dog looked up at him with appreciation.

"Be careful, Perdiki. Stay out of sight until I come for you. Look how quickly they found you in the last place. It might take a day or two, but I'll be back. Just be sure you're still there."

"Just a boy and his dog."

"If you hear a soft whistle, it will be me. Otherwise if you hear anything, watch this big dog." He patted Argos's head. "Because he has no politics he smells everything. He will let you know if anyone's coming long before you see them and hopefully before they see you. If you see anyone, cut diagonally through the vineyard and head North over the mountain to the other side of the island." Zev looked off down the terraces before he spoke again. "Once you get to the other side of the island go to Pharaoh's house. You can trust him, he's the same as he always was. Do you remember his house?"

"I'm sure I can still find it. And I remember that Pharaoh was always as solid as the rock above his house. Don't they call him Pharaoh because his father was Egyptian?"

"No, it's because he looks like he came out of one of those Egyptian tomb paintings."

"After all those times they tortured him, isn't he a little crazy?"

"Only sometimes. Like the rest of us. Except Argos. He is always dog." He scratched behind the big Newfoundland's ears.

Zev turned back to Perdiki, saying, "Stay with Pharaoh and he will get word to me. If you don't have to run, I'll see you in the hut above here in a day or two. Now, I'd better leave. I know another way out and I'll leave a bit of a track so if we were being followed, it will lead them astray."

Before Perdiki could respond, Zev was gone, heading quickly along the terrace where they had been standing and within a minute he was out of sight, hidden by the wind-whipped olive trees. Perdiki waited to catch his breath and then started up the steep mountain trail that was hidden behind the pine trees. Argos followed behind, as man and dog picked their way up a trail that was overgrown in places by thick brambles and bushy pine saplings. The big Newfoundland leapt over the low ones, while the man carefully picked his way around, trying to obscure his passage as much as possible. The wind was a constant, which made the dust they stirred up with their feet swirl back at them. Although he was tired and out of breath, adrenalin kept the musician moving without stop until he was in sight of the small hut Zev had described.

It was an exhausted Perdiki who sighted the hut. He sat on a boulder behind a clump of *skinya* with Argos lying beside him chewing at a thorn wedged between the pads of one of his forepaws.

While he rested, he thought about what a reviewer had said, that he was the soul of Greece. The irony, he thought, was that in his case the soul had to wander away from the body in order to survive. He knew he'd have to leave. Not just leave the island, but get out of Greece, entirely.

With that thought, the words for a song whose melody had struck him on that last night with Athena began to form in his mind and he dug out his notebook to write them down before they fled. The hut could wait a few minutes more.

Athena calls when I am crumbling like old bread.

And yet she still calls.

A sudden noise made him quit writing to look up at the cabin, but though it was only a shutter flapping in the wind, it was enough to make him close the notebook and carefully pack it away in his shirt. Stiff from the long climb, he stood and walked bent-over the last few meters to the tiny, stone hut.

The hut sat alone on one corner of a large swath of flat land, beside thick gnarled grapevines that stood in rows and columns for a hundred meters up the mountain slope. They'd been pruned back for maximum sun and air on the grapes and the leaves were so few that it looked like an orchard of small, green marbles on the gnarled and twisted old vines.

Inside the stone hut was a wide wooden bench with a mattress hung above it by a rope to protect against rodents. Across from the bench was a small counter with a single-burner camp stove and a sink that had a drain hose that led out through a hole in the wall. On a shelf above the counter he found a couple of bowls, two plates, a few foggy-looking glasses, a briki, two tiny cups, a can of Greek coffee and a dented canister half full of sugar. As a Greek, he thought, what more do I need? As if in answer he noticed a hinged table that was now folded up parallel to the wall and held in place by a clip. It had a hinged leg that lay flat against it that would swing down when it was set up. The table reminded him of the ones he'd seen on small boats. Probably a fisherman built this place, he thought. It had that feel and efficiency.

Perdiki went outside to pump water from the well into a jug that he'd found under the sink. He'd brought out two bowls, as well. One he filled with water and the other with some of the dry dog food that Zev's niece had brought to the cave house. Argos bounded like a puppy and pounced on the food bowl, gobbling the kibble and stopping only for a second to look up at Perdiki with gratitude.

"*Tipota*, it's nothing," said the man.

Back in the cabin Perdiki brewed himself a cup of coffee and brought it outside so that he could sit on the ground hidden behind a big boulder to watch for any signs of his pursuers. A drooling Argos came to lie beside him, dropping his dripping chin onto Perdiki's lap. He pushed the dog's head away and wiped the drool on his trousers with his sleeve. "You're not perfect, after all, dog. I already know that you snore and you probably have other disagreeable characteristics and since you're male like me. I know how you'll act around female dogs first time one lets out her scent." He ruffled the fur on the Newfoundland's head. "But you're a good one. Maybe one of the best."

An hour later, hunger drove Perdiki back into the hut. He undid the clip that held the table pinned to the wall and lowered it on its hinges so that the leg swung out as a support. He ate the bread and cheese that Zev's niece had brought to the cave-house and thought of her with a darkness, knowing that anything might have happened to her since she was captured. It was his fault, his guilt and there was nothing to be done but try not to dwell on it. They might not have known of her connection to him, or they might know everything.

As he lowered the mattress from where it was hung above the wooden bed, he thought of Athena in a studio somewhere in Paris with a candle burning beside a chair like the one where he'd sat for her in Athens. If there were someone else she was painting, he wanted it to be a woman because an unreasonable jealousy crept through him when he thought of another man in that chair.

When he finished eating, Perdiki rested on the mattress with images of Athena flickering though his mind. He had never been to Paris although he was aware that his recordings were played in

France, knew because of the royalty checks that came occasionally when he still had an address. If he joined Athena in Paris, there would be concerts and friends and freedom, writers and artists, dancers and musicians. Musicians … he would be with other musicians again, free to learn and experiment. Free of Greece. Free of the damn military junta that had seized his country and was now wringing the life out of it, unhappy with its soul, unhappy with him.

He wanted to be working right now, to pull out his notebook but he knew nothing would happen. If he didn't already hear the words beginning to form in his mind, they wouldn't suddenly come out just because the notebook was open and a pen was held tensely in his hand.

The music, well, the music. Sometimes he wrote the music when it came to him along with the words. He wrote to the rhythm of it before he knew the notes and then they just began to be heard as the words flowed out. When there was no music, when the words stood too much on their own, he would send out a call for his friend, Stratos, who would arrive with a bouzouki, a guitar, and an ancient lyra that he played late at night when his fingers were sore from the bouzouki.

He'd met Stratos the first time he'd been exiled to Mythos. Perdiki had attended a village party where Stratos was playing and hadn't noticed him at first. He'd sat quietly and almost anonymously, barely noticeable, with a couple of other musicians but once the others set the beat and laid down the supporting chords, Stratos's playing penetrated the air with brilliance and light. It soared through the village square where the villagers were sitting at long tables and feasting on roasted goat and drinking wine as if it were water. Stratos' bouzouki inspired the villagers to get up and dance. and when he played the lyra, its ancient whine nearly brought everyone to tears.

When Perdiki had finally been released, he'd contacted the extraordinary musician and convinced him to leave the island to tour and record together. Stratos came to Athens when Perdiki called, but when they were done writing or performing together, he would return to Mythos and the village life that he preferred.

Stratos had been bald since his early twenties, with only a fringe of hair, an inch or so above his ears, surrounding the circumference of his head. His nose was broad and large and resembled a small potato pasted to the front of his face. Above the potato were two bulbous eyes that moved slowly toward an object of interest and then focussed on it to the exclusion of everything else. But as serious as the rest of his face appeared, that broad mouth of Stratos's kept hitting the high notes of a smile that was remembered by everyone who met him.

His fingers moved so rapidly and smoothly on whatever instrument he happened to be playing, that they seemed to be pulled magnetically to the strings. His fame might have surpassed Perdiki's if he'd had any inclination in that direction, but Stratos lived in the one-on-one only. If he spoke to you, he talked until you had a holographic image implanted in your mind of whatever he was trying to convey. You couldn't win an argument with him because he had every base covered and the stamina to bring it home every time. When he lived with a woman, he lived only with her until she disappeared into herself and fled for her life from the intensity. In Mythos, he was just another villager and spent time harvesting his olives and making wine with his friends. He still showed up with the band at village parties, but otherwise played only for himself.

When Stratos was writing music with Perdiki, nothing else existed. They would stay together for days, drifting off to their rooms when their energies failed. It was always late at night when they wrote, the words and music fighting to get along and find each other. It was something that could not be done in daylight because the sun is too bright and you can only stare for so long, but at night when the view is everlasting there is a chance of writing something that is eternal or at least worth singing for a while.

Stratos was a man who could wring a melody from a coffee can and a sonata from whatever else was in the kitchen. When they talked, he invariably had the guitar under his arm, so that there was always music underlying their conversations. It was background and punctuation to every thought. As they spoke, his extraordinary fingers ran along the strings and the bits of tune that emerged naturally moved into whatever they were writing together.

Perdiki sat at the battered old Steinway in the living room when they worked. They would stop to eat and drink and wind up with grease on piano keys and guitar strings and tzatziki on the score and they just kept going. If it was going well, they'd get up and dance the zeibekiko together, with the joy of it. "All this for one song?" Stratos would shout, and then pick up the lyra, a tiny version of a violin that he stood on his knee like a miniature standup bass, and play something so ironically poignant that they would laugh and then get back to work.

When they performed together onstage, Stratos never danced. He was always shy, preferring to let his instruments talk for him, with Perdiki spotlighted at the piano, but when they were writing together, he was as expressive as an actor, shouting out his ideas or whispering them conspiratorially, his face gritting or grinning or puzzled as he spoke. If he hadn't always been holding an instrument, his hands would have been in constant motion, waving thoughts up from the air, but instead his fingers constantly moved on the strings.

Early on, they had decided to avoid all contact with each other unless they were writing or performing so that they would never fall into the discord that happens with so many teams. It wasn't difficult because their writing sessions were so intense that they were weary of each other by the end of each. Stratos would return to his life on Mythos and wouldn't hear from Perdiki until it was time to tour, record or write together again.

Onstage it was a matter of not being caught by the fame. Stratos avoided it entirely but Perdiki couldn't escape the impact of his words. The left embraced and lionized him because his lyrics touched the essence of their beliefs.

Still, it was Stratos the police tortured after the night Perdiki was arrested in Athens. Athena had already left, but Stratos, not knowing the situation, came to her apartment to be greeted by a man in a suit, surrounded by uniformed police. They tortured him after dragging him down the stairs of Athena's apartment.

They only exiled Perdiki because he was too well-known, and they were afraid of repercussions, but they tortured Stratos because he was not famous enough to draw world attention.

When Perdiki forced himself to stop thinking about Stratos, everything buzzed in his head as he confronted his current fear, loneliness and the knowledge that he had to leave Greece, leave everything. But what was he leaving? He couldn't perform, couldn't make public his new songs or sing the old ones that everyone knew. The government was scared of him, scared of what he could say in his songs in words that could never be pinned down. How do you prosecute a metaphor? They knew he could convey a message that they didn't want heard so they forbade his music and made it a crime to own or play his records. Everywhere Perdiki's mind turned there was only danger for everyone he touched. How many people had suffered because of him, because of his music, because of his support of causes that were lost every time?

"Enough!" he said aloud causing Argos to jump to his feet, frantically searching around for what had caused the outburst. Seeing that nothing was out of place and assuring himself that there were no new scents, the big Newfoundland dog lay down again beside the bed where Perdiki was desperately trying to rest.

The longer Perdiki stayed in Greece the more friends would be pushed into hiding and some would be caught and tortured to tell the police what? That they understand the meaning of his songs, the hidden messages and the call to arms?

No more concerts in Greece, he thought, no more danger for anyone. He couldn't let himself be responsible for any more pain. There was no reason. He was just a songwriter, just a musician, an entertainer. He wasn't going to change a damn thing.

Finally, his body's exhaustion won out over his mind and he drifted off from the present into a restless sleep where vague dreams kept him near consciousness for the next several hours. When he woke, it was dark in the stone hut. Argos heard him moving and pushed himself up, shook his furry body and grumbled that he needed to go out. Perdiki opened the door for him to a night full of stars. There was a slip of a moon in the distance but in the complete dark of the mountain it was barely noticeable. The Milky Way was as bright as he'd ever seen it, a white swath across the sky hiding the millions of individual stars within it, like an audience at one of his concerts.

The big dog slipped past Perdiki and disappeared into the shadows of the vineyard. The wind had stopped and with it the background rustle of vegetation. He was startled by the strange screech of an owl and laughed at himself for his fear. The owl made him think of the goddess Athena who sometimes took its form when she came to earth, and then his thoughts turned to his own Athena and although he'd never heard her screech she growled when they made love and it was something he longed to hear again.

He waited outside for the dog to return, breathing the clear air and letting the bright stars ease his thoughts. For such a big animal Argos moved quietly and suddenly appeared at his side as if he'd just materialized. The dog pushed against him as a greeting and let out a groan that turned into a soft growl as he turned his head at something that had caught his attention.

"Already?" cursed Perdiki to himself as he quickly grabbed his small sack of things from the hut, threw out the coffee, cleaned up any signs of occupancy and ran diagonally through the vineyard with the big dog following closely behind. There was as yet no sound of pursuit, but he knew they were somewhere back there.

CHAPTER 8

The Old Man and Spiro

"The hut where Perdiki stayed so briefly was like the cabin of this boat," the old man said as he took a final sip of his coffee. "He'd been around boats and would have been comfortable there for a while."

"But he had to keep running."

"They wouldn't let him perch anywhere. But enough of this story for a while. I need tsipouro and my voice needs a rest. You've been as quiet as a stone, so you should have plenty of voice." The old man took two thin glasses from the cabinet above the sink, pumped a couple of strokes of water into each and then poured it down the sink. "That should be enough *nero*," he said, "Now the *Tsipouro*. Did you know that tsipouro was first made by monks on Mount Athos in the fourteenth century? I think of it as the true holy water." He half-filled each glass with the clear liquid from the plastic coca cola bottle, and handed one to me. "Stin ighia sou," he said as a toast and clinked my glass before we each took a long drink. The Tsipouro burned my throat, then my stomach, and as a finale planted a pain in my chest.

The old man coughed and stamped his hand, hard, on the counter. He shook his hand, complaining, "Now my hand hurts, but at least it distracts from the pain of this devil's idea of Tsipouro. It has no relation to what was made by monks." He reached up into the cabinet for two more glasses and filled them with water. "Drink this," he choked, handing me one of the water glasses. "It won't stop the pain but it will make it easier to finish the rest of the Tsipouro." He held the plastic coca cola bottle up close to examine it. "At least there's nothing dead floating in it."

"Will this kill us?" I asked, holding my drink up to the lantern to peer through it. The old man quickly grabbed my hand and pulled it away.

"You don't want to get that too near the flame."

"What do we do?"

"We don't have a choice," the old man said. "If we pour it overboard we might kill all the fish." He clinked his glass against mine. "Good luck to us," he grunted, and finished the rest of his drink. Seeing that I hadn't followed suit, he pushed the lip of his glass against the bottom of mine. "Drink," he said.

It was terrible. This time it made me breathless and I had an immediate headache that only receded when I took a gulp of water. When I could finally breathe normally, I realized I'd become instantly drunk.

The old man said, "Tell me about you, Spiro Glaros."

At first, everything was blurry and it was difficult to start. Finally, I managed to croak out, "I thought you already knew."

"Don't be funny with me. I know who you are but I don't know why you have suddenly appeared on this island. Did you come straight to Mythos from Canada?"

"*Ochi*, no," I answered. "I was in Athens for a year. It was difficult."

"Poh poh poh," he said raising an eyebrow with a sense of irony, "Difficult? What kind of difficult in Athens? Did you trip on one of our cracked sidewalks? Difficult? What is it that you do for a living that you have so few words?"

"I'm a writer."

He poured two more drinks from the plastic coca cola bottle. "Stin ighia sou," he said, tipping back his glass and taking a cautious sip. He noticed that I hadn't picked up my drink and frowned. "Drink, damnit." He shook his head. "Panagia-mou, a writer who doesn't talk. What's next, a politician who doesn't steal? Drink and tell me your story."

CHAPTER 9

Spiro
The Situation

It was cold in the little apartment in Athens that winter because no one in the old building was paying the tenant's fees that went for oil. We huddled in our little flats under blankets, waiting for spring and not much else. Occasionally, I visited retired old Doctor Markopolis, on the third floor, but otherwise I only saw my neighbors in the hall, and when I asked how they were their response was always, "You know, the situation."

The cold always woke me early in the morning, and I'd rush down the street to the bread bakery, trying to keep warm in a thin summer jacket and lightweight jeans. The fish market next to my apartment building would still be closed and even the café on the corner where the old anarchists had their morning coffee wouldn't have yet opened. But there was always new graffiti on the walls because the street artists worked at night. The young anarchists took up the most wall space, with stark, black and white posters about meetings, memorials and demonstrations. Some of it had slashes of red for the blood that was being shed in the streets.

Occasionally, I'd find a saying or symbol sloppily spray-painted on a wall, but mostly the graffiti was well executed because it wasn't a particularly messy anarchy. At demonstrations the anarchists were the ones who were always as prepared as an army going into battle. They carried gas masks and their pockets were filled with packets of soothing cream to hand out to anyone caught in a wave of tear gas. They knew where to run and hide as surely as cats in the jungle.

Although the anarchists put up a lot of graffiti, it was a movement mostly without words. There was no message, just the knowledge that Greece was back in the hands of the Germans and people were starving in the streets. It hadn't been like this since the last time

Germany came to visit. If you were an anarchist, you threw rocks and yelled and maybe somebody would notice and do something about the situation. In the meantime you survived.

In the bakery I'd buy a round ring of sesame koulouri for breakfast. When I paid, the woman behind the counter always handed me something to sample. She assumed I was hungry. Everybody was hungry that winter. Hungrier than me because I didn't have to be there. I was in Athens because I'd saved a few bucks to get from Vancouver to Greece, planning to work part-time in my cousin's bar while I finished writing another book. I wasn't making much on the sailing novels because the genre was slipping out of fashion, but I kept churning them out because they were easy to write and paid the bills. I'd spent so much time around boats that the words slipped out without much reflection or even planning. In an instant I could summon up the feeling of bringing the Haiku into port in the late evening, with only the channel lights and a misted-over moon for guidance. Once I'd gotten that far, a plot would reveal itself as clearly as the course on a chart.

When Cousin Manoli offered me a job in his bar, he'd thrown in an apartment in Athens as part of the deal, and it looked like the perfect course for the next year of my life. A few hours of work a day and the rest of the time I could be writing or wandering Athens. But just as my plane touched down at Venizelos airport the Greek economy collapsed and along with it my job. Manoli was fighting to keep his business alive and was taking most of the bartending shifts himself. He'd already laid off two waiters and was barely affording the three who were left. But he let me have the apartment anyway because there was no one to rent it.

I had half of the advance on the new book, but I wouldn't see the balance until I delivered the completed manuscript to the publisher and that was months off, so I left most of the money in the bank back in Vancouver and lived on as little as possible. I was trying to stretch out my funds because once the book was done, I planned to spend some time on the island of Mythos, where there was a family house where I could live rent-free. Once I was on the island I didn't want to be tied to any work, even though that was currently all that kept me anchored to the ground.

I'd drifted away from my friends in Vancouver or maybe it was just that I had nothing left to say to them. Things happen, the world doesn't necessarily spin the way it's supposed to and it had turned me into a distant planet floating high above everything, so high that for a while I was barely an observer. By the time I left Vancouver, my ties had become so tenuous that I wasn't sure whether anyone would know I was gone except for my agent. Harold knew everything and he was the one who'd told me to get out of town.

We were sitting at a dim sum restaurant in Richmond, near enough to the airport for him to have lunch with me between flights. "You need another world, Spiro," he said. "This one's gone sour on you." He looked down at his plate. "Seriously. Why not write the book somewhere else?"

I'd travelled to Greece on that suggestion and Harold had been right. I was slowly feeling less numb, less clamped down. In the evenings, I'd sit in my cousin's taverna and take notes for the next day's writing, or watch people engage with each other. Although I couldn't usually hear the words, their expressions often showed a bitter resignation and a simmering anger that slipped out into the air. It was part of living in a nation that was economically defeated. But I didn't feel part of it or part of them. I could see, but it didn't penetrate. It was as if I were watching an old black and white film that flickered and popped on a screen just above the stage in an old theatre. But, the movie made no sense except as a visual display.

There was a night, though, when the moon must have risen oddly or the stars slipped out of place because I could feel a release as I locked the door of the apartment behind me and stepped out into the hall with a camera in my pocket. I heard explosions outside, but instead of being scared I felt enervated. The night street was roaring with the noise of a demonstration. I had no business being in the midst of it but I needed to try to feel what was going on. I needed to feel something.

The police stood in the street like storm troopers, carrying big plastic shields, tear gas canisters and guns. They couldn't fight off the creeping poverty so they fought the students instead. The burnt-plastic smell of tear gas was immediately in my throat and my eyes streamed with tears.

The demonstration raged in front of me in the cobbled streets between the old buildings. Something boomed a few blocks down Harilau Trikoupi, followed by a flash of fire and then a mob of students ran toward me. I'd expected to photograph only the facelessness of the police hiding behind their masks, but instead my camera caught the demonstrators running down the side streets and ducking into cafes and restaurants where the proprietors hid them amongst the patrons. A girl fell as I took her picture, her face searing its way onto the digital frame as surely as if it had been burned there. It was the indelible tattoo of the frustration of a revolution with nowhere to go.

She hit the pavement and slammed into the pitted marble stairway in front of my apartment building. I shot three rapid frame pictures as the girl fell, then stuffed the little Leica into my pocket and knelt to help her. With a tissue, I wiped away a slow trickle of blood that was running from under her black toque. When I tried to remove the knitted cap she grabbed my wrist and spoke rapidly in Greek, "There is no time for that. If you really want to help me, please just get me to my feet. I can't stay here."

Down the street, blue lights blinked on top of a prowling police car. Most of the demonstrators had vanished and the street was nearly empty except for the smoke from tear gas canisters. But the police needed arrests as retribution for the Molotov cocktails that were hurled by the black-clad anarchists at the head of the crowd and they'd grab whoever they could find.

I put an arm around the girl's waist and pulled her to her feet. She leaned heavily against me, hanging onto my hand while trying to support herself.

"Anything hurt?" I asked.

"Everything hurts but if I can walk that's enough." She let go my hand and pushed herself away but immediately threw an arm around me as she nearly collapsed. Her full weight landed in my arms and I held her in an embrace to keep her from falling again. The blue lights twirling on the top of the police car were flashing along the nearby buildings. From the police car a bright spotlight was being shone in the doorways as they hunted for someone to arrest. If we didn't move quickly it would be us.

"My apartment is right here," I said. "In this building. If we get inside, you can clean up and rest until you feel better."

"I don't know you," she said hesitantly.

"Don't worry," I glanced toward the approaching police car. "I'm a lot safer than them."

"Yes, okay," she said. Her forehead wrinkled, somehow out of synch with her words as if her thoughts were miles ahead of what she was saying. "How far up is your flat?"

"Ground floor. It's easy. Just these stairs."

"You will have to hold me."

"I know. We'd better be quick."

"I need to know your name," she said. "In case I don't make it up the stairs I want to know whose arms I died in."

"Spiros Glaros."

"Spiro," she said. "You are dancing with the bleeding Anastasia Milonas. You may call me Anastasia because you are holding me so closely." She attempted a laugh, but didn't seem to have the strength. "Let's go, Spiro," she rasped in a voice filled with pain and fear. "I need to lie down."

Anastasia was small enough for me to bear most of her weight as we climbed the stairs. She moaned softly with each step and when I reached in my pocket for the key she nearly fell and I had to wrap both arms around her for a few seconds until she regained her balance. I let go with one arm long enough to get the key into the lock, push the chipped black metal door open and close it with my hip.

As the door closed behind us and we were finally safe, Anastasia suddenly ran out of strength and I had to carry her to the old sofa. She was pale and shivering as I pulled off her toque to see the source of the trickle of blood that was again trickling down her forehead. There was as much sweat as blood.

Out in the street the demonstration must have started up again because through the window we could hear the sound of thuds as Molotov cocktails hit their storefront targets.

I covered Anastasia with a blanket from my bed and wet a clean washcloth from the bathroom. When I wiped away the blood on her forehead it revealed a small gash. I used antiseptic cream and a bandage from my travel pack to patch the cut and then held her hand trying to reassure her.

There was shouting from the alley behind my building and a scream that came from someone's intense pain. I tried to ignore it and keep my attention focussed on helping the girl.

"Spiro," she asked between chattering teeth, "my hero, do you have any brandy or whiskey?"

Her forehead showed a wrinkle that was out of place on such a young girl and her skin was that light green that olive skins turn instead of pale. I worried about shock but decided to go with my instincts and half-filled a small glass of Metaxa from the bottle I'd bought when I first moved into the apartment. Anastasia held out her hand to take the glass, but it was shaking so hard that I had to hold it to her lips so that she could drink without spilling the brandy. She held her hand around mine as she drank, as if it were she who was steadying me.

"Nothing," Anastasia whispered to herself, as the explosions continued. "Nothing at all."

"Does that help?" I asked.

She looked at me quizzically.

"The brandy, is it calming you down?"

"Oh, yes, thank you. It is just what I need." Her big, nearly-black eyes studied me. "I don't know you and I can't see into you. Your face, I don't know. Who are you? What do you do besides save me?"

"What if we take care of you, first? Then we can talk and I'll have some brandy, too."

"I just want to lie here until the world settles down."

"I understand but we need to take care of your injuries first. What is hurting you?"

"My side, maybe my ribs, I don't know. My leg is sore, too, on the knee and more. I need to look but ..."

"I can go into the other room."

"No. That's not it. I'm just a little scared to move. Would you be embarrassed if I asked you to help me?" She stared straight into my eyes as she spoke, weighing the effect her words had on me, wondering whether I really wanted to help or simply get her out of my apartment quickly.

"Of course I'll help you. And, please, relax. You can stay here as long as you like."

Those eyes, again. "How did you know what I was thinking? You are reading me. I don't understand how that's possible when we know nothing about each other. At least tell me something about you."

"I'm a writer."

"Are you a serious writer?"

"They pay me."

"What do you write? Are you a journalist? Is that what you do?"

"Ah, Anastasia, this is going to be a long story, so let's see first if you need a doctor."

"Are you going to write about me?"

"I'm not a journalist. I write novels."

Another huge explosion went off in the street and a new round of loud voices and screams followed. I clearly heard a policeman shout, but his words were made incoherent by a series of small explosions and when they ceased, all I could hear was cursing. I lifted the blanket off Anastasia, looking closely for the first time at who had landed on my doorstep. Once I got past her huge dark eyes, I saw a girl with a face that was still forming. She appeared to be in her early twenties, early enough that her cheeks were still losing the last vestige of teenage puffiness that would settle down to flatter planes in time. Everything on her face kept leading me back to her eyes. Above them sat eyebrows that were thick, young thick and not yet shaped. There were dark shadows under her eyes. Her mouth was small and had the barest brush of lipstick on it.

She was wearing a thick black sweater that hid much of her shape but hinted at full breasts and a slim waist. The slam against my doorstep had ripped her black jeans at the hip and knee and the skin that showed through was raw and bloody.

"We need to take care of this," I said.

"I know. Help me take these pants off, please. This is no time for modesty and I'm a woman, not a child." She unsnapped and unzipped her jeans, then lifted her hips, with a sharp cry. "Please. Pull them off."

Carefully, I worked her pants down over her legs trying to hold the material so that it wouldn't scrape her wounds. There were three places where the skin was raw and bloody, the ones that I had seen on her hip and a small one on her upper thigh. Her panties had shifted to one side at the crotch and I tried not to look at the dark patch of hair as I covered her again with the blanket, "Stay for a minute," I said. "Those scrapes need to be cleaned. I have to turn on the hot water and while it's heating we can see what else is hurt."

"My side," she said. "It hurts like hell and so does my arm."

"We'll look at those in a minute. Hold on," I said, hurrying to the kitchen where the switch for the water heater was located.

"Can you help me sit up?" she said when I returned. "I need to get this sweater off. If you pull it up from the back and over my head I won't have to raise my arms too much."

"Of course." With my arm behind her for support, Anastasia moved as little as possible as I took off her heavy, black sweater. Under it she was wearing a light tee shirt that had a small blood spot just below her right breast. When she rolled the shirt up far enough to reveal the source of the blood, I could see that it was only a small cut.

"Another minute or two and the water will be hot," I said. "Then we'll take care of all of it. So tell me something about you. Do you live nearby?"

"I did until I lost my apartment. Now, I'm staying with my sister in Pireas."

"Do you need to call her? I have a cellphone."

"Only if you want to get rid of me."

"Relax, Anastasia. I'll help you and if we need a doctor there's an old retired one who lives upstairs and he's a friend. I was just concerned that your sister would be worried about where you are."

"She doesn't keep track of me or anyone else. My sister just seems to float along oblivious to everything."

I'd been inhabited by the same feeling for the last year, but I kept the thought to myself. Instead I asked, "What does she do?"

"She's a dancer, always in class, always dressed the part."

"And you, Anastasia? What do you do?"

"I make noise. Greece is broke and the Germans are helping by choking us like so many chickens. So we make noise. It's the situation. When I was in school, I was a painter. A good one, a really good one. But now, I make noise."

While she was talking, I filled a bowl with hot water and found a clean wash cloth on the shelf in the tiny bathroom. I let her keep talking as I cleaned the small cut just below her right breast. It had already stopped bleeding and only required a small band aid.

There was some kind of chanting outside, something that sounded like what you would hear in the Greek Orthodox Church. It made me expect to smell incense. Instead all I caught was a whiff of tear gas, so I left the girl for a minute to close the window.

"Why are you really here?" she asked. "Why Greece and why now?"

"I came here to become invisible for a while so that I could finish the damn book I'm writing. I'm not here for the revolution or whatever it is that's going on outside. That was all starting to happen just as I arrived. All I really want to do is finish the damn book."

"What is this damn book?"

"I've been writing a series of novels about sailing. That's how I make my living." Another explosion rocked the street. "It doesn't seem very important in the midst of this."

"Don't you like to write?"

"Most of the time, but I'm tired of doing these books. I want to write something different, maybe better. I just don't know what yet."

"Think you'll find it here?"

"Not in Athens. Or at least I didn't think so until tonight. My plan is to finish this book and then head to the island of Mythos. Do you know it?"

"Everybody knows that island. It's where they sent the exiles. They say the people there are backward and that they're all political."

"Careful with that. I have family from Mythos."

"Are they backward and political?" Her thick eyebrows raised as she laughed.

Anastasia suddenly pulled the blanket away from her legs. "Finish with me," she implored. Her hand grabbed my arm. "I want to be done with this and sleep for a while. Please, Spiro."

"Of course," I said.

As casually as I could, I pulled her panties back over her triangle of curly black hair before I began, which made her smile and pull me down to kiss my cheek. "You're a sweet man, Spiro," she said.

It took only a few minutes to clean her scrapes and anoint them with antiseptic cream. "Let's not bandage these yet," I said. "First I want to see if there's anything else. Do you think you can stand?"

"With help. I'm a little shaky."

I put an arm behind her back and guided Anastasia to her feet. She held on while I turned her around to look for other injuries. There was one further scrape on the back of her thigh that I cleaned and smeared with antiseptic cream and then I got her to walk while I steadied her to see what else was wrong. She was able to limp and it was obvious that it was painful. She said her ribs hurt on one side, and I felt for anything obviously broken, but found nothing. The arm that she was favoring was badly bruised but to my untrained hands it didn't seem that there was anything broken, just the pain of a bad slam.

A series of shouts penetrated the closed window and then it grew very quiet.

"I think you're okay," I said, "but I don't really know very much. It would be a good idea if I let my friend, the retired doctor, take a look at you tomorrow just to be sure. It's too late now to call him."

"Are you inviting me to stay here tonight?"

"If you're comfortable about it."

"Comfortable with you, Spiro, my hero? You saved me and you don't even know me. Maybe you should be scared of me."

"Scared of a pretty girl in her underwear? What kind of hero would I be?"

That absurd moment when I was laughing with this bruised stranger in her underwear in the little apartment in Exarchia, with the demonstrations raging around us in the streets and the police and everybody out of control, and Greece flailing and reeling, and my goddamn book not done, it was this beautiful, strange girl in her underwear in my life without warning, it was at this honest moment that I was in love.

One minute later, the loud knocking began and I was back in Greece, in the middle of a night of demonstrations, with the police at my door and the strange girl they were probably looking for in her underwear in my apartment. And still I was in love with her.

CHAPTER 10

The Old Man and Spiro

While I'd been talking to the old man, a wind had come up, one of those wild Aegean winds that slash their way down the mountains, corkscrewing through the ravines and stabbing the sea with tremendous gusts clockwise, then anti-clockwise, so that a boat couldn't sit comfortably, even behind the breakwater. The wooden fishing boat, where we were sitting, rode better than a modern fiberglass hull but it wasn't immune to the sudden onslaught of waves that came in around the breakwater whenever the wind shifted. When the old man saw that I was completely at home in the rock and roll of the sea, he laughed.

"So you really do know something about boats," the old man said. "I wondered because I've heard it sometimes happens that writers fill books with things they know nothing about."

"I lived on a sailboat in a marina near Vancouver for several years and sailed the coast of British Columbia."

"But now?"

"Now I'm here."

"That simple?"

"Nothing is that simple. You know that."

"What about the girl, this Anastasia?"

"Tell me more about Perdiki first."

CHAPTER 11

Perdiki

The musician and the big dog made it to the Northwest side of the island before morning. They waited and watched for four hours, hidden in the dense brush near their destination, watching and listening to be sure they hadn't been followed. Man and dog leaned against each other for warmth watching the stars dim out and the sun begin to add structure to the lightening sky. The trees blackened and the clouds greyed long before color highlighted the horizon and the world became distinct enough to make out the lines of Pharaoh's odd house.

Its roof was a huge, flat boulder that shot out from a cliff face twenty feet above the ground. The back of the house was the face of the cliff, Stone walls had been built around the perimeter of the boulder and in front there was a huge wooden door that was half the width of the house. The door opened a crack as Perdiki and Argos approached.

"Inside, quickly," a voice called from within. "What the hell is that?" he asked as Argos passed into the house behind Perdiki. "They didn't tell me you were travelling with a monster. Watch out for the …" Before he could finish his sentence, two, scrawny, grey cats shrieked out of the house and disappeared into the brush.

"What the hell, I wanted them out for a while anyway. They were getting far too fat and complacent." His voice was high-pitched, with a light crackle. "Let me get a light going so I can see you." He struck a match, illuminating his own face, which was out of an Egyptian tomb painting. It was all sharp angles, with high cheekbones and long, planar cheeks, with a nose chiseled to an isosceles triangle. When the lantern was lit, it revealed that Pharaoh was a wiry man dressed in faded brown pants and a blurry-grey shirt. He walked with a limp that was a souvenir from the torture he'd undergone during the Greek Civil War.

He spoke again with his crackled high voice. "Brandy," he said. "Then food. I made a stew last night and there should be breakfast enough for your monster, too." He looked warily at the huge dog. "Does it bite?"

"Not yet." Perdiki patted the dog on his head. "His name is Argos. We jumped ship together."

"Is he a communist?"

"He is a dog and knows only what smells good."

"He's smarter than us then, isn't he?" Pharaoh laughed. "Sit down and let's eat. See that tin bowl on the counter? Can you ladle some stew into it for Argos?" He looked over at Perdiki with a grin. "I can see that he is smart but he doesn't eat at the table, does he?"

"He eats on the floor so that we can't steal his food. Once he's finished, though, he may demand a seat so he can steal ours."

"Does he drink brandy?"

"Ask Argos. I'm not his interpreter."

They both laughed and greeted each other in the traditional way, repeating the phrases that are always said. "It's good to see you again, Perdiki, my friend. *Kalo sorises.* Good arrival. Well landed."

"*Kalo sas vrikame* …Good to find you."

"I've heard you became very famous. They always said you could sing."

"And you can see how well I'm living."

"*Veveo*s, truly. It must be wonderful."

"And you, Pharaoh?"

"Bigger boat now, but it's the same. Fish or no fish."

"Your wife?"

"Gone to Athens to help her mother die."

"How is she doing?"

"Not much success, it's been two years and she's still alive."

Pharaoh poured two short glasses of brandy from a tall, rope-covered jug he kept on the floor beside the table. Raising his glass, he hesitated as if he were about to make an elaborate toast but instead said simply, *stin ighia sou* and they both drank.

They talked so little while they ate that the loudest sound in the room was Argos slurping his dinner. Finally, when they were done with the food and having a second brandy, Pharaoh turned to

Perdiki. "So what now, my friend? I can get you off the island to Samos, but after that what will you do?"

"Are the twins still in the same place?"

"Yes. Lonnie got married and lives with his wife in Samos. That's who you'll see. He's building boats in Agios Isidoros with his cousin."

"And his brother?"

"Working with him as far as I know."

"Lefteri's okay, but he's always been a little …"

"Goofy."

"Yes, goofy. But he's okay. Depends on what you want him to do."

Their conversation was interrupted by Argos rising from where he'd been resting after dinner. He stood at the door, staring at it.

"Does that mean anything?" asked Pharaoh.

"I think he just needs to go out."

"Let me make sure we're alone." Pharaoh pushed the big dog away from the door and Perdiki held him while Pharaoh opened it a crack. When he saw nothing, he swung it open the rest of the way and stepped outside. "Let your monster go," he called in to Perdiki. "But you stay inside. This is making me very nervous."

Argos disappeared immediately into the brush as if he knew that he had to stay out of sight. Pharaoh could hear him rustling around, and then was silent for a minute or two before reappearing a few meters from where he'd entered the brush. Pharaoh slapped his hand against his side and the dog ran up to him. "Go, go," he urged, pushing Argos back into the house and closing the door quickly.

"Now my friend," he said to Perdiki, "I have to leave to be out fishing. It's not everyone who can spend his time running away from the police. Some of us have to make a living. Besides, if I vary from my routine someone might notice. I'm already late, but that happens sometimes when I'm a little hung over, so it won't be noticed."

"I understand," said Perdiki. "I need to get out of here before I fuck up your life. I'm the hottest of potatoes."

"*Veveos*, truly." Pharaoh shook his head. "We need to get you off the island before you become fried potatoes. You can rest here, today while I'm out fishing, but when it's dark you need to leave." He took a last sip of brandy before continuing. "Listen to me, my friend," he said. "Do you remember the old tower, the one they call Drakano?"

"I remember it well. The ancient signal tower on a hill above the sea. Built in 500 BC they say."

"Can you find it easily?"

"Yes, I know the path. We picked thyme and sage there in the summer."

Pharaoh continued, "When you reach Drakano, if it looks safe, work your way down to the cove at Agia Paraskevi. Someone will meet you at the dock. If there's been a problem and no one is there, take Thoma's boat. It's the blue one on the end. He broke his leg so he won't need it right now. Thoma leaves the key under the seat in the cockpit. Go straight out a mile so you miss the rocks, and then head East North East so that you come up just west of Karlovasi. From there, continue up the coast to Agios Isidoros."

Pharaoh put his hand on Perdiki's shoulder. "Don't get caught, my friend. The only real solution is to leave Greece until things change. We'll find a way to get you out. You can probably be able to get more done for the cause outside the country than in." Before Perdiki could object, he laughed and continued, "I know, I know, you're not a member of anything, but your songs do more than anything the rest of us seem to do."

Perdiki slept through most of the day but began to grow restless before nightfall. He felt trapped inside the house. Having been built against a cliff, there was no back way out. Argos seemed to pick up his mood and began pacing back and forth in front of the door.

"Better we wait outside for nightfall," he said to the dog. "If we were found inside this house there would be no way to run." He rubbed behind the big creature's ears. Argos groaned with pleasure.

"I don't know what would happen to you if they caught up with me, Argos," the musician said. "You jumped ship with a convicted songwriter and now you're on the run with him. There must be some laws against that. Are you a communist like the rest of my friends?" Argos cocked his massive head as Perdiki spoke, which made the man laugh. "My sentiments, exactly," he said.

Perdiki checked that his notebook was under his shirt, grabbed his little sack of provisions, opened the door and said, "Let's go. If they're waiting out there we're already caught. No sense in hesitating."

They moved quickly along a goat path that began a hundred meters from Pharaoh's house. When they finally stopped, it was to hide in the midst of a series of large boulders along the edge of a cliff that looked out over the sea. Drakano was visible from there, a tall cylindrical tower built of huge square stones. It was mostly intact, with only one corner blown away when the Turkish navy hit it with a cannonball during target practice in the nineteenth century.

Surrounding the tower was an archaeological dig that was slowly unveiling a small city that had existed somewhere in the distant past. Lengths of wall had been unearthed and the corner of what had been some kind of building was emerging. Work had stopped on the dig when the military junta took over the country and there should have been no one around, but Perdiki thought he saw movement beside the tower and at first hoped it was just a few of the goats that wandered free on this part of the island.

But goats don't wear uniforms and shout in voices that carried up to where Perdiki and Argos were perched. "They can't know where I am," he whispered to the dog. "It doesn't make sense. Even if they caught Pharaoh they wouldn't have gotten anything out of him. He didn't talk when they tortured him during the Greek Civil War and if anything he seems even tougher now. No, whatever they're doing, I don't think it has anything to do with us, Argos."

Perdiki gave him a few nuggets of dog food that were in the bottom of his sack and found an apple for himself. "We'll wait them out. You, dog, can contemplate whatever it is that dogs contemplate and I will think and maybe work for a while." He ruffed up the fur on the big Newfoundland's neck. "I wish my friend Stratos was here. Know anything about music, Argos?"

The air was sweet with the smell of thyme and Perdiki saw that he was surrounded by clumps of its purple flowers. He was reminded of the few days when he and Zev's daughter, Kiki, roamed the island searching for pleasure and finding it everywhere. They'd swum at the beach below Drakano and found bits of ancient pottery trapped in the reef that ran out from the shore.

He'd met Kiki the first time he'd been exiled to Mythos, when he'd been assigned by the authorities to live with a family in a small village. Dimitri and Vaso Pastis were good people and treated him as one of the family. They fed him, gave him advice and listened to his political ideas by the hour. Their three children jumped around him and made him their friend. Sometimes, when they'd close the windows and shutters, he'd play an old guitar and sing his songs for them, but softly because his music had been outlawed. It was on one of those nights that he'd first met their neighbor, Zev, the man who would meet him on the shore twenty years later when he jumped ship along with the big Newfoundland dog. With Zev was his daughter, Kiki.

Once a week along with the other exiles Perdiki had to report to the government officials in a building that was in a town on the other side of the island. It was a rough 20 kilometer hike over the mountains. The trail was steep and hung out over treacherous drops in places along a path that had first been forged by wild goats. Where there was no natural ford, it plunged straight through streams and zigzagged its way around huge boulders. The building where the interrogations were held was grey and rundown. He would be brought into the plain room, the one with nothing other than a chair for him and a table and chair for the officer who kept asking for names that he didn't have. It was unpleasant, but it was only once a week and nothing else seemed required of him until the day they started ringing the bell. The officer in the black suit, the one called Xenos, rang the bell each time Perdiki didn't answer a question, just before the iron bar struck. He remembered the second before the pain, before the heavy bar smashed an arm, a leg, an ear. He never knew where it would strike, only that damn bell announcing impending pain.

But that was in the past and it was the present that concerned the musician. Down below at the tower, the uniformed men were still milling around with no indication of what they were about, but at least it didn't seem as if they were actively searching for Perdiki. Feeling a little more secure, he lay back using Argos as a big pillow under his head intending to wait for the rest of the day to pass. He tried to think about the song he was writing but found himself dozing intermittently throughout the afternoon. Just before dark, he woke and saw that the uniformed men were no longer in sight. In case they might be travelling up the path, he worked his way deeper into the brush, with Argos following closely behind.

But the soldiers never appeared, and after a half hour of staying hidden he was convinced that they'd taken a different path, the one that ran along the coast. He was about to make his way through the brush back to the boulders when he heard someone softly whistling one of his tunes. Perdiki cautiously made his way out of the brush to where the man was waiting.

"You leave a trail like a bulldozer," a crackled high voice called.

"And you make more noise than one."

"I wanted you to hear me."

"You could have just shot off a cannon."

"That might have damaged Drakano," snapped Zev and then his expression became serious. "They still have my niece. They were tracking her when she brought your food. I guess they know that we're old friends and that I might be helping you. They were probably watching a lot of people, but this one paid off for them. They grabbed Maria just after she climbed over those big boulders that block the path. They'd seen her heading up into the hills with a sack and coming back without it. That's how they knew you were up there."

"And now?"

"They have Maria alone in a cell. You remember how they start. No food, the light never goes off, they wake you every hour."

"Anything else?"

"Not yet. So far, no torture. But it's coming. He's coming."

"How do you know all this?"

"My cousin is a guard. Today is his day off."

"And?"

"We're going to get her out. My cousin won't be there because we don't want him caught up in this. We need him to keep working at the prison. He's our only source of information."

"We?"

"There's always a we, and we have people to help get her out of the jail. Your part is to take Maria to Samos with you."

"Is Pharaoh going to take us?"

"No. They would notice he was gone and then his life, here, would be over. Once we break Maria out of prison, if any of us leave the island at the same time we can never come back while this government is in power."

"Then you could become a songwriter like me. I'm not safe anywhere in Greece."

"You, Mister Songwriter, will need to take the boat Pharaoh told you about, the one that belongs to Thoma, the fisherman with the broken leg. You know where the boat key is?"

"Pharaoh told me. But the big question is where in Samos should I land?"

"Not in any of the big towns like Vathi, Pythagorion or Karlovasi. Too many people, too many police. Do you know Agios Isidoros?"

"The boatbuilding village?"

"That's the one. It's Southwest along the coast, after Karlovosi. No one lives there anymore, but there are still two brothers who drive down from their homes every day to the bay to build boats."

"The twins?"

"Yes, those two. They can hide you until we set something up to get you out of Greece."

"Do you know if there's a chart of Samos onboard?"

"Not likely. Thoma has been a fisherman all this life. His chart is in his head."

"I guess I can head for the lights of Karlovasi and then follow the coast. But how will I know Agios Isidoros in the dark?"

"Stay as close to the shore as you dare and watch for channel markers. There are two other bays you'll pass before you get to Agios Isidoros and they all look the same in the dark. At the entrance to each bay there are two lighted markers. The traditional red on the right and green on the left. As long as you count and head into the third bay you should be okay. If we can get a message to the twins, one of them will set a white lantern beside the red light at Agios Isidoros and that should help. If there is no extra lantern, it just means we couldn't get through to them. Hopefully, you'll be in the right bay. If no one is there, tie up to the dock and when the brothers show up in the morning tell them who you are. They will help you and they'll also find a safe place for Maria."

Zev stopped and thought for a minute before he continued. "Once it gets dark, make your way to the boat and wait there until I bring Maria to you. We will break her out of jail late tonight. Just keep low and be ready to leave as soon as we arrive." He looked up at the sky. "I think the weather will be with you, but the wind is fickle and can turn nasty without much warning. If it gets bad, when you get to Samos you can duck into the first bay but we don't have anybody in that one so you'll be on your own."

"Thank 'we' for me."

"You'd be thanking yourself."

CHAPTER 12

The Old Man and Spiro

"Now, it's your turn again," the old man said. He stood slowly, unkinking his body and adjusting it to the night. "But we need to walk a little because my glue is setting and soon I won't be able to move at all."

The wind had settled down as quickly as it had come and the night was now nearly still. We walked along the waterfront, past a dozen small boats and a ferry that was parked for the night. A fishing boat came into the harbor, its engine thumping slowly as it pulled alongside the dock. A young boy jumped off with a line in his hands, expertly looped it around a bollard and then ran to the stern to catch another line thrown by the captain.

"That was me as a boy," the old man said. "My father took me out of school when the fish were running hard."

"You were a fisherman?"

"Yes and some other things as well, but there is only so much of this night and I want to hear the rest of your story. Later, maybe, I'll tell you mine." He made a face. "Is there any more of that awful tsipouro left? Let's go back to the boat and see if we can poison ourselves further before you begin."

CHAPTER 13

Spiro

It began with the pounding on the door growing louder and Anastasia hiding her ripped jeans under a cushion and sitting back on the couch with the blanket pulled over her bare legs. Athens had been roaring around us all night, but this was the loudest sound. There were shouts of "Open the door," and more pounding with what sounded like a stick.

I'd been living too quiet a life to be prepared for any of this. The last time I'd felt this kind of fear was in the middle of a storm in the Haiku. We were trapped in a narrow passage between an island and the mainland of British Columbia with the wind coming head-on, forcing me to tack back and forth every couple of minutes.

But there was no tacking against whatever was pounding on my door in Athens. I finally unlocked it and was pushed to the floor by the fury of the charge of two policemen. They were dressed in riot gear that let them barely fit through the doorway. They wore helmets with face shields, bulky armor and each carried a large, wooden baton. "Who are you?" they demanded, but before I could answer they turned their attention to Anastasia. "That one," the taller of the two policemen said. "She was right in the front."

He turned back to me. "You," he snapped. "Who are you?"

"I'm a Canadian," I said, holding up my passport as if it were a shield, as if it gave me some kind of immunity. "This is my apartment. What do you want?"

"Who is this girl?"

"What do you want?" I insisted, remaining the outraged foreigner.

"Shut up," the other uniform spoke up. "You answer the questions."

"My name is Spiro Glaros and I'm a writer."

"Journalist?" asked the shorter of the two policemen, suddenly wary of me.

"Yes," I lied. "For the Globe and Mail. It's a Canadian newspaper."

"Are you here to write about the demonstration?"

"All that noise outside? I'm not interested unless it affects my life." I looked at him, pointedly. "Is it about to affect my life?"

"What about the girl?" he demanded. "She was in the demonstration, right at the front throwing Molotov cocktails."

"That's not possible," I told him. "She's been here with me all night."

"Shut up," the policemen snarled. He stared at Anastasia for a long moment before he spoke to her. "What is your name?"

"Anastasia Milonas," she answered trying to keep her voice steady. "I've been here with my boyfriend all night." A note of anger rose in her voice. "Is there something wrong with that? Do you want to know what we did, too?"

"Get up, you're coming with us."

"No, I'm not. I'm a Greek citizen and I have rights. I don't have to go anywhere with you. I haven't done anything wrong."

The shorter of the two policemen grabbed Anastasia's injured arm and roughly pulled her from the couch. The shriek she let out of pain gave away nothing because the yank on her arm was vicious enough that it would have been a natural reaction even if she weren't injured. She managed to keep the blanket around her lower body so that her scrapes were hidden from view.

"Leave her alone, you bastard," I shouted as I stood up. "What the hell's the matter with you?"

The taller of the policemen shoved me against the wall and pinned me there with his club against my neck. "Shut up," he said, "Mister Canadian."

"I guess I will write about the demonstration, after all. You'll have to let go of me so I can get my notebook. I wouldn't want to misspell your names."

"You can write whatever the hell you want," the policeman said, "She's under arrest and Mister Canadian, you're under arrest too. Write that!"

"Asshole," I mumbled under my breath, but not softly enough. The club suddenly was released from my neck and though I saw it coming I couldn't duck fast enough to miss its swing at the side of my head. And that was it. I was out.

Then there was a long blank, a sense of intense pain and nothing until someone was calling my name from far away. When I tried to move there was a sharp pain just above my right ear and as my mind began to function everything seemed blurry. There was an annoying sound I couldn't identify until I opened my eyes and saw a young man in an expensive grey suit, tapping a pencil against a notebook, which was probably deliberately done to awaken me. I also saw that I was in a jail cell.

"Are you Spiros Glaros?" He asked when he saw my eyes blink open. "My name is Peter Eaton and I'm from the Canadian consulate," When I didn't react, he took an exasperated breath and repeated everything, slowly and deliberately.

"Yes," I finally managed to say. My words came out like porridge, slurred and soupy. "I'm Spirolas Glaros and I'm from Vancouver. Do you need an address or anything? My passport is in the apartment where I'm staying." It felt as if I were talking in slow motion.

"Not a problem," the young bureaucrat said. "The police showed me the ID in your wallet. We can deal with the formalities later."

"I need a doctor," I managed to force out. "I was hit on the side of my head with a club and I think I have a concussion. Can you get me out of here?"

"Already taken care of. As soon as you can stand up, we're gone."

"There was a girl with me."

"Um, yes, isn't there always," mumbled the young bureaucrat, to himself. "She called us," he said aloud, "that's how we knew about your um predicament."

"Is she here?"

"Bailed out, I think. Said she would contact you. That's all I um know."

"Am I being charged with anything?"

"No. They just um held you without charges for a while."

"They can do that?"

"Apparently so. Best not to um bring it up to them. Just be neutral and get yourself checked out of here. Anything we need to talk about can wait until we're on the way to the hospital. I'm taking you straight to emergency, unless you object."

"Of course not, and thank you."

"Let me give you a hand up. I can't stand the um stink of this place."

I had barely noticed my surroundings, the grey, streaked walls and the bars penning me in. In the porridge that was still my brain I hadn't quite accepted that I was in jail. But the door to the cell was open and with the young bureaucrat's help I managed to stand and after a minute of dizziness and nausea, was able to shakily walk back into the world.

CHAPTER 14

The Old Man and Spiro

As we returned to the boat after a short walk, the old man shook his arms and wiggled his fingers. "Everything has to be constantly reminded that it is important to keep in motion. Your agent understood this when he told you to find a new place. If you don't keep moving, it's too easy to get stuck."

We were about to pass a very big fishing boat, the kind that actually makes money. It was probably a third larger than anything else on the dock and stood with its empty hold high in the water. Once it was filled with fish it would sit a lot lower.

"My moving could use a little lubrication. Let's stop here, for a minute," the old man said. "This is Tony Mouganis' boat and I know there's always a bottle of brandy in the cabinet beside the outside wheel." Beckoning me to follow him, we stepped aboard. The old man opened a battered wood cabinet on the outside cabin wall beside the wheel. He withdrew two cloudy-looking shot glasses and a three quarters full bottle of three-star Metaxa brandy. "This is the cheap stuff they give out at funerals," the old man said. "But it's a lot better than that tsipouro that was trying its best to poison us." Placing the glasses on top of the cabinet he carefully filled them with hands that were remarkably steady for a man in his nineties. "I've been out on this boat with Pavlo many times. He won't mind if we take a little of this."

He held up his glass and indicated for me to do the same. "To the jailbird," he said, with a phlegmy laugh, clicking his glass to mine. "Drink up," he said. "You must need it after that long stretch in jail."

The brandy was rough, but after the damage done by the tsipouro I barely felt its burn.

"Now," the old man said, "let's get back aboard our own boat and I'll tell you about Perdiki in motion.

CHAPTER 15

Perdiki

The weather held until the sea turned choppy and the wind picked up enough that Perdiki and the girl had to hang onto the rail to keep from being thrown off their seats. It was a pitch-dark, starless and nearly-moonless night and they were bouncing so much that they could only see the lights of Karlovasi on the upkicks. It was enough, though, for Perdiki to occasionally get a bearing and then steer mostly by the dimly-lit compass. Its hand swung back and forth as the small fishing boat was bounced around by a sea that grew rougher with every passing minute, but he could still get a sense of their direction.

They were in the pilot house of the old ten-meter wooden fishing boat that they'd "borrowed" when they fled Mythos. Argos was stretched out at Perdiki's feet, comfortably back in the environment in which he had been raised. The girl, Maria, was huddled on a bench and had been quiet until the sea turned rough and then she began to hum softly to herself. When she finally spoke, it was as if she were coming out of a trance. Above the noise of the storm she shouted, "I'm okay and this doesn't scare me."

"Well, it scares me," Perdiki called back, grimly, as he fought to keep the boat on course.

"You should write a song about it."

"There are two kinds of songs, the ones in which you survive and the others. I can only write the first kind about this adventure."

Maria gave a forced laugh that had a catch to it and then she suddenly began to spew words as quickly as possible as if she were anxious to get rid of them. "I was very scared," she said. "They had me alone in a cell with no lights and they took away my clothes and there was no food or water and then the lights came on and someone would be staring in at me and I was naked and then the lights went off again and there were rats, I know there were rats. And they were going to rape me. They told me that. But first, they said, I needed to meet Xenos so that I could hear his bell." There was a sudden catch in her breath before she plunged back in. "Everything I'd heard could happen was about to begin." She stopped to breathe slowly and continued, "Then my uncle Zev and his friends, they came late at night when Xenos wasn't around and they were wearing masks and they tied up the guards and no one was killed or hurt and they got me out. They let out a lot of other people too. Uncle Zev gave me his shirt because they had taken my clothes and then we ran. The others scattered, but my uncle held my arm and we ran to the boat and then you and that big dog were here and Uncle Zev left and the engine started and maybe I am a little scared." She shivered. "I'm cold, too. And very scared. But not of this boat. I like this boat. It's just like my uncle's."

Perdiki had been so caught up in taking care of the boat that he hadn't thought about the girl and hadn't noticed that she was still wearing only Zev's shirt. Her bare legs looked cold and she was struggling, unsuccessfully, to hold a flap of the shirt between her legs for modesty. "I can't let go of the wheel," he said, "but look around. There might be something you can wrap around yourself." He thought for a minute and realized all that he wasn't saying. "Maria," he said, swinging the wheel away from a too-fast-approaching shore, "it's hard for me to talk because I have to concentrate on the sea and the boat, but I've been listening to everything you've been saying." He smiled, in case she could see it. "I'll save up all my responses until we reach the shore. Is that okay?" Before she could say anything, a huge wave broke over the bow and showered water over the windshield.

Perdiki turned his attention back to the boat and focussed on getting through the storm. When they finally neared land, with the lights of Karlovasi growing brighter, Perdiki held off changing course as long as possible until he finally swung the wheel, allowing the sea to throw a wave against the side of the boat that nearly swamped them. He was forced to turn away from the island to take the next big wave head on, so that the bow broke its way through and then he swung the wheel back toward the island. The sea smashed against the stern quarter of the boat as it rushed back toward the land. When he drew too close to the shore he swung the wheel again and headed back out. The maneuver was repeated again and again as he tacked back and forth, working his way up the coast. The lights of Karlovasi quickly faded until there was nothing to be seen besides water and dark shapes. Each time he'd swing in toward the island he'd look for the lights of the first of the three bays that Zev had described. He could make out the occasional dark shape, but no lights were visible. Perdiki worried that he would miss all three bays and he'd never thought to ask Zev about what lay beyond.

The girl managed to find a tarp to wrap around herself and as she warmed her body, the scenes that were flashing through her mind began to disperse. Almost everything she'd been warned could happen had almost happened. She'd heard the stories at home about the man with the bell. Their faces always changed when they spoke of him and they would grimace and twitch. Their thick eyebrows would press down and their eyes would grey and even their hair would seem to sag.

Sensing her distress, Argos pushed up against the girl and laid his big, woolly head in her lap. She rubbed behind his ears and even smiled when he gave out a sound that was somewhere between a soft growl and a groan, but the smile didn't last and the scenes kept returning until Perdiki's voice broke through her thoughts.

"Help me watch for lights," he called out over the sounds of the engine and wind. "Your uncle said there are three bays and the one we want is the third but I'm going to put into the first one we can find. It's too rough to be out here."

"I've been on this coast before," Maria called over the sound of the struggling engine. "I've even been in the first bay as well as Agios Isidoros. It was with my uncle when he had some work done on his boat."

"What do you remember?"

"Before we reached Agios Isidaros we stopped at the first bay to fix something on the engine. There are big rocks you have to watch out for in the middle of it. You can't see them, but they're in the center of the bay."

"Any houses?"

"Nothing. We needed to drop the anchor."

"Do you remember anything about the entrance to the bay?"

"It's very narrow with a marker on either side. Once you're past the markers it's straight until you hit the rocks."

"And if I don't want to hit the rocks?"

"Stay along the port bank and we should be okay. I don't know of any landmarks that we can pick out in the dark, so you'll have to do it by feel." For the first time, she looked up at him. "Do you want me to take us in? I was at the helm when I came here with my uncle."

"It's pretty rough."

"Not now. When we get through the entrance to the bay where it should be calmer you can give me the helm. I think I'll be able to find where we anchored my uncle's boat. There was a stump on shore where we tied a line to keep the boat from swinging when the tide changed. We can probably find it by starlight."

They said nothing more for the next half hour as they tacked back and forth along the coast searching for lights. The storm blew ceaselessly, mercilessly colliding with the boat on every quarter and there was nothing to be done about it, no magic cure, no place to pull over, no relief.

Only Argos didn't feel the strain. He was snoring as he slept pushed up beside the bench on which Maria sat huddled. When Perdiki finally saw a glimmer of red light in the distance, he called to Maria, "Better be alert. Wake the dog, too. He's pretty smart and he'll smell things we can't see."

"He makes me feel safe," she said in a voice Perdiki could barely hear. When she shook the big dog he stood, grumbling until he found his balance. His big black nose tested the air and found a feint smell of sage and pine that let him know they were approaching land, but there was nothing alarming on the wind and he settled back down again.

Perdiki spotted a flash of red as the boat pitched and rolled and the waves obscured the shore. "Can you see it … the light?"

"Yes. I think so," Maria called in a voice growing more confident in its tone. "I don't see the green one yet, but they never show up as well as red lights at night."

"Sing out when you see it," he called back. "We need both."

Perdiki fought the sea, trying to avoid another tack, but the waves were pushing the boat too rapidly toward the shore and he couldn't yet see a green light. The only hope was to bear slightly off to port of the red light, but he really wanted to see both lights, one on either side of the entrance before heading through the near-invisible gap.

There! The slightest hint of a green light appeared much closer than he'd expected or needed. He was much too near to it to be able to take the waves on the rear quarter of the boat as he'd planned, and if he didn't change course, they'd be hitting the side and pushing the boat into the shore. There was no choice but to tack out again away from the land, but also away from the lights, and when he was finally able to tack shoreward again, the lights were gone.

"I guess that was the first bay and we missed it," he called out to Maria.

"The second one is pretty close," she yelled over the sound of the storm. "Probably easier to head for it than go back."

"Have you been in there?"

"No. I know nothing about it."

"How far from there to Agios Isidoros?"

"Not much further."

The sea had gotten nastier and now each time they tacked, the windows were awash in seawater. For Perdiki and Maria, there was no getting comfortable, there was only hanging on. It was a solid boat, though, a seaworthy one and Perdiki regretted that he had not bothered to look at the transom to find her name before he boarded back in Mythos. It would have been comforting to be able to address the boat by name when imploring it to hold together and stay above the waves.

There. A light. This time a green one and a moment later a red one and he could see that the two markers were perfectly lined up.

"Better wake up Argos, again," he called. "I want to know if he smells something as we head in. He'll know if there are people or animals around."

There were no lights, only the green and red channel markers on either side of the boat as they passed between them. Ahead there was nothing. It was almost pitch black with only the barest of shadowy outlines on the starboard side of the wooden fishing boat to indicate land.

The swell quit as they entered the tiny harbor and it was suddenly very quiet. Perdiki throttled the engine back to a near-idle and they slowly glided through the dark night.

"This must be the second bay," Maria said, her voice now softer. "If it was Agios Isidoros we would be seeing anchored boats by now."

Perdiki let the boat move slowly toward the shore trying to peer through the dark sea for rocks until Argos suddenly rose and went out on deck. He held his massive head up to a wind that within the shelter of the bay was now just a soft breeze.

"I think he's found land for us," Perdiki laughed. He put the engine into reverse to stop their forward motion and then into neutral. "This is good enough because there may be rocks closer to shore. Can you hold the helm while I throw in a leadline to see how deep it is? There's no depth sounder on this old boat, so we have to do it the old-fashioned way."

While Maria sat at the wheel, Perdiki threw the weighted line over the side. When it stopped sinking, he pulled it back up, counting the knots that marked each meter of depth.

"*Endaxi*, we're okay here. I'll drop the anchor and then you put it in reverse to set it."

"I know," she said. "I've done this many times with Theo Zev."

When the anchor was set, they relaxed for the first time in many hours. The bay was completely deserted with no lights in sight. There was barely a ripple in the dark sea and nothing clearly in sight.

Argos began to get agitated and Perdiki realized he hadn't had a walk in hours. With a sigh, Perdiki undid the lines that held a small dinghy on top of the cabin and lowered it into the water.

"Are you okay for a few minutes if I take my big beast to shore for a quick walk?"

Her voice was hesitant. "I guess, but please be quick. I'm a little scared." He looked at her and realized that she still had the tarp wrapped tightly around herself and looked very small.

"See if you can find some clothes in one of the cabinets. Your uncle might keep something around."

"You're scared, too, aren't you?"

"Go find some clothes. We can talk when I get back."

"But you're scared. Right?"

"Maria, I'm scared. I was scared yesterday and the day before. It's how I live these days. But right now I'm more scared for you than for myself and I feel guilty as hell about this. It's my fault you're in trouble, that you've had to leave home and risk your life with me. For what? For my songs? Your life is more important. You... what do you do?"

"I don't know. I make cheese, I cook, I swim, I am alive. I appreciate. Doesn't all art need someone to appreciate it? That's me. I'm an audience."

Perdiki laughed. "Right now my audience will have to wait because my dog needs a walk. But when I come back, I just might entertain you with my answer."

Maria smiled, which made the musician more comfortable about leaving her alone. He hooked the steel ladder onto the rail and climbed down to the little dinghy. Argos jumped down to join him and nearly swamped the little boat when he landed. Maria was still laughing as Perdiki pushed the big dog to the stern of the dinghy and settled himself into rowing.

When the little boat was no longer in sight, Maria dropped the tarp she was wearing and took off her uncle's shirt which had somehow become soaked, although she didn't remember it happening. She stood naked, looking out into the dark night, pointing her body at Perdiki, knowing he couldn't see her but wishing it were otherwise.

CHAPTER 16

The Old Man and Spiro

"How do you know all this?" I asked the old man. We'd finished the dreadful tsipouro and he'd been brewing coffee while he talked.

"It's a small island," he said. "This is our information. It's more than history. Mythos, this island itself, plays a part, too. You'll see."

He handed me a cup of Greek coffee. "Try it. It couldn't be any worse than the tsipouro. *Lipon*, listen," the old man said. "This island is alive. I may have already told you that but now you have to think about it. You need to understand that if you're going to live here."

"I'm not living here. I'm just staying for a while."

"You're not the one making that decision."

"I'm not making any decisions."

"That's what I'm saying. Mythos will decide it for you. And maybe I will help."

CHAPTER 17

Spiro
The Wail of the Clarinet

After the arrest, everything changed. Although I still went out in the early morning I no longer looked at the latest graffiti and the woman at the bakery had quit giving me free cakes. The demonstrations had burned themselves out and the streets were quiet and hopeless.

There was still no heat in the apartment. Funny, I hadn't noticed the cold the night Anastasia crashed into my life, but after they let me out of jail it felt like a walk-in freezer. Because I knew that the end of the book was drawing near, I finally let myself spend a little money and bought a small electric heater. The stuff I was churning out wasn't great, but it would be acceptable and I could see the second half of the advance drawing into sight.

I moved the table in front of the window so that I could look out at the balconies of the neighboring apartments when I took a break from writing. It was still too cold for anyone to sit outside and the balconies looked forlorn with their awnings rolled up and bagged in tattered plastic. Two or three minutes of staring at them was usually enough to drive me back to work.

The words rolled out and the days evaporated. In the late afternoons, I'd walk through the cracked streets, past the ratty little art galleries, the used book shops, the piano rental store and the luthier who somehow made a living crafting traditional rembetika instruments. Down in the square where the students and anarchists hung out, there was a café that had big heaters beside the tables and served very strong, Greek coffee that I drank sugarless and bitter. I'd sit there and watch people drift through the square. Mostly I looked at the young girls, but I wasn't ogling them, it was a search for one particular girl. I had no idea if she ever came there but I had no other place to look. I hadn't heard from Anastasia since the arrest and had no other ideas on how to find her. Maybe I was looking in the way least likely to produce results because I knew she could have knocked on the door of the apartment at any time and hadn't.

I even found myself wishing the demonstrations would start up again, because that might bring her back. In my more rational moments I was astounded that I could be this obsessed with a girl I'd met so briefly. It had only been a couple of hours and then we were carted off to jail.

In the evenings I'd be back at the keyboard working on the book. At that time of night, I would hear my neighbor practicing Greek clarinet, that wailing erotic sound piercing even my closed window. It brought a stab of emotion, of desolation, longing and loneliness.

There were people I could have visited in Athens, my uncle, a few friends and even the old doctor who lived upstairs in my building. But I stayed alone, excusing myself that I had to remain focussed on the book, knowing that if I saw anyone I'd have to talk about Anastasia and then I'd be lost because they'd most likely suggest elaborate ways to search for her when all I really wanted was for Anastasia to find me. Strangely, I felt less isolated than I had in the past year, as if just waiting for her to reappear finally gave me something to which I could feel attached, about which I could feel. It kept me clear of why I left Vancouver, of what had happened to drive me out.

When the cold weather passed, I turned off the heater, opened the window and worked through the day with a light breeze coming in. In the mornings I'd smell the sharp scent of my neighbor's coffee and when it began to grow dark, there would be the wail of the clarinet and it was like an Odyssean siren.

One night, in the midst of the clarinet's call, the door buzzer rang. Anastasia looked thin and tired as she stood in the open doorway. Her hair was long and stringy and the last of the teenage puffiness was gone from her cheeks. Before I could speak, she put her arms around me and started to cry.

"Where have you been, you look …" I stopped talking before I could say words like weary, tired, drawn out and older.

"They put me in jail," she said. "I had no way to call you. I didn't have your phone number and I had no way to get it. There I was. In jail. Me."

"But you called the Canadian embassy. How did you do that?"

"That was my sister. I was still in jail when she did it. I phoned her as soon as I was arrested. She said she would call the Canadian embassy for you but that she'd use my name because she wanted to stay out of it."

Although Anastasia had been in my arms when I helped her into my apartment the night of the demonstration, I'd never really held her before, never felt her entire presence pressed up against me, never caught the scent of her hair or felt her electricity.

"I thought they'd killed you at first. You weren't moving and the other cop started to yell at the one who did it. Even when you started to move and open your eyes they were still yelling at each other and didn't notice me at all. I grabbed my pants and pulled them on under the blanket." She sniffled. "Your eyes were closed again so they picked you up and made me follow them to their car."

"I didn't know if you'd ever come back," I said. "If I'd ever see you again."

She kissed me lightly on the lips and stepped back and away. "Here I am. I'm out of jail and they didn't kill me or rape me or do much except keep me locked up until yesterday. Can you make me some coffee or do you have any of that Metaxa left?"

"I have new Metaxa, now," I said, feeling suddenly light. "I finished the other bottle while you were away on vacation."

"Let's have a drink from your new bottle of Metaxa, and then I have to go to see my sister and thank her for helping you. Then I have to find a place to live."

"You can stay here," I said without considering the implications.

"Spiro, I don't know what happened between us when I was here, but I want to find out. Just not so suddenly."

"I looked for you every day."

"Let me guess. In the Exarchia square?"

I started to laugh.

"With all the druggies and the students and the musicians?"

"Don't forget anarchists."

"Of course. You thought I'd be there in my black beret and ski mask. How would you recognize me in a ski mask?"

"Don't forget, I've seen you in your underwear."

"So. You figured I'd be walking through Exarchia Square in a ski mask and underwear and you'd be able to pick me out in the crowd?"

"In a minute!"

She came back into my arms, held herself against me and held her lips lightly pressed against mine for a long minute before we merged into a kiss. She pushed herself away, suddenly. "Spiro, I have to leave right now. I need to find a place to live."

"If you don't, come back and stay here tonight. I can sleep on the couch."

"As if that would happen." She touched my arm. "But it's very sweet, nonetheless." She thought for a minute. "I think I'll just check into a hotel tonight."

"If you need any money …?" I let the question hang.

"Money is never an issue for me," she said. "I'll tell you about that, but right now I have to go." She suddenly looked at me and said, "You make me feel good." Then she continued her list. "I have to see my sister and get some clothes that I left and get your phone number."

"And I need yours."

"I also need to buy a new cell phone. Mine disappeared that night. I'll give you my sister's number. And I'll call you from whatever hotel I stay at to give you the number."

"Can't you stay at your sister's place?"

"Her boyfriend moved in and it would be very uncomfortable. I don't like him and it's hard to pretend otherwise. Easier just to stay someplace nice and not have the tension."

We exchanged phone numbers, she kissed me on both cheeks in the Greek style, then pressed her lips against mine, slipping her tongue into my mouth for a long moment and hurried out the door.

The apartment was suddenly empty again except for the phone number on the pad on my desk and the wail of the clarinet in the night.

CHAPTER 18

The Old Man and Spiro

It was the dead middle of the night in a small Greek harbor far from the rest of the world, far even from the rest of Greece. "Do you remember my mentioning Stratos, the one who played all the instruments and wrote songs with Perdiki?" the old man asked.

Our boat rocked as a fishing craft came in, throwing a small wake as it headed to the dock. I didn't say anything because I knew he'd continue without a prompt.

"I want to tell you something about Stratos," he said.

"I know about him."

"Of course, you do, but I don't think you know very much or how it all connects."

"You told me they tortured him."

"It was worse than that. They tortured him and when they let him go he was dead. Not buried yet, but dead. When his friends took him to the hospital, the doctors cleaned up the stump where they'd cut off the middle finger of his right hand and they spent hours setting the two other fingers from the other hand that had been smashed and broken. He wept as they tried to repair what made him a great musician. The American girl, I didn't know her name then, took him home and nobody saw him after that. I don't know why she stayed with him because he was a dead man."

"I never knew any of that."

The old man lit the stove to make us another cup of coffee and it was halfway done before he again spoke. "Eh!" he said. "He stopped performing … he couldn't perform. His fingers were no good. Perdiki knew all this but there was nothing he could do. What could anyone do? Stratos chased away everyone who came to see him, even me."

"I didn't know you knew him."

He stopped for a minute and seemed to drift away and when he returned he looked sad. "Afterward, after the torture, I went to see him and the only part of him that was alive was being kept so by the American girl."

The coffee was poured into two cups and the old man lit a cigarette, letting the smoke drift over his eyes. "After a while," he continued, "when anyone knocked on his door he would yell that he was dead and that they should put flowers at his door."

The old man blew over the top of his cup to cool it and took a first sip. "It made him crazy, but there was nothing to be done. That American girl took care of him or he probably wouldn't have fed himself. She was a physicist I think, and when she cooked it was like a lab experiment. A lot of what she did was like that, but she sure took care of what was left of him. I liked her. She approached everything as a problem she was solving. But I didn't see how she could do the math with Stratos." The old man stared into his coffee cup. "They did that to him and he wasn't even political. It's true that Stratos knew everyone but the only thing he belonged to was his music and they took it away."

"I know part of that."

"Of course you do." The old man put down his cup, stood up and stretched and sat again. He sipped his coffee and stared at the lantern for a minute before he spoke again. "I heard Stratos play twice and each time it changed something in me. The first time was at a concert in Athens when he was there with Perdiki and the second time I'll tell you about later." He shook his head. "Enough of that for now. Let me tell you about Athena because she is very important in this."

CHAPTER 19

Athena

While Perdiki is on the run in Mythos, Athena is in her studio in Paris, painting feverishly. The walls and the floor, which she had always kept clean, are now splattered like used palettes with every color that has flown from her brushes for the past month. She has paint in her hair but she cannot stop. Somehow, she eats, does what is necessary, sleeps when it is unavoidable and refuses to talk to anyone.

The painting is a massive piece of work that fills an entire side of the studio and sits up off the floor on a huge easel. Painting on such a scale is an athletic feat of five-foot-long sweeps of the brush and thousands of little strokes. Supplies vanish nearly as quickly as the art store can deliver them. Empty paint tubes, squashed down tubes of titanium white, ultramarine, burnt sienna, cerulean blue, Naples yellow and hooker's green fill a large garbage can that sits at the far end of the studio.

Like the paint tubes, her body collapses when she runs out of color and she thinks of her bed as a trash bin, where she throws herself when she is done. But unlike the paint tubes, somehow there is a miracle that refills her through the night. In the morning, she drips paint on her nightgown and coming out of the bath she stands naked at the canvas with flecks of paint on her nipples as if she were a pointillist painting.

There are no individual days and the only sense of time she has is when she leaves the studio and finds the stores closed or the cafes not yet open. There are probably church bells on Sunday, but the music in the studio keeps her isolated even from the church.

The music never stops and it is all Perdiki. In the mornings, she plays his early work, the formal symphonies and the short, classical pieces, but as the day progresses, she puts on recordings of the songs and concerts that drove the government insane. Most of the time her mind intertwines with the music so that it becomes part of her and part of what goes on the canvas.

In all of the recordings, Perdiki's friend, Stratos, can be heard on guitar, bouzouki and the little lyra, soaring with the melody and extending it beyond itself in his solos. When Stratos and Perdiki performed together she envisioned them as two birds winging around each other in flight.

On the afternoon when it had been whispered to her that Perdiki dove off the ship and escaped, she roared through Paris, pushing people out of her way, not noticing the streets or the rain or friends who recognized her. Nothing. She splashed through puddles, soaking her feet without notice and moving until she finally, somehow, accidentally arrived at her own door. When she couldn't find the key, she kicked and pounded on the door until the lock finally gave way. She shoved the tall loft door closed behind her and stuck a chair against it to keep it closed.

Still dripping from the rain, she measured the far wall of the studio and phoned the art supply shop to demand that they stretch the enormous canvas for her immediately and with it, deliver paints, brushes, everything she could think of to work on a massive scale.

Nothing was logical, any more than her belief that she could keep Perdiki alive by painting and she wanted the work to be as big as possible to give him enough room to survive. As close as she could come to thinking about what she was doing was to say to herself, "Ah, Athena, you dumb fool," and then she would push everything out of her mind, turn up recordings of Perdiki's music and paint with her entire being. If you could get close enough to ask, she would not be able to explain what she was painting because she did not know how to describe what it was. Once when she was in Taiwan, she spent an afternoon at the National Art Museum on the outskirts of Taipei. Room to room she roamed through the enormous buildings of the museum absorbing two centuries of art of that had been smuggled out of China when Mao's horde was at its most destructive phase. Finally, she entered a room with a small bench and only one painting. She stood in the middle of the room and was completely overwhelmed by a painting that was two thousand years old and astonishing in its power, so much so that she felt herself blown off her feet and onto the bench. At the instant that she landed, a small,

Chinese man landed beside her. They looked at each other and burst out laughing because they realized that they'd had the exact same experience.

Athena could tell the story, but she could not explain what there was about a simple painting of a white monkey that gave it such immense power that it endured across cultures for two thousand years. It would have been the same if she had tried to describe and explain what it was that she was now painting.

Perdiki had been similarly engaged in his music and it was always art and never intended to be political. The left had adopted him as one of their own because of the themes of his songs, but he hadn't been actively involved in their political maneuverings since his youth. "I had politics once," he had told Athena. "It was like the flu, and I was lucky to survive."

But politics pursued him and she painted that too, grasping to understand it on a visceral, painterly level because that was what she knew and her mind was just a dummy. She could no more understand her art than she could explain the power of the painting of the white monkey she'd seen in Taiwan. Somehow within her she begins to connect Perdiki's survival with this painting. It must be everything to give him enough room. All of Greece must be in it, and that only as the background. All of his music must be there, all of his life, every face that she's heard or seen of him except the women. She will not paint the women. He never talked about them anyway, except once he told her about a girl in high school.

He had been sitting next to a redheaded classmate in the library. She was willowy and had light green misty eyes that gave away nothing. They sat close, reading a book together.

"Is it okay if I put my hand on your leg?" he asked.

"For starters," she answered.

When he told Athena the story he laughed and would not say more.

Athena will leave it there. She will allow herself one conceit. She will be the only woman and every woman. She will even have green misty eyes and will grab him back.

And so she paints. The garbage can of used tubes has to be emptied. And she paints. She needs to work and eat and shit and sleep and work again. And only when the music goes off does the world sneak in through dreams and nightmares that are gone with the dawn. And she paints.

CHAPTER 20

The Old Man and Spiro

The old man reached for the bottle of tsipouro. "Do we dare drink any more of this?" Without waiting for an answer, he put the bottle back under the counter and lit the stove to make another pot of Greek coffee.

On the street beside the dock a motorcycle broke the stillness with its harsh muffler. We sat and listened to it curve up into the interior of the town until the sound receded and the silence of the night was restored.

The old man was looking tired and I wondered whether he could continue. It had been a long night, long for me in my thirties and much longer for the old man. But he seemed to want to unroll the entire story and I wasn't going to stop him because I needed to hear it.

He stared into my eyes as if he knew what I was thinking. "We can't stop, either of us, until we reach the end of our stories … where they meet and what this all means, if life ever means anything." He paused to pump water into the briki and set it on the stove, where he added coffee and sugar. "You need to hear this story and I need to know who you are … who you've become."

When the coffee boiled up the old man poured for each of us, careful to evenly divide the foam at the top of the briki between the two cups. When he was done, he coughed, took a long drink of water and began speaking again.

CHAPTER 21

Perdiki

When Perdiki and Argos returned from their walk onshore Maria was dressed in an old shirt and pants she'd found in a cabinet, and sleeping peacefully. Argos stretched, sniffed, and settled onto the floor. Perdiki lay down on the bunk opposite Maria's and fell asleep listening to Argos snoring.

Perdiki woke at first light to take the big dog to shore for a quick walk before waking the girl. Back aboard, he got the engine running and pumped the bilge. Maria awoke in the midst of the noise and took the helm while he hauled up the anchor. Two seagulls were the only sign of life as they motored quietly out of the bay. The air had an early morning sea-dampness that brought its scent and weight to the atmosphere. The sea was calm, with little more than light, feathered ripples on its surface and it was as if the storm of the previous night had never happened.

For breakfast, they shared the last of the cheese and bread. Afterward, Perdiki fed Argos and pumped water into his bowl. He made coffee on the small gas ring in the galley with ingredients he found in a cabinet above the sink. He brought it up on deck, handed a cup to Maria and sat on a bench sipping his coffee, watching Maria steer the boat with the skill of someone raised to the sea.

"How far do you think?" he asked the girl.

"Probably a half hour or a little more."

The morning opened up as they worked their way up the coast, looking for the entrance to Agios Isidoros. The sun rose to a high cloudless sky that burned the moisture out of the air and reflected itself in the water and turned it a brilliant blue. A school of fish broke the surface, leaping into the air, a silvery presence on a very quiet morning.

The appearance of a small military boat shattered everything. It came up suddenly with its brash engines churning the calm water with its wake as if to announce its importance, its dominance, its presence and the inevitability that Perdiki and the girl were about to be apprehended. The loud engines sounded angry as if mirroring the attitude of its Captain and crew.

There was nothing Perdiki and Maria could do except continue on their course. Their boat was hopelessly slower than the powerful military vessel and there was no way to outmaneuver it. They could only proceed as if there were nothing abnormal, hoping that they were not its target.

"They're too far away to see how many of us are aboard," said Maria. "You should hide below because you're Perdiki and everybody can recognize your face. I don't think any of the guards will be on the boat and nobody else knows me."

"What will you say to them?"

"I'll identify myself as my cousin and tell them that this is my father's boat and that I'm bringing it to Agios Isidoros for repair."

"Are you strong enough?"

"After yesterday, yes." Her eyes stared darkly at Perdiki, nearly black in their anger and intensity. "I can do it because we are going to live."

Maria ruffled the fur on Argos's head. "I don't think they know about your big friend." she continued. "He can stay below so that if they start to look in the cabin maybe he can scare them. He's big enough, but can he look mean?"

"I don't know," answered the musician. "I've only had him for a few days, but he seems pretty smart so he might just smell danger on them and react to it."

Maria scratched Argos behind the ears as she continued. "If this boat is like my uncle's, there's a secret hold where they sometimes smuggle things. My uncle was involved in that last year. I don't know exactly what he was up to but when I came to bring lunch one afternoon my uncle had the secret hold open and that's how I found out about it. He told me that I should forget it existed. But of course I didn't. There might be one like it on this boat. The secret hold in my uncle's boat was up in the bow in the cabinet under the berth. The cabinet had drawers that were short with a false bulkhead behind them. If this is like my uncle's boat the false wall lifts out and there will be enough room for you."

Argos grumbled and stared at the compartment as Perdiki fitted himself into it, and looked fretful when Maria put the false wall and the drawers back in place. She patted Argos's head and scratched behind his big ears to calm him.

"Lie down, Argos," she told him, patting the floor in front of the cabinet. "He'll be okay, you just stay right there."

Maria went back up on deck to untie the wheel and stand behind it. Five minutes later the military boat pulled alongside and a voice called out to her to cut the engine. A deckhand threw a line which she caught and tied to a stanchion on the bow of her boat. He threw a second line which she tied off to a cleat on the stern.

From the cabin of the military boat a man in a uniform emerged. It was obvious by his bearing that he was in charge even before he began shouting orders, to one of the crew to board the fishing boat and search it. "Get the girl and bring her to me, first." he added.

Maria knew there was no point in struggling and boarded the military boat on her own, waiting for whatever would come next. The uniformed man was obviously aware of her presence when she stood beside him, but he ignored the girl, keeping his focus on the fishing boat. She wondered, briefly if he was the one they called Xenos, but she wasn't about to ask him. What gave her hope was that Xenos was based on land and this one was obviously a nautical creature.

From below, Argos stood and watched while the boat was searched. When they came down into the cabin, he lay in front of the cabinet behind which Perdiki was hiding. The dog was casual about it, not in any way indicating that he was guarding anyone or doing anything but resting.

One of the crew poked his head out of the cabin and called to the official on the deck of the military boat, "There's a dog down here, sir. Biggest I've ever seen, sir. It's a beast."

"Is it threatening you?" called back the official.

"He's just lying there," called the crewman.

"Then don't worry about him. You're not scared of a dog, are you?"

"No sir. But the dog's in the way of some drawers."

"You think Perdiki is hiding in a drawer? You couldn't hide a cat in a drawer in one of these old fishing boats, you idiot. We've wasted enough time. I'm sending the girl back across and then we can get out of here. She's nobody."

Maria hung onto the helm and began to shake. The uniformed man had shoved her in the direction of the boat, and she'd barely avoided falling into the cockpit. Without a glance into the cabin, she untied the lines, started the engine and slowly pulled away from the government boat. Everything, even releasing Perdiki from the hidden compartment, could wait until they were far enough away.

It was a still, peaceful morning, with a smooth sea and the sun reflecting the blue sky in the water, but Maria was aware of nothing but the receding government boat and the sound of her own engine. When the government boat was finally out of sight, she throttled the engine down, tied off the wheel and went below. Argos jumped to his feet when he saw her and watched anxiously as she pulled out the drawers and removed the panel that hid Perdiki. He emerged slowly, stiff from his confinement.

The boat rocked as he stepped into the cockpit, blinking as the direct, bright sunlight of early morning assaulted his eyes.

"Could you hear any voices?" she asked. "I just wondered if that was Xenos?"

"Was he wearing a black suit?"

"No, some kind of uniform."

"Then it wasn't Xenos. If it had been him, he would not have let you go. And he would have found me. I knew him, you know. Far too well."

Maria interrupted. "Up ahead, just between those two big rocks, my uncle showed me a hidden little niche," Maria said. "It looks much too shallow for a boat to get through, but it's not."

Perdiki twisted and stretched, trying to work out the kinks in his body after being confined to the hidden compartment. "Can you get us in there?" he asked. "I don't think we should take the boat into Agios Isidoros. If we find a way to get there by land it would be a lot safer."

"I think I can get us through the little passage," Maria said, hesitantly. "But I don't know if there's a way we can reach Agios Isidoros by land from there. I'm pretty sure there's a road up above the cove. If we can get up there, we can follow it to the turnoff for Agios Isidoros. But getting up to that first road is the problem. I don't know if there's a path of any kind and it's a pretty steep climb."

"We can't motor straight into Agios Isidoros right now, anyway," said Perdiki. "So it's still best if we duck into your hidden bay. Maybe we'll find a path or worst case, we can stay hidden for a few days, until they give up looking for me. There must be something else they need to do."

The boat scraped against one of the big rocks on the way in and the bottom thumped ominously a few times as they passed over hidden boulders. Once they were past the rocks there was a narrow channel that veered off to the left and ended abruptly at a crumbling, old dock. The boards were rotted and it sagged nearly down to the water but enough of it was intact that they were able to tie off to one of its posts.

They didn't speak or move for the first few minutes after landing. It was as if they didn't dare or the next catastrophe would be called down upon them. Maria stood on the dock, staring at Perdiki, whose face had turned blank and whose eyes were unfocused. Argos broke the mood when he leapt from the boat onto an edge of the dock that crumbled under his weight. He spluttered his way to the shore with such an indignant look on his face that Perdiki and Maria laughed beyond the humor of the dog's situation as they let go the tension of the past two days.

"I think we should just do nothing for a little while," Perdiki said. "We're finally safe and we should savor it."

They were in a nook that was surrounded by spindly trees that gripped onto the rocky earth. Down the shore from the dock was a small pebbled beach. Argos had already found it and was sniffing at the sea life along the rocks and shuffling his big feet in the water. Halfway along the beach he stopped, looked carefully around and walked slowly into the water, like a reluctant bather. Once he was immersed, his face lifted and he swam with delight to the middle of the channel before paddling back to the shore and shaking off.

Maria stood up and called to Perdiki, "I think I'll do the same. Try to wash off some of today and yesterday and even tomorrow. I just want to swim and stop thinking."

"Go ahead," he called back. "Argos will watch out for you. I'll stay here and see if there's a fish to catch. Then I'll bathe and maybe we can have something to eat."

Maria waved, changing if only for an instant back into her light self, her original self, the only one she'd known before the weight of her life had changed.

Argos charged up to her, sensing her mood and became almost puppyish, bounding up and down, stretching and scratching his hind legs against the pebbles. The water flew from his back each time he stopped to shake. Maria found a thick stick and threw it far down the beach for Argos to fetch, but he simply stared at her as if trying to communicate that this was beneath his dignity.

Maria laughed and then slowly began removing the old clothes she'd found in the boat's cabinet. Aware that Perdiki might be watching, and partially hopeful that he was, she turned her back to the boat as she dropped the baggy trousers. Naked, she turned toward the sea and carefully made her way into the water, feeling with her toes for sharp rocks before placing weight on each foot and sensing that Perdiki's eyes were on her small breasts and dark blond patch of pubic hair.

CHAPTER 22

The Old Man and Spiro

The old man suddenly quit talking and stared out at the town beyond the dock. There wasn't much to see of the dark buildings and the quiet streets but he stared anyway as if there were words to be found there. Finally, he said, "I used to run up the mountains like a *katsiki*, a goat, and now look at me. Bah! I am old enough to know that I can't escape any of this. Sooner or later everybody is a casualty of life."

He pushed himself up and paced inside the narrow confines of the cabin, slowly moving his arms to regain their flexibility. "I was on a ferry back from Athens a few years ago," he said. "And there were two girls with a dog like Argos. It was midday in the summer and very hot. They'd set up a blanket for him as a sunshade in a corner where two rails met. Those girls took care of that big beast as if he were royalty." The old man gazed at the dark town again as if trying to find something there. "Some dogs are like spirits you care for, and some, like the one that adopted Perdiki, are spirits that take care of you."

He lay back on one of the benches along the bulkhead, coughed, and looked old. His eyes were ablaze but the rest of his face was skeletal and the skin of his cheeks hung slack.

"I need to listen for a while," he said. "Your turn, *pethi mou.*"

CHAPTER 23

Spiro

Anastasia telephoned the day after she appeared at my door to say that she needed to visit her parents in Thessaloniki because they'd been worried when they heard she'd been jailed. She would be back in two or three days and would be living in a temporary, furnished rental. "I don't want you to be scared that you'll lose me again," she said and gave me her new address.

While I waited for her return. I kept writing. As it grew warmer and I opened additional windows, I could hear the music of the neighborhood and it found its way into my work. The rhythm and texture of the book changed the more I listened and it was turning the novel into something far better than I'd expected. I'd been grinding it out as a chore, relying on the plot to carry it. I knew that if I threw in enough nautical terms and kept the readers aboard that would be enough. But what came wafting through my window in that old Athens neighborhood wouldn't let it stand at that. I breathed in the aromas of a nearby restaurant and the day passed with the sharp scents of Greek coffee in the morning, souvlaki through the afternoon and wine and Greek salad at night. When it rained, the damp brought out the smell of old mortar and aging cement and when the sun baked it dry again, the bricks of the buildings emitted the dusky scent of an ancient city.

While I wrote, taxis rumbled and scrambled in the street and motor scooters and motorcycles buzzed and roared, rising in volume and discordance at rush hours until the city was filled with a solid mash of sounds. In the late evenings, when things quieted down, lone motorcycles blared out like broken-reeded saxophones in solos that wavered through the night as they drove past the corner of Kalithromiou and Harilau Trikoupi, heading into the center of the city. There was no resisting the imposition of all that sound into my writing. It brought staccato, crescendo, grace notes, sudden key changes and texture to the novel. It forced me to go back through all of it, right back to the beginning to raise everything to the same key and rhythm.

When the writing was at its best, it came straight out of me without a thought, as if I were at the piano. When I'm playing an instrument, music comes out of my fingers without thought or hesitation. It's harder to achieve that state when I'm writing and I'm always reaching for those times when the words come the same way as music does from my fingers.

Maybe it's because music was with me long before writing. My mother said I was picking out tunes on the piano when I was two or three. I learned to read music when I barely knew the alphabet. By the time I was in my early teens I could pick up any instrument and after a few minutes, make music out of it. The high school band leader got a kick out of this and constantly moved me between instruments for the hell of it. He put me inside a sousaphone for marching season, had me breathing into a bassoon for woodwind quintets, and wailing away on the tenor sax for the dance band. When we accompanied the school musical play, I jumped between bass clarinet, flute and oboe. Mostly, I'd follow the score but once in a while I'd just riff on my own, making up my part as I went along. When the band leader caught me at this he just laughed.

I never seriously considered becoming a musician. Mostly, because my father had been a great one, and I couldn't compete with what he'd been. But I wanted to do something similar. So I kept music alongside my life like a close friend and put my life into writing. Even in Athens, my old guitar sat beside the table where I wrote.

Writing was always something I had to chase. When it came as easily as music it made me think that I could do anything, but the rest of the time I worked a brick at a time, with half the bricks faulty. But eventually I made a living at it. I was like a musician gigging his way along while putting in enough hours to get it all way beyond right. At first I did it by freelancing for sailing magazines. It was easy money, if not a lot, but it gave me the freedom and time for my own work. In lieu of paying rent, I lived on the Haiku, an old Ericson 34 sloop that I'd bought with a small inheritance that came to me when my parents were killed in an automobile accident. I built up enough of a readership through my regular appearances in boat magazines that when I wrote a sailing novel it was quickly taken by a specialty publisher and I'd never had to do anything else since. One book followed another in a formula that I'd set up in the first of the series.

For a while, I tried to write something serious, but the bread and butter brought in by the sailing novels gave me less and less time to indulge myself and when I tried it didn't seem to go anywhere. The problem was that I wasn't sure what I believed in or whether I had anything to say, so all that hit the page were words.

In good weather, I cruised the Haiku along the coast of British Columbia, working from wherever I dropped the hook. Usually alone, I'd beat my way up the coast, anchoring in a bay or tying up at a marina when I wanted to fill up the water tank, gas up, and buy supplies. At night, when I was anchored out in a remote bay, I wrote by the light of a hanging, brass oil lamp and during the day I charged the batteries of my laptop by running the engine for a while.

Along the way I had a few friends who had a slip where I could tie up. When they'd invite me in for dinner, I'd bring my beaten-up, old guitar to sing for my supper. It had been my father's guitar and I treasured and kept it in a case designed to help it withstand life on the water.

My most frequent stop was at the marina of a small coastal village where the girlfriend, as I always thought of her afterward, lived. The girlfriend's parents were both disabled, and the small lunch place she owned was their sole support as well as her own. Mondays and Tuesdays were her days off and we spent as much of her free time together as we could. I would pull into a slip on a Sunday evening and she'd join me when the shop closed.

Mostly we'd sail, and if life were just sailing it would have been enough. But onshore there was really little between us. I don't think I ever loved the girlfriend. Or maybe I did and want to forget that along with her name. I try not to remember the storm, either. I try not to remember anything. But there she is, with her quiet brown hair and strangely thick eyebrows, her broad face, not traditionally beautiful except in its uniqueness. There was something about her look, though, her visage, a wistfulness and a quietness that drew me.

I think it might have worked out, but she was like everything in my life, too convenient. Too easy. As it was with music. I wanted my life to be beyond that and I felt like I was coasting.

The storm was like a symphony at first, with roaring wind, rushing water, the rattling of the sails and the slam of the hull into the waves as we headed through Welcome Passage. We were beating our way, tacking back and forth against both the wind and water washing over the bow and pouring into the cockpit. The girlfriend and I immersed ourselves in the sounds and laughed to each other in lieu of being able to speak above the wind and our fear. As it intensified, I realized I'd made a terrible mistake. What had been fun became increasingly more dangerous as the storm showed its true strength.

A sailboat isn't like a car. If the weather's too rough, you just can't pull over to the side and wait it out, especially if the shore is as rocky as that stretch of the Strait of Georgia. You have to keep going until you can find a sheltering cove.

I'd made a bad choice. Welcome Passage is between the open waters of the Georgia Strait and a small, rocky island. Although it may be windy within the passage it is protected from the seas that build up in the Strait in stormy weather so it's usually the safest course. But when the wind is blowing up hard from the south and the tide is running against you, it can grow quickly dangerous and once you're in Welcome Passage there's no turning around, not when you're running against the tide in a sailboat.

I should have gone around outside the passage. It might have been rougher but there would have been sea room rather than the confines of what had become an unwelcome passage. We tacked back and forth between the jagged rocks of the shore and the sheer side of the island, with the mast slamming under the force of the wind. Each time we tacked, the tiny storm jib slapped wildly against the shrouds until we could get the sheet tightened on the winch. We were soaked from slashes of water that flew up over us from a sea that kept building.

On the last of the tacks, just as we were nearing the end of Welcome Passage, there was a huge puff that drove the nose of the Haiku way off course as she was about to pass through the wind. I couldn't get the boat around enough to make the tack and we slammed into the jagged shore with such a jolt that the girlfriend was thrown overboard onto the rocks.

I abandoned the Haiku, which was jammed into the rocks, and half-swam, half-staggered to shore. By the time I reached the girlfriend she wasn't moving and her eyes were open, still and empty. The water around her held rivulets of her blood and when I looked at her eyes I knew she was gone. Although I gave her mouth to mouth for what seemed like hours it was hopeless. There was no pulse and there never would be again. Finally, I used my cell phone to call the coast guard. Then I waited it out.

CHAPTER 24

The Old Man and Spiro

The old man was studying me in the cabin of that small, wooden fishing boat. His eyes sought mine and held them until he finally spoke. "So that's who you are. You know something about the sea and about the world after all. Something about something, *neh*? Maybe you are a writer." His old eyes stared into my own and wouldn't let me escape. "There is nothing I can say about what you've told me. Your cousin described your condition to me when you first came back to Greece to work in his restaurant."

"My condition?"

"That you were," he hesitated looking up at the roof, "quiet," he finally said.

"But how did you speak to my cousin?"

"He called from Athens on the phone. We have them, you know."

"But how do you know my cousin?"

The old man ignored my question and looked up toward the town. "We need some food and there's a café that opens early for the fishermen. Maybe we can get a cheese pie or a koulouri. Stories like this require food."

We walked together through the sleeping town, toward the one café with a light. It was early, even for the fishermen. There were only two ancient men settled at separate tables, staring out to sea and the past. The old man gestured toward them and said, "They've reached the final stage, they've outlived sleep."

We went inside, and gave our order to a proprietor with folds over his eyes the same shape and color as his grey drooping moustache. We took our coffees and a couple of *hortopites* to a table outside and like the other patrons of the restaurant, stared into the past for a few minutes until the proprietor brought us a couple of glasses of water and the old man began to speak.

"You told me about yours," he said. "Now I'll tell you about Perdiki's. We all carry one, you know." He looked away and I could see blood and tiredness in the mottled whites of his eyes.

CHAPTER 25

Spiro

The girl was standing naked up to her hips in the sea when the government boat roared into the bay. She tried to run through the cling of the water as she forced her way to shore and was conscious of the crew staring at her body as their grey boat neared the crumbling dock. When she reached the shore, Maria stooped as she ran, grabbing her clothes and sandals, and ran barefoot for the trees and beyond to the hills that led to the interior of the island. After a few meters on the hard, thorny ground, she slowed enough to slip on her sandals and continued toward the tangle of trees and boulders that stretched up into the hills.

Perdiki had been fishing off the stern of the boat when he heard the government boat approaching. He dropped his line and jumped off the fishing boat onto the crumbling dock, collapsing more of it as he landed and having to struggle across its cracked and tilted boards. When he reached the shore, he ran in the opposite direction of where Maria was headed, sprinting toward the cliff that formed a solid wall fifty meters to the West and appeared unclimbable. As he ran, he shouted to try to divert attention away from the girl, figuring it was him, not the girl, they were really after, but the soldiers on the ground ignored him, assuming that he'd be stopped by the cliff and would be trapped. Where the girl was headed, escape looked possible and they'd been ordered to arrest both of them.

The big dog, Argos, stood his ground beside the dock, barking ferociously and threatening the crewmen on the approaching government boat until one of them lifted his gun and took a poorly aimed shot at him. Argos growled and then turned and ran to Perdiki and past him, finally waiting at the foot of the cliff for the musician to catch up.

As Argos and Perdiki began to climb, the musician continued shouting to draw attention to himself, but still the soldiers ignored him and focussed their chase on the girl. The climb was far less difficult than it appeared from the distance, easy enough that Argos had no trouble remaining at Perdiki's side as they made their way up. They found footholds on the small pines that clung to the cliff and pulled themselves along on exposed roots and rocks. Finally, they reached a narrow rock ledge where they could turn and look down at the soldiers. Two had finally split off and were headed for the cliff and the rest he could see were in pursuit of Maria. She was a fast runner and was nearing the shelter of the tangled trees and boulders but the soldiers were drawing closer.

There was nothing Perdiki could do to help the girl. He could only hope she would outrun them and somehow make it to safety. He began to climb again traversing behind a line of twisted pines that somehow clung to the cliff until he found a hidden ledge behind a rock wall that he could crouch behind. It reminded Perdiki of the wall in front of the cave house where he'd stayed that first night on Mythos only days ago. There were even a few cracks where he could watch for the soldiers' approach without being seen.

Maria's screams began just as he had hidden himself and Argos behind the rock wall. Trying to shut out the sound of the girl's anguish he gathered a mound of baseball-sized rocks and waited for the two soldiers who were pursuing him to draw closer. When he could see them a few meters below where he was hidden, he began to throw the rocks. The first one connected with the soldier to his left and knocked him loose from his perch on the cliff. He could hear his shouts as he fell, then a crash at the foot of the cliff as the soldier landed. When the second soldier called down to him there was only silence. The second soldier remained crouched out of range directly under the spot where Perdiki and Argos were hidden but quickly lost patience and began to try to circle around them. As soon as his head appeared, Perdiki threw a rock that connected with the soldier's shoulder but he managed to maintain his grip and continue climbing. The next couple of rocks missed, but the third connected solidly, smashing the soldier on the top of his head and toppling him off his perch. He fell several meters until his fall was stopped by a clump of trees. Dazed, he stayed where he fell, unable or unwilling to move.

He feebly managed to call down, again, to the soldier who had fallen, but his voice was weak and he heard nothing back.

Instead of continuing to climb, Perdiki now made his way along the ledge, until he found a way down, half sliding and scraping against rock and exposed tree roots until his arms and legs were bloody. Argos stayed beside him, sliding and tumbling until the pair reached the foot of the cliff. The base of the cliff at that point was shielded by thick brush that completely covered Perdiki and Argos as they worked their way through it to get close to where Maria was screaming.

There was no sign of movement from either the soldier who'd landed at the base of the cliff or the dazed one clinging to a tree halfway up. For the moment, Perdiki was safe. Without waiting for the man, Argos pushed ahead, forging through the brush and finding a path between the trees. Perdiki crouched as low as he could and followed. When they were parallel to the line of trees where he'd seen Maria, he kept going until he was a few meters in before turning toward where he assumed she was being held. Her screams had turned to defiant shouts of "Don't touch me you pig."

Perdiki and Argos concealed themselves in a copse from which they could see that Maria, had not managed to get her clothes on and was now tied to a tree. A soldier stood beside her and was running his gun over her body, lingering at her vagina and laughing. The other soldiers watched and laughed with him.

Perdiki had no idea what to do. He was a musician, not a fighter and even with the help of Argos, was vastly outnumbered. A well-thrown rock wouldn't help him as it had on the cliff. He was saved from further fretting when the soldier he'd left dazed halfway on the cliff managed to shout and attract the others. There was a great commotion and suddenly the majority of the soldiers began to head toward the area of the cliff Perdiki and the dog had climbed.

They'd left only the soldier who was running the gun over Maria's body to guard her. Before Perdiki could react, Argos rushed through the brush and threw his great weight at the soldier, knocking him off his feet. The gun fell from his hands as he hit the ground and the giant dog pinned him down with his jaws on his throat.

"Don't move," Perdiki shouted as he reached them. He threatened with no basis other than his experience so far with Argos. He had no idea what the dog would really do. "The dog will eat you if I give him the signal," he bluffed. Argos retained his grip and the soldier lay still while Perdiki picked up the gun from where it had fallen and pointed it at the soldier. "I'm going to leave my dog holding you while I untie the girl. If the dog doesn't eat you, I'll shoot you if you try to stand up."

Holding the gun vaguely pointed in the direction of the soldier, Perdiki untied the ropes holding Maria. She quickly put on the clothes she'd been carrying. When she was dressed, before Perdiki could say or do anything, Maria picked up a huge rock and smashed it against the soldier's head. His eyes rolled back as he lost consciousness and fell, and blood flowed freely over his face.

"I'm not taking any chances with this *malaka*," the girl said.

Perdiki shook his head at her spirit, and might have grinned if he weren't worried that she'd killed the soldier. It reminded him that the fall from the cliff may have been the death of the one he'd knocked off his perch with the rock he'd hurled.

Through the trees and brush they were able to see that the military boat was tied off against the crumbling dock with its engines still running. The captain and crew were on shore, running to help the soldiers heading toward the cliff where they thought Perdiki was still hiding. They'd left only one crewmember onboard. He was at the stern of the boat looking out at the empty bay, smoking a cigarette.

"We have only one chance and if he turns around and has a gun …" the musician said to Maria, leaving the thought unfinished.

She was staring at the soldier on the ground, whose eyes were now completely covered in blood and ignored Perdiki's words, asking instead, "Do you think I killed him?"

Perdiki looked closely at the man's head. Without knowing whether it was true, he comforted her by saying, "No, it's just a deep cut and eventually the bleeding will stop." He put his hand on the girl's shoulder. She was beginning to shake as events caught up with her emotions. "Be strong," he said. "We have only one chance."

"Yes," she agreed, beginning to control herself. She patted the big dog who was now standing beside her. "Please tell me, though, when I can stop being strong." She scratched the big dog's ears. "But we have this secret weapon, your dog, the magnificent Argos."

"He isn't my dog. He's his own dog, but he chooses to stay with me."

"How long has he been with you?"

"Only a few days."

"This breed must grow very fast."

"We need to run now. There is no sense in waiting," Perdiki said. "We need to run flat-out to the boat and try to get the crewman before he turns around. Argos is much faster than us, but I don't know what he'll do. We'd better count only on ourselves." He searched for a minute and came up with two thick limbs they could use as clubs. "This is the best we can do," he said as he handed one to the girl.

When they ran, Argos stayed alongside Perdiki, with Maria a few steps behind. Just as they reached the boat Maria tripped and with an involuntary gasp, she fell a few meters from the boat. At the sound, the crewman whirled around and fumbled to get his pistol out of its holster. Argos struggled with boarding the boat from the crumbling dock, his big paws sliding on the surface, as Perdiki leaped on the boat and swung his makeshift club at the crewman. It only glanced off his arm and he pulled out the pistol and pointed it at Perdiki.

"I don't want to kill you," he said, "I know who you are and like your music. It touches me, and I have nothing against you, personally, but I have orders. Just stay still and tell the girl to come here. They tell me you are my enemy."

"Because of my music?"

"No, your politics."

"I only write songs, not politics."

"I know, I know, but I also understand what you are saying in your songs. I still have to do what I have to do."

That was the last he said before Argos leapt at him, knocking the crewman to the deck. The girl was right behind him, with the club in her hands but before she could swing it, the gun went off and she fell to the deck.

Perdiki kicked the gun from the crewman's hand, picked it up and pointed it at the him. The dog tore at the crewman until Perdiki managed to pull him away. Maria lay unmoving, with blood pouring out of the wound where the bullet had entered her forehead.

"Get overboard," he shouted at the crewman. "Go swim to shore before I shoot you." As the terrified man dove off the boat, Perdiki let loose the lines and pulled the throttle all the way back on the powerful government boat. It roared out of the bay until Perdiki shoved the throttle into neutral and bent to help the girl. Beside her, Argos whimpered, pressing his body against hers. But she was gone.

CHAPTER 26

The Old Man and Spiro

The old man became very quiet. We finished our coffee, brushed the hortopita crumbs from our shirts and walked slowly back to the boat, neither of us talking. The town was silent and the stars had not yet been squeezed out of the sky but we could feel dawn approaching. There was too much I needed to hear for the night to end quickly. It felt as if I only had this one night to fulfill the old man's promise and know everything.

The old buildings that fronted the shore were shadowy in the sparse light and there was no one else on the limani. It felt as if we were walking on a stage set where we were the only visible players. It was too early for the fishermen. Their boats, wooden, traditional caiques, with high bows and huge rudders, were empty as we made our way along the dock toward our boat.

Finally, when we were back aboard, the old man settled onto a settee and began to speak. "And so it was Perdiki's turn," he said. "You don't stay immune forever." His old eyes stared deeply into mine. "As you know. As you most surely know."

CHAPTER 27

Spiro

It was one of those days when I could do the trick, when the writing was flowing from my fingers without the conscious imposition of my brain. Although I normally work in the afternoon, something had awakened me early in the morning and after a cup of Greek coffee, I began to write. The sounds of the morning rush were loud and brash at exactly the moment when I needed to insert that tone into the book. I wrote page after page before I was done for the day. The tension of the writing overwhelmed me as it flowed out, but as soon as I stopped for a break, I felt nothing but exhilaration.

Although my relationship with Anastasia was still just a promise, the prospect of being with her again had lifted me. When I walked into the bakery the woman behind the counter must have sensed it. For the first time in a couple of months she handed me a cookie along with my fresh loaf of bread. And for the first time I thought of music again.

My father's old guitar had survived the wreck of the Haiku better than its current owner. I'd brought it along to Greece more as a habit than with the expectation that I'd be playing again. But I picked it up one night when my neighbor was wailing away on his clarinet and began to play along, strumming chords and even doing the occasional run on the strings. Later, I played long jazz riffs to accompany the sound of lone motorcycles roaring through the night.

The next morning, when I thought of Anastasia, I picked up the guitar to try to play her voice and the rhythm of her speech. I'd spent so little time with her that there were gaps in my playing because I didn't know enough yet. I wondered if she could sing and tried to play her voice in song but my fingers couldn't find what my ears had yet to hear.

One morning when I'd returned from the bakery and had a quick breakfast of fresh bread and cheese, I picked up the guitar and played until there was a loud thump on the door. I opened it to the sight of Anastasia bumping her body against the door with her hands and arms full of bundles and over her shoulder a Greek stringed instrument called a baglama. She dropped everything on the couch and put her hands on my shoulders, holding me away from her body to look at me closely. "I could hear you through the door. Music, too?" she said, laughing. "Are you truly everything my hero?" Then she drew me close and whispered in my ear, "I want to stay with you tonight."

"Because I play music?"

"All of it. Have you been writing?"

"Yes and it's the best I've ever done."

"Have you been waiting for me?"

"Yes, every minute."

"See. All of it."

She kissed me deeply, pressing me close against her body for a long time until she suddenly broke away and said, "I brought a bottle of wine and some food. Let's open the wine."

Late in the night, as she slept beside me, a fear of the peace that I was feeling descended on me. It was much safer being numb, as I'd been when I first arrived in Greece. The change in my being had been so sudden that it felt temporary. I wasn't sure it could be trusted.

But eventually I fell asleep and in the morning, when I was awakened by the sound of Anastasia softly picking a tune on the baglama, everything else faded. She was wearing my shirt from the night before and a smile that reflected what I felt at that moment too.

She was playing rembetika, the music that came straight out of the outlaw soul of Greece. In the nineteen twenties and thirties there were rembetika cafes in Pireaus and up North in Thessaloniki. They served Turkish hash in waterpipes while rembetika musicians, drifted in and out, stopping to play and sing, two or three songs and then wandering off again. Late at night, a man might stand and do the zembekiko, his own dance, the one that put everything about him on the floor.

The women of rembetika sang in warbling tones that could break your heart with their pain and love. Like theirs, Anastasia's voice took on a slightly hoarse tone when she sang. It was barely noticeable when she spoke, but her singing brought it out and gave her the sounds I'd heard only on old rembetika recordings of the nineteen- twenties.

But the music coming out of Anastasia's baglama wasn't one of the old tunes. It was light, tickling and filled with our lovemaking of the night before. I watched as much as listened to her play while I made our coffee. As soon as the briki boiled and the coffee was in the cup I didn't wait for the grounds to settle, but took a sip while it was still gritty and picked up the guitar.

We played the music I knew from recordings I'd heard in my parent's house. I don't know how long we played, but we finally stopped when she sang a song with the lyrics;

Like an Orthodox Christian, in this society
I prepare myself for the ceremony
I shop for tobacco ends, and a piece of hashish
And I set out for the village
I go into the church, into the round rooms,
And I start puffing as if I were lighting candles
The archangel suddenly appears
He's got high from all the smoke
He says, "Listen Christian, it's not a sin
To come into the church for your little ceremony."
But, suddenly, a monk speaks to me, "Get out of here! It's my turn
To have a drag," he says.

It had us laughing so hard we couldn't keep playing. We spent the rest of the morning back in bed, luxuriating in each other. Every touch was sensual and even later in the afternoon when we went for a walk and stopped at a taverna it remained that way. We sat at a table under the spring sun and let it warm us while we drank wine so bad we had to laugh at it.

"Tell me about your parents," she said. "I want to know more about who you are." Her hand caressed my knee under the table as she spoke.

"It's difficult," I said, not wanting to break our mood. "And will take a long time. Tell me about yours first."

"My parents understand me," she said. "I guess that's the opposite of what most people say." She squeezed my knee. "They know how

I feel about the current situation in Greece and understand it, although they are very distant from it, very distant from everything except what interests them."

"And what's that?"

"That's the problem. Their only concern is the minutia. They have a lot of money and don't have to do anything, so they don't. They do care about me and their way of expressing it has been to continually put money into bank accounts for me from the time that I was born and now there's so much I don't have to do anything, either." She let go of my knee and grabbed my arm. "So that's it. That's my parents. My sister is like them, only she at least has dance as an obsession." She reached across the table and kissed me lightly. "There's nothing more. No great mystery." Her expression turned serious. "Now, what about you? Besides being a writer and my hero and your music, I know nothing else."

"There's a lot," I said, hesitantly. "I'll tell you about my parents … and especially my father later.

"We have time," she said. "I'm now in your life, this life and not your past. I'm not going to disappear again and you'd better not vanish from mine." She stood and came around to my side of the table and gave me a deep kiss, smiling when she stepped back. "For now, we need some lunch and then I want to go back to your apartment and make love with you again. Afterward, I want you to write while I make dinner for us. You don't even know that I'm a great cook."

It should have gone up from there. And for a while it did.

CHAPTER 28

Perdiki

Once Perdiki was clear of the island, he headed the big government boat aimlessly out to sea because he had no idea what to do. The big dog, Argos, still huddled against Maria as if to protect her lifeless body, sighing as he lay there. Occasionally, the radio would squawk, but Perdiki ignored the noise and finally turned it off.

"What do I do, Argos?" he asked, as if the big dog could answer him. "Maria needs to be properly buried and I need to reach Zev to tell him, but I don't dare use the radio." He throttled the engines back while he thought about his dilemma because there was no sense in wasting gas to head nowhere.

The sea was remarkably calm, with barely a ripple on the water and only the faintest hint of wind to stir the air. There was something wrong with everything being so damned pleasant, he thought. He knew that he'd better make a decision soon because by now the government people and the troops back in the bay would have been in touch with their bases and there would be other boats searching for the one Perdiki had stolen. He needed to abandon this one as soon as possible, but he couldn't simply leave Maria's body onboard.

Finally, he reached the only decision that made any sense. He would head for Agia Paraskavi near Drakano, where he'd taken Thoma's boat. The priest in a nearby village had been part of the underground in the days when Perdiki was exiled to the island at the close of the Greek civil war. Perdiki hoped to leave Maria's body with him and head the boat back out to sea. It wasn't much of a plan, but he couldn't think of anything else. He would tell the priest everything that had happened and ask him to pass it on to Zev. After that, Perdiki had no idea where he'd go but at least he would have done the best he could for Maria.

With the decision made, he turned the boat toward Mythos and pulled back on the throttle until the powerful boat fairly leaped out of the water. Argos left Maria's side long enough to nuzzle up beside Perdiki as if to give him encouragement, then resumed lying beside Maria's inert body while they raced toward the island.

Perdiki didn't worry about the few fishing boats that he flew past because he knew they would find nothing remarkable about a government boat scurrying somewhere. As long as he avoided official vessels, he would be safe.

Pharaoh was in the harbor about to go out fishing and was just letting go the lines when he saw that it was Perdiki at the helm of the big, grey government boat. As Perdiki drew nearer he could see a deep sadness and fright on the musician's face and knew that he was about to hear of tragedy.

Perdiki threw the gear into reverse to slow the boat as he approached the dock, then threw a line to Pharaoh. Neither man spoke until the bow and stern lines were secured and the engine switched off. Finally, Perdiki stepped down onto the dock before Pharaoh could come aboard and see Maria's body.

"Don't speak," began Perdiki. "I'll tell you everything as quickly as I can because I have no time. I have to get this boat out of here." He quickly told Pharaoh what had happened, which left the man stunned for a few seconds until he shook himself free and began making decisions.

"This minute, we need to move Maria's body onboard my boat and then get the hell out of here. You take that big boat and head straight East until you are out of sight, then wait for me. We have to sink that boat and then you and Maria will spend the day fishing with me and just hope that we don't run into anybody looking for you. If we survive, we will come back late tonight and we'd better have fish in the hold so that nothing looks out of the ordinary. The fish will be on top of Maria's body so that if anybody boards it will be hidden. There is a place where you can hide, too."

"I know the hiding place," said Perdiki, "I've already experienced it. I can tell you about it all later. Right now, let's get out of here as fast as we can."

They wrapped Maria's body in a tarp and quickly carried it to Pharaoh's boat and hoisted it aboard. "Forgive me, Maria," said Perdiki as they lowered her body into the fish hold.

"Don't think," snapped Pharaoh. "Just get that boat out of here. Remember … straight east."

Perdiki boarded the government boat and started the powerful engines. Pharaoh undid the lines and quickly threw them on deck as the big grey boat backed out of the slip, turned and roared out of the cove.

CHAPTER 29

The Old Man and Spiro

The old man's voice had a rasp to it by the time he finished telling of Perdiki landing back on Mythos with Maria's body. His eyes were red and teary from the long night, and filled with veins and blotches and years of wear. He seemed to be aging as the night wore on.

"I think it is your turn now," he said. "You ended on music and love but what happened then? Where is this woman now and why is she not with you? When I first saw you in the cafenio this evening … and it seems long ago now … you were not a man in love, or at least not the good part of it. You … the son of my old friends … tell me the rest, for it can be no harder than what I'm about to tell you next."

The old man, settled back on the bench along the starboard side of the wooden fishing boat and waited for me to begin. I was quiet for five minutes while he stared impatiently at me and I think he was wondering whether I was going to speak at all.

The truth was that I didn't know where to begin. Events sometimes seem so scattered and have no inherent meaning until they all unroll and then they connect hard enough to create lightning and explosions and sometimes even meaning and if not meaning, then confusion.

CHAPTER 30

Spiro

Sometimes writing is like hiding. When it's really going well, you're gone for a while, and when you return you have to find your place in the world again.

Athens was napping that afternoon and I was finished working for the day. It wasn't that I was dry, I was full and content with what I'd already done. Anastasia made coffee and sat across the table, waiting quietly as I came back into focus. When she thought she had my attention, she leaned forward on her elbows and asked me to tell her something. "Anything, everything. I want to know all of you. Tell me about your father. Are you like him?"

"That's difficult to answer because I never knew him well enough to be able to answer that question."

"Was he away a lot or were your parents divorced?"

"No. He was always around. But it's very complicated. My father was Stratos," I said, watching her face show puzzlement across the table. "The musician."

Anastasia's broad eyebrows lifted and her dark eyes flashed with surprise. "You mean Stratos who played with Perdiki? Is that where you get your music?"

"And my guitar. My mother gave it to me after his death because she said I should have it," I answered, without elaborating further.

Anastasia responded, carefully. "I imagine it's difficult being the son of someone famous, or at least acknowledged to be great by his peers. I don't know what to say. My own parents are rich, but ordinary. Very ordinary. I can't imagine your life … how you grew up. What was he like?"

"He was home most of the time, I don't know a lot about him because he didn't talk. Wouldn't talk. He was missing one finger and a couple of the others were crippled, so his musical instruments sat in their cases against a wall. He never tried to play and when he spoke, it was never about his life as a musician."

"Do you remember anything he said?"

"Only a few things that have stuck with me but they're just scraps and so enigmatic that I'm still puzzling over them. Once he mumbled that he didn't need to play any more because the last time was enough, but he never explained what he was talking about. I don't know anything about a last time or a first time. I don't even know how or when his fingers became crippled. He never talked about any of it. You may know more than me about that part of his life because I grew up in North America where he wasn't well-known. Here, in Greece, people have heard of him."

When I paused to think ahead of what I was going to say, Anastasia nodded her head and didn't speak while she waited for me to continue.

"Perdiki was the one who was world-famous," I continued. "Who didn't know of Perdiki after the movies that won all those awards? There was a time when everyone knew his music. He was a romantic revolutionary figure like Che Guevara, and his image, the one painted by that artist who calls herself Athena, became a poster that you saw in every college dorm room. Maybe you've seen it, with the line, 'We are not yours.' I don't even know where that line came from or what it means."

"I've seen the poster and I've been to museums where Athena's work hangs. Did you ever meet her?"

"I knew her enough to call her *Thea*, Aunt, and not just out of respect. She was a real aunt to me. She took me to museums to look at paintings. She was nice but she was very different. I mean, aside from always having a bit of paint on her clothes or in her hair. When we were out for a walk, she would sometimes become quiet and stare at everything intensely. Whenever that happened, she would always go straight to her sketchpad when we returned to the house. She told me that if I wanted to be an artist, any kind of artist, I would sometimes just have to stop talking and watch everything around me very carefully."

As I spoke about Athena, I realized how much I missed her. "She would sit in the living room with my father and mother without a word being spoken. Once, I looked in and saw that there were tears running down her face. Yet they never seemed to say anything. They just sat together as if they were waiting for someone else to show up, or maybe they were already with him."

"What else about her?"

"She was always very caring with me, and never came to visit without bringing me armloads of art supplies. I trusted her more than anyone I knew and one day, I broke down and asked her why my father wouldn't talk to me."

"Your father was a great musician," she said, very carefully. "But now his hands are hurt and he can no longer play. He's very sad and that's why he doesn't talk to anyone. Including you. I'm sure that he loves you and cares about you but he's just too sad to say anything. I want you to know that he is a great and very brave man, but I can't tell you any more about that until you're older."

Anastasia reached across the table for my hand and asked, "How old were you when she finally told you?"

"She never had the chance. Thea Athena died a couple of years after we had that talk, so I was never old enough to know. Not even now, I guess."

Anastasia stood up, walked around to my side of the table and put her arms around me from behind. "You were in the middle of so much, my Spiro, my hero. Tell me a little more and then I'm going to take you for a walk."

"There was never a poster of my father," I continued, "because he was not the same as Perdiki. Everything he had to say was with his fingers. I think that when they were gone, that was it for him. He'd always stayed in the background where he wanted to be, so I'm not sure how many people noticed when he was gone. He was a musician's musician and those who listened to those famous recordings he made with Perdiki always talk about him. But most people, at least outside of Greece, seem to be unaware of my father. I listened to the recordings when he wasn't around, but he'd locked himself away from it all and wouldn't have them on when he was in the house. Mostly, he just sat and looked tired. I think he'd used everything up and didn't have anything left for me."

"Didn't he work? How did you live?"

"My father and Perdiki wrote a lot of music together that was used by the movies, so there were large royalty checks. And other people recorded their music, so there were those royalties, too. There was also my mother's salary from the university. Money was never an issue in our house. We were comfortable if we could ever manage to get comfortable."

"What did she teach?"

"She was a physicist. Although she taught a few classes, mostly she was occupied with theorizing and writing papers. I think she was trying to organize the entire universe. Nothing else would have satisfied her. That's just the way she was. She approached everything as if it were a science experiment. Even when she cooked it was that way and always had to prove a thesis."

"Is that how she raised you? Like an experiment?"

"Maybe. I've never thought about it that way. Maybe that's why she always spoke to me in Greek, although it was a second language for her. That's why I'm bilingual. She was fluent in Greek, but sometimes my father corrected her on a word or phrase. And occasionally he'd do the same with me."

"What were they like together?"

"I think they shared a complicated life early on but all I knew was that their life together was an isolated one because my father wouldn't socialize and never left the house. They would often sit close together, holding hands and it felt like they were in communication, although they barely talked to each other. It was as if everything had been already said and understood."

"And you felt left out?"

"Maybe that set the stage. I've always felt outside of everything until I met you." I stopped, hesitating because I hadn't meant to say that much, but Anastasia leaned across the table and gave me a long kiss.

"I feel the same way," she said, smiling deeply into me. "But let's not say anything else about that yet."

"But I want to talk about something else right now, since I'm saying so much already. I need to tell you. I had a girlfriend before."

"And I thought you were a virgin," she laughed.

"No," I said, trying to laugh with her but not succeeding. "There was a sailing accident and because of my bad judgement my girlfriend died."

"What happened?" she asked, taking my hand and squeezing it.

It took a minute before I could talk and then it all began to come out too quickly until Anastasia stopped me by putting her hands on my shoulders and saying softly, "Enough. You don't have to tell me everything at once. Be in the present with me now, instead."

"I just wanted to …" I began, but she stopped me again until I said, "It's all connected you know."

"No, I don't know, but I think we have lots of time to discuss it. Take me back to your apartment and let's just be in the present."

And that's how it was until I emailed the final draft of the book to my agent and waited for a response. Meanwhile, I searched for what to write next and kept coming up with a blank. I'd promised myself that I'd write something different this time, but nothing came to mind. A month later, my agent called to let me know that the publisher thought the new book transcended its genre and had the potential to become a best-seller. They were going to put some real money behind its release to try to make that happen. "Are you ready," my agent wanted to know, "to talk about the next one?"

Anastasia thought I should write about what Greeks were calling the *katastase*, the country's current fiscal crisis, the devastating effect it was having and the uprising of the people in demonstrations in response. I didn't want to tell her that I didn't believe the demonstrations would lead anywhere, even though I loved the spirit of the demonstrators. The country wasn't in political turmoil, it was just broke. It needed a boost of spirit, not a revolution. But I couldn't say any of this to Anastasia so I ducked the issue. When she eventually realized that I wasn't about to write about her cause, she said, "I don't care, Spiro. You don't need to find a revolution, but you need to find something."

As the weeks passed, I could feel myself growing increasingly remote as I became lost in where I wanted to go with my writing instead of in the work itself, I felt uneasy, unsettled. It was a miserable feeling, especially since I knew that I could easily commit to another sailing novel, and my agent was telling me I'd get a much bigger advance for it.

Long ago, when I was making a few extra bucks playing guitar in little, obscure clubs, I ran into an aging singer who'd been on the circuit far too long. Tony once said to me, "Spiro, you know you can be lying in bed next to the most beautiful woman in the world, in a fancy hotel room, in the money, you know what I'm saying, on top of the world, but somehow you have to go out sometimes and do something else, as if to prove that nothing can be that good. Do you understand what I'm saying to you? Listen to me, I'm being serious here. You've gotta watch out for that stuff."

That's what scared me.

CHAPTER 31

The Old Man and Spiro

"S he's right," the old man said. "I don't think you need to find a revolution right now, either." He laughed. "But you should be comforted to know that there's always one waiting when you're ready. Let me finish telling you the rest of the story. Then you'll be prepared to find your own revolution, if that's what you want."

The boat rocked as a fisherman motored out of the little harbor. "Too early for the fish," the old man said, "He must be coming back from his girlfriend's house." He chuckled, then resettled himself on the bench.

"Perdiki suffered the consequences of putting his spirit on the line in his songs," he said. "I was political. Pharaoh was political, god knows, Pharaoh was political. We believed the communist nonsense because it made sense. That's what we thought, or maybe were told to think. But we all knew Perdiki wasn't political. He was something else, entirely, but his words could be applied to our politics so we claimed him as one of our own."

The old man stared at me out of his teary eyes. "He was the opposite of you. He'd always known who he was, as much as anyone can be when they're caught up in the events of history. But the death of Maria, was the end of that for him. He could handle being a victim, but for someone else to die because of him was more than Perdiki could bear and his spirit broke."

CHAPTER 32

Perdiki

Perdiki was back in the cave house where he'd spent his first nights on the island but now it was as if he were invisible. There was no reason for anyone to suspect that he was living in the abandoned village or even in Mythos. As far as he knew, the police weren't searching for him because they had no idea he was on the island. As long as he stayed out of sight he was safe.

He sat on a patched-together chair at an ancient table that was thick with layers of faded, old green paint. The chair's wicker seat had long ago fallen apart and had been replaced with two roughly-finished boards that made for a hell of an uncomfortable chair. It could have been less spartan with something soft to pad the seat, but Perdiki couldn't be bothered to make it any better, though he sat there for hours every day. He thought bitterly that the splintering seat was his version of a hair shirt. The bench along one wall, where he slept, wasn't much more comfortable, but at least it didn't leave splinters.

In the middle of the table sat the notebook that had somehow managed to survive. He had opened it several times and read through what he'd written just before he'd jumped off the ship taking him to Mythos but there was nothing new he could write. All of his lyrics, even the laments, had always contained an element of hope and he just couldn't do it. There wasn't much left of anything and even the sounds of everyday life that always inspired his music had deserted him. The abandoned village where he was living was too far from any of the other villages for him to hear their sounds so his isolation was complete. He could peek at a few rooftops in the distance, but they were too far away for any sounds to carry. and he desperately missed the sounds of daily life, the chickens in the morning clucking loudly as they were fed, children yelling to each other and motorcycles roaring off into the distance. When he was in a city, he hated the cacophony of discordant noise but now he would have even welcomed that.

Along the rough, back wall of the cave house was a long counter, made of flat slate and supported by piled stone supports. At its center was a stone sink, and above it a grooved stone spout set into the rock wall that poured out an endless stream of water. It had a splash as it hit the sink and was the only sound he heard aside from Argos's occasional grumble when he was hungry.

On the floor, in a corner of the one-room house, was Argos's water bowl, and beside it another large bowl used for the giant dog's food. Whenever the dog was hungry, aside from grumbling, he would nudge Perdiki's leg to get his attention. Otherwise he stayed quietly beside Perdiki wherever he went, remaining as unobtrusive as possible for a 150 pound dog.

When Perdiki wasn't at the table, he brought his chair outside and spent his time in front of the cave house, drinking coffee and gazing at the land below through a spyhole-sized gap in the wall that hid the house from view. Below there were huge boulders that had collapsed to block the only easy path that led up to the abandoned village. Above the house were nearly unclimbable cliffs and it made him as secure as possible, but that didn't keep him from nervously watching for any signs of activity.

He knew that he had to get out of Greece if he were to survive and have any kind of life, but that would require help and he couldn't, wouldn't, endanger anyone again. So, he sat in suspended animation, unable to head in any direction other than the blackness of his guilt.

His only companion was Argos who rarely left his side and then only for a moment or so to scramble behind some boulders to relieve himself.

There was no one to talk to except his guilt and try as he could to focus his thoughts elsewhere, he always returned to Maria's death. He tried to imagine what happened as a many-sided object but never could arrive at a perspective that didn't find him at fault for her death.

Maria's funeral had been sad, all the more heartbreaking because it was done in secret. The priest, a trusted one, picked up a shovel and along with Zev and Pharaoh, helped bury her body after a service for a congregation that included only the three of them. Perdiki stayed away until the end, when he stood hidden behind some trees and watched her coffin and her life disappearing under the dirt.

Every few days, Zev brought food. He came by the rough trail on the cliff behind the house that he and Perdiki had used to escape when they were cornered by the police. It was a tough and dangerous route and he did it as rarely a possible. Zev would put the groceries on the table as quickly as possible and leave. He might pause to scratch Argos behind his ears, but he never said a word to Perdiki, who was equally as silent.

It went on like this, weeks of this limbo, until one afternoon Argos suddenly rose, fully alert, as if waking from a long sleep, and gave a low growl, so low that it was almost a whisper. He looked up at the cliff above the house, his big body so tense that he shook and then with a speed that was surprising in a dog of his bulk, he suddenly bolted and ran to the end of the abandoned village, turned up toward the cliff, and disappeared from view.

Argos had never budged when Zev brought the groceries, so there was something wrong. Perdiki waited, listening for any sounds that might indicate where the dog had gone and whether he'd found someone approaching. Unless Zev had been followed there was no reason for anyone to know his location and if any of the authorities did, then he should be already on his way down the path that led to where it was blocked by boulders that had to be climbed. But, he just couldn't move. What was the point?

His thoughts were broken by a familiar voice from somewhere above the house. "Easy, dog. Argos isn't it? You remember me, Argos? You were my houseguest. Oh, you're just trying to say hello? Okay. Don't lick. Yes, you're a good dog."

Five minutes later, Perdiki saw Pharaoh and Argos emerge at the far end of the abandoned village.

"I just happened to be in the neighborhood," called out the man with a face that looked as if it had been copied from an Egyptian mural. "I thought I'd drop in. You need a better walkway, Perdiki. You musicians are always so impractical. How is your public ever going to find you?"

Pharaoh dropped a familiar-looking pack on the ground when he reached Perdiki and took his hand and clapped him on the back. "Zev hurt his leg and asked me to help feed his animals. You were on the list. The sheep were easy. You? Not so much. Zev almost sent me to my death with this pack full of musician food."

Perdiki remained silent, brooding and not feeling fit for company.

"What? You're not going to thank me for risking my life to bring you this food? Bah! You are one rude musician. Do you have a couple of glasses? I brought some tsipouro and I can see that we need to open it right now. I'm a fisherman, not a mountain climber. I almost got killed getting here, and then your giant beast showed up and scared the hell out of me, so don't expect me to leave anytime soon. Let's have that drink."

Perdiki remained silent as he fetched two glasses and a second chair from inside the cave house.

"Aren't you talking to me?" Pharaoh asked as Perdiki handed him a glass. "Are you angry or something?"

The musician stared expressionlessly at Pharaoh for a full minute before finally speaking. "I'm done. That business with Maria took it all out of me. I was responsible for her death. You and Zev both know that."

Pharaoh's sharp angled face turned stern. "I don't know that and neither do you. What I do know is that Zev blames himself, too. So, which one of you was it? Which one is going to be Jesus and take on all our sins for himself." He waited, but when Perdiki didn't respond, Pharaoh continued. "Things happen in a war, my friend, and this is a war and they shot one of ours. It is us and them and sometimes we lose one and when we do it's all of us who lose that soul, that person. Are we all to blame? Should we all just capitulate and let the other side win?"

Perdiki filled their glasses with tsipouro without a response to Pharaoh's fundamental question. In exasperation, Pharaoh finally shouted at him, "Hey! Pay attention to me. I'm very serious. Tell me, again, if you think we should all just quit because there's guilt along the way?"

"Quit what? I'm not part of a side. I'm not in your politics. I'm just a musician who writes songs."

"You are what carries us. Your songs make us think there is hope that maybe the struggle is worthwhile."

"What struggle? Communism you mean? It failed, you know."

"I haven't been a communist since I realized that long ago."

"So what side are you on now?"

"The side that doesn't silence musicians and kill their friends and allies."

"They don't have to silence me now because I can't do it any more. I have nothing to say."

"That's strange for you who have always been so full of words."

"Well … I've run out."

"Rolling around in your guilt doesn't become you, Perdiki."

"How, do I erase this if you know so much?"

"You don't get rid of anything, you just swallow the bitter shit like we all do and get on with it. That's the way life works. I thought you knew that."

"I only know how to write songs."

"Shut up! You're making me angry. Don't you know, yet, that everybody carries one? Are you that self-centered? Why should you be exempt?"

"What would you do if you were me?"

"If it were me, I would get in my boat and go out and catch fish. That's what I know."

"I have to invent my fish and they're just not running right now. Maybe never again."

"Then do the other part."

"What do you mean?"

"When the fish aren't around, I carry things for people in my boat and sometimes I carry people. If you can't write, you can always perform, damnit. You don't have to write anything new for that."

"Perform where? How? Are you forgetting my situation?"

"I'm not forgetting anything. Everyone on this island, this Mythos, knows that Maria was shot. Did you know that?"

"I thought …"

"You didn't think. There are no secrets on Mythos. Everyone knows that Maria is dead and nothing is happening about it."

"So what can I do?"

"Give a concert to honor Maria. Speak truth."

"And then the police will kill me."

"No, because we'll have the international press there."

"You didn't just think this up by yourself, did you?"

Pharaoh looked down before he spoke again. "Zev didn't hurt his leg. He asked me to talk to you. That's why I came in his place. But it was all Athena's idea. Zev spoke with her on the telephone to let her know you were in hiding. She thought of holding a concert and said she could bring the press. You think anybody could ever stop Athena from doing what she wanted? Even you, so you better start thinking about what you'll perform."

"How can I do this? Everyone will be at risk just being in the audience. I can't be responsible for another death."

"It is the police who are responsible for deaths. You are responsible only for songs. Everyone has his position."

Perdiki tried to interrupt, but Pharaoh wouldn't let him.

"Just shut up for the next hour and pour us some tsipouro. Better yet, two hours, or when I finally get bored of this. Nothing else. No words. Just drink with me and think about what I've said. Think. Don't be a donkey's ass because I know that if you try to argue with one all you get for your troubles is a bad smell and a pile of shit."

The two men sat drinking tsipouro through much of the afternoon, taking turns at the spyhole. Every time Perdiki began to speak, Pharaoh shut him up, until finally he said okay and Perdiki managed to burst out, "How can I write music here? It's too damn quiet. I need to hear the sounds of life, other people … all of that."

Pharaoh laughed so hard he spilled some of his drink and had to refill the glass, topping up Perdiki's at the same time.

"Listen, Mr. Bird Man," he said when he'd gotten control of his laughter. "I mean … listen. I may not be a musician, but I've heard recordings of all kinds of music and I'll tell you what I've heard. I hear the seagulls in the morning when I set out to sea, the cicadas buzzing together in the heat of the day when I'm in my garden, and the wind when it rattles the olive trees. I've heard bird songs in Mozart and in jazz. I hear the dekaochto bird' song in the old Greek island music. I know that's where it all comes from, and what do I know? I'm a fisherman."

In the shadows of the late afternoon sun, Pharaoh's sharply angled face looked ancient. He lifted his arm in the air. "I think I've said all there is to say. Now I need to find out if you've gone deaf."

The musician raised his glass. "This is empty."

"Easy enough to fill," said Pharaoh, as he poured enough of the clear firewater to nearly overflow the glass. "I think I'll have one more, myself," he said, filling his glass to the top. "What shall we drink to?"

"You figure it out."

CHAPTER 33

The Old Man and Spiro

Daybreak was coming slowly, but already I could begin to make out shapes more clearly and almost see the ripples on the water that lapped against the hull of the boat and caused a faint rocking. The old man had sat very still for a long while, shoulders against the bulkhead, a bit crouched and obviously tired.

"Maybe we'd better stop," I said. "We can always continue tomorrow."

The old man pushed himself upright, shook his frail shoulders and said, "I'm alright. Just resting for a minute." I could feel my own tiredness and was surprised that he was willing to keep going.

"It's true that I'm getting tired, though," the old man said. "So I am going to tell you more right away because if you are going to understand anything, you need to know the people of this island." Petro leaned closer to me as if he were imparting a secret. "I told you before about how the villages were hidden but in one of them their salvation came through the Church. When the pirates arrived in their village, the people rushed into Agios Demetrios, closed and barred the big doors, and prayed at the top of their lungs. Being a superstitious lot, the pirates wouldn't bother them while they were praying, and besides, it kept everybody out of the way while they looted the village.

"One by one, the villagers made their way up to the alter and then beyond, to where there was an exit that was normally hidden by panelling. It led into a cave that ran all the way down to the sea. At the very last, Papa Stelios, chanting throughout, quietly turned the key in the back door to unlock it so that the pirates would assume they'd left that way and somehow slipped past their guards. Then, the old priest entered the cave, carefully closed the hidden panel behind himself, and followed the last of his flock through the underground passages and down to the sea.

"When the pirates finished gathering up the few things in the village worth carrying away, they were a very disappointed lot. All they had to show for the rough passage to the island and the tough climb up to the village were some jars of olive oil that was too old for anything but soap making, a few leaky pots and pans, and three small coins that had been dropped by a child rushing to the Church. Determined to at least be successful in the rape portion of pirating, since they'd failed so miserably at the pillaging end, they stormed the Church and found it empty, with the back door open. Aware that somehow the villagers had eluded them, they headed back to the sea, only to find their boat stripped of everything of value, and the villagers nowhere in sight."

The old man began a laugh that led into coughing and breathlessness. He thumped his hand on the table, waiting for his throat to clear enough to allow him to take a drink of wine. Finally, when he could breathe clearly again, he continued his story.

CHAPTER 34

Perdiki

Perdiki was alone with Argos in the cave-house. After an afternoon of drinking tsipouro, Pharaoh had slept for several hours, before he awoke suddenly sober and ready to leave. Argos accompanied Pharaoh part of the way along the path and then came ambling back after a few minutes to grumble about some food and fresh water. It reminded Perdiki that he hadn't eaten except for a little bread and cheese with the endless rounds of tsipouro that Pharaoh had forced on him. He shook some kibble into one of Argos's bowls, and filled the other under the spigot of ever-running water.

With the big dog happily slobbering down his meal, Perdiki looked through the supplies Pharaoh had brought. He found a package of well-cooked lamb, wrapped in wax paper. Cooked in with the lamb were potatoes and carrots. He spread it out on the table, along with a chunk of the coarse loaf of village bread, a piece of feta and a ripe tomato. It was the first full meal he'd had in many days. There were also three chocolate bars, a tin of pulverized coffee, and a few cans of beef stew and sardines. Under it all was a fat bone for Argos. When he gave it to him, the dog nearly swooned.

Still reeling from the hours of drinking with Pharaoh, Perdiki chewed slowly on the lamb to avoid disturbing his aching head and washed down the meal with cup after cup of water from the ever-running spigot. As the food found its way into his system he recovered quickly and was left feeling well, but very tired.

When he slid the food scraps from the wax paper into Argos's bowl he felt a pain in his chest and realized that it was a physical reaction to his deep exhaustion. He hadn't stopped running since he'd, literally, jumped ship and landed on the island. He knew he didn't dare let the emotion of it all overwhelm him. He lay on the bed, feeling the pain in his chest recede as he relaxed until he felt himself slipping into a dreamless, deep sleep thinking "at last" just as he lost consciousness.

In the morning, he woke to Argos's insistent nudging of his shoulder as the dog lost patience with waiting for a chance to get outside to relieve himself. Perdiki stumbled out of bed, barely awake, and opened the door to sunlight so bright he had to turn away and slowly let his eyes adjust until he could see well enough to step outside to peer through the spyhole at the empty world below. After a minute, the need for coffee drove him inside, though he left the door open to let in light and fresh air.

As he stirred the coffee in the briki and waited for it to boil, he heard the call of the dekaochto bird, with its familiar tones and cadence that made it sound like someone singing the Greek number for eighteen … deka ochto. The third or fourth time it repeated, he remembered what Pharaoh had said, laughed at himself, and rushed to the table where he'd left his notebook. He grabbed the pen that lay next to it, and quickly wrote the tune for the song of the decca octo and as soon as he did, lyrics began to flow. By the time he looked up, the coffee was boiling over.

He would have gone on working but his thoughts suddenly turned to the memory of the soldier he'd knocked off the cliff and the one Maria might have killed with a rock driven into his head with the force of intense outrage and anger. Both were on him and he'd be hunted down for them. It was no longer a matter of just his music, they would find him guilty of murder. If they weren't looking for him on the island at the moment, they were searching elsewhere and eventually their thoughts would turn back to the island and then they'd flush him out. If he went through with the concert, he'd be doing the job for them. It would be a lot simpler to slip out of Greece, rather than expose himself at the concert. He would disappoint a lot of people, but he would be alive.

He cleaned up the mess from the boiled-over coffee and prepared another cup, watching it carefully this time while he tried to muffle his thoughts and succeeded relaxing again. Something was settled in his mind, but he wasn't yet sure what it was.

CHAPTER 35

Athena

Athena roared as she painted. It was early in the morning, so early that the sun hadn't risen and her neighbors were barely abed. She didn't give a shit. The music was up loud enough to drown out their shouted complaints and when they pounded on their ceilings or floors, she just added the rhythm into her work as accent marks. The paint flew in all directions, and her hair, uncut and wild for months, collected color like a prism. Squeezed-out paint tubes filled the big metal garbage can in the corner to overflowing, and drips of color were all over its outsides and the floor.

One morning, there was a pounding on her door, louder and more persistent than most and it just wouldn't quit. Finally, she picked up a piece of two by six from her pile of scrap wood, and headed for the door, ready for a confrontation. When she swung it open, instead of irate neighbors, she saw Stratos and the American girl looking disturbed and impatient.

When they saw the mess of her studio, they dragged Athena to a nearby café that had grown used to her paint-spattered appearance and the waitress automatically showed them to her usual table on the street, set apart from any others.

Stratos said nothing, spending most of his time staring at his hands. Finally, Athena asked, "What are you doing here?" She glanced at the woman sitting with Stratos. "I know who you are, but I'm not sure about your name."

"Everybody always referred to me as the American girl, so I'm not surprised. I'm Emma Huntington. Now it's Emma Glaros."

"You're married?" Athena's smile broke through the drips of paint on her cheeks. "If I wasn't so fucking wrapped up in myself I should have seen that in you." She reached across to kiss Emma on both cheeks. "I wish great joy to both of you."

Stratos looked up from his gloom long enough to give a shy smile, then went back to staring at his crippled hands.

"There's more," Emma said, returning the smile, "or there will be more in a few months."

"Congratulations even more," said Athena. "Let's have a bottle of wine and celebrate this." She signalled the waitress. "And some food right away."

"First, we should tell you about Perdiki," said Emma.

"Have they captured him?" Athena's breath caught as she said it.

"No. Not as of yesterday," said Stratos, raising his eyes to Athena.

"Then what is it?" she asked.

"They're saying he killed two soldiers," Stratos said.

"I don't believe that."

"Of course, he didn't," broke in Emma. "All we really know is that he managed to get to Samos, but something happened there and they're blaming him. Zev was in touch to tell us. The police are searching all over Greece for Perdiki, but Zev says he's actually back on Mythos."

"They'll find out, soon enough. Someone will slip," said Stratos, staring down at his hands again until Athena spoke.

"This is my fault," she said. "I brought this on him with the concert. I thought it would help him get past his guilt over Maria's death. But, shit, getting him out would be a lot easier if we could just slip him away now, before the government figures out that he's on Mythos."

"I know," said Stratos, "but now Zev says he insists on the concert. He won't leave, otherwise. We should still be able to get him out of the country, but it will just be harder. We are going to have a very fast boat pick up Perdiki after the concert and take him to Turkey, which is less than fifty nautical miles from the island. I have friends who can easily get him from there to Paris."

"Why does he have to do this concert? Isn't his life worth more than one performance?"

"It was your idea, Athena," said Emma with careful calm.

"Jesus. Shit. Fuck. Damn. I know it's my fault!"

Emma continued, "No it isn't Athena. It was a good idea and if it all works you'll get a Perdiki in Paris who is a whole man."

"Give me strength!" Athena groaned ironically and harshly. "I don't want to be this good. I just want him back."

"Don't pull that shit, Athena," snapped Emma, raising her voice. "He says he needs to say goodbye to Greece. Maybe wants to make some kind of statement. Maybe he just wants to be a martyr. I don't know. I have my own things to look out for."

"I'm sorry. You're right, of course. Let's celebrate because you and Stratos are here now and so am I and soon you'll have a baby. Perdiki is crazy, I know because I'm crazy. And crazy people always survive, right?" Tears ran down her face, across the paint drips and the hollows that were left from no sleep and only work and worry. She wiped at her tears with her sleeve and said, laughing, "But my work is going great."

At the end of the meal, Emma told Athena the rest of her news. They were leaving in a few days for America where there were doctors who might be able to help Stratos with his hands and she had an offer from a university that would let her do the kind of work she wanted. "I'm a physicist and it's time I got back to work. I also have some family left that I'd like to see and introduce to Stratos," she said.

"I thought Stratos might play with Perdiki."

"He tries every day, but the pain is too great, as is the frustration."

"Can you still bring him to the concert? You know what it would mean to Perdiki. It's just a few days away. Are you able to get back into Greece?"

"Yes, they've already done to Stratos what they wanted, so they no longer care about him."

"Then will you come?"

"I'll try," she said looking at Stratos meaningfully. "We'll try. Okay Stratos?"

"Yes. Okay," he mumbled. "We'll try."

When they were gone, Athena made her way back to her studio, thinking of how to organize everything. If she failed to get the international press at the concert, the police could break it up, unnoticed. With live cameras rolling and reporters ready to interview government officials, it was unlikely anything would happen until the concert was over, and the press dispersed.

She decided to wake even earlier every day, so that she could paint before confronting the dilemma of getting the press to Mythos without prematurely revealing the impending concert to the world. If the Greek government got word of the event they would probably send troops to surround the concert to capture and arrest Perdiki at the end of the concert. There might also be additional troops to guard the ports if he somehow slipped away. If the ports were blocked, there was no escape. That's what scared her the most. The idea was to keep the police presence limited to those who were already on the island because there weren't enough of them to cover everywhere.

Perdiki's flight from the authorities and his current situation had not appeared in the media anywhere in the world and Athena took the task on herself. She needed to build awareness and world-interest in Perdiki before the concert so that when news of it did get out, it would have a greater impact. She also needed to arrange for the concert to be recorded because once interest was stirred up, she wanted people to hear the concert and Perdiki's music.

In order to entice TV news crews, and awaken world interest in the musician, Athena had leaked to three different American news shows that Perdiki had escaped the clutches of the government and was now on the run. She promised that in the next few days she would set up interviews for them in a secret location. No mention was made of the concert.

A friend in New York, who was the art critic for the New York Times, put her in touch with Heleni Tsimbides, a features editor who could be trusted because she was Greek and was obsessed with Perdiki and his music. The prospect of an article from the perspective of the famous musician's lover, a well-known artist, had Heleni willing to agree to any conditions set by Athena, including absolute secrecy. If she maintained absolute discretion, Athena promised a secret interview with Perdiki and told her to be ready to fly to Greece at an hour's notice.

When she could no longer think about the details, Athena would pick up a brush and become lost in the detail. She had added another panel and the work had evolved and was now clear and luminescent, with the spectre of immense failure still overhanging it all, but diminished in evidence. She was excited by the work and didn't want to stop. But the telephone would ring and it would be a friend who was helping, or supporting, or offering money, or simply making noise, and the brush would grow stiff lying on the palette.

She contacted the head of the recording company in New York that produced Perdiki's albums. He was so excited at the prospect of recording the concert that he insisted he fly to Paris to meet with her.

"I'll be there on Thursday," he said. "Mark it on your calendar," and then hung up the phone before she could put him off.

Athena threw a cup of coffee across the studio where it smashed against a wall and left a blotch of dripping coffee stain. "Okay," she screamed, "now, it's on my calendar."

CHAPTER 36

The Old Man and Spiro

The old man insisted we walk again. "If I stay still for too long, my body might forget it's alive and I'd be gone," he said, "Then who would tell you the rest of the story, eh Spiro?"

It was a false dawn. The stars were dimmed out, but the sun would be a while yet in rising. They walked up from the docks to a road that ran along the coast and quietly made their way to the skeleton of a failed café, someone's dream that was located too far out of town to attract anyone. One of the windows was covered with a big sheet of plywood and the other had a drawn curtain. But half of one side of the building was wide open and blackened, where a fire had eaten it away.

"Everything isn't always perfect. Even here in paradise we have fires, terrible fires," the old man said. "A few years ago, eleven people died. In the summer, it gets too hot and then everything is dry and one day, boom! You look up the hill and there is a black cloud of smoke and flames just starting to show. You can either get out of the way or die. All you can do is run for the sea and hope the fire doesn't overwhelm you. Regardless, the houses will survive because unlike you, they're made of stone. But I'll tell you the surprising one, olive trees. They regenerate. An old tree will get burned right down to a stump and in a few years a ring of new trees will grow around it."

CHAPTER 37

Perdiki

Perdiki barely noticed that he had been alone for the past two days. He'd been sitting at the old table, writing in his notebook, so engrossed in his work that the hours passed without notice and only Argos's occasional nudges for food or a walk broke the spell. He'd finally relented and put a chunk of his rotted-out mattress on the patched old chair and now could sit for hours without fear of splinters. The sounds of his environment, the buzzing of the cicadas in the heat of the afternoon, the small birds in the morning and the dekaochto when it called its mate all found their way into the music that he was writing.

Pharaoh had left enough canned food and cheese to last for a week, so Perdiki wasn't really expecting any visitors for a while. The bread might run out, but he wouldn't go hungry. They'd drunk all the tsipouro, but that was just as well. There was all the running water he could drink and enough pulverized coffee and sugar to keep him going for a long time.

He scrubbed his clothes, and laid them on some boulders behind the wall that hid the cave-house and then washed himself and stood naked in the wind to dry. The wind and the hot afternoon sun had his clothes ready within an hour. When he was done, he washed Argos, a pot of water at a time. The big Newfoundland dog revelled in it and stood patiently while Perdiki fetched pot after pot of water and scrubbed with a piece of the soap he'd had in the sack he'd been carrying since his first visit to the cave-house. While Argos was busy rolling in the dirt to dry his fur, Perdiki heated up some water and shaved.

Afterward, he opened a can of sausages and put half on a plate and half in the big dog's bowl. Argos gave a groan of pleasure as he slowly savored each morsel. When he was finished, he sat beside

Perdiki, put a giant paw up on his knee, and looked up at him with an expression that Perdiki read as "Why the party, chum?"

He ruffled the black fur on the dog's massive head and said, "We're alive, which means I guess we're winning." Argos rolled his eyeballs up to meet Perdiki's gaze and then twisted around and licked him on the cheek. "I guess you agree," the musician said, laughing.

The work continued until dark. He would not risk the light of the lantern leaking through the door, so he slept when it was dark and woke at sunup. At night, he rose to step outside to peer through the spyhole, but there was never a threat from the path below and he went back to sleeping soundly.

On the third morning since he'd seen Pharaoh, he poured kibble into Argos's bowl and put the cheese and the remaining half loaf of bread on the table. He brewed coffee and let it cool while he ate and wrote in the notebook.

He might have missed the sound of rocks falling from the cliff were it not for Argos suddenly jumping up and giving a low growl. When he opened the door, the big dog shot out, raced to the end of the village and tore off up the cliff. A moment later there was a scream, a thud, and the frightened curses of a man in pain. Argos came back into sight and ran to Perdiki, stopped in front of him and looked back and forth until the man understood and followed him. On a narrow ledge just above the cave-house, he saw a man clinging to a stunted tree and in obvious distress.

"Who are you?" shouted Perdiki.

"Michaeli. They call me Mickey."

"Why are you here, Mickey?"

"My brother is in the hospital."

"Sorry to hear that, but what does it have to do with me?"

"He is a soldier. The one you threw a rock at and knocked off a cliff."

"He would have captured me."

"That was his job."

"And my job was stopping him. Is he badly hurt?"

"Fractured skull."

"Sorry to hear that, Mickey."

"You'll be sorry," he snarled back.

"Not so far. You are stuck up there and I am down here. What did you hurt?"

The man tried to move and gave out a shriek of pain. "I think I've broken my leg."

"Are you a soldier?"

"No, I'm too young."

"Who sent you here, then?"

"No one. I came on my own. I knew you'd been here before. My brother told me that they almost caught you here the last time. I figured I'd check if you'd come back. Guess I was right."

"Yes. You've got me, Mickey. Nice chatting with you but I have to get back to work. See you later."

"Wait, you can't just leave me here."

"Tell me, what about the other soldier who was hurt?"

"Somebody hit him with a rock but he's okay and already out of the hospital. I heard they sent him away somewhere. Now will you help me?"

"I didn't put you there, Mickey. Why should I get you down?"

"Because you can't leave me up here like this."

"What would you have done if you hadn't been stupid enough to fall?"

"It was your dog. He ran at me and slammed into me. That's why I fell."

He patted Argos's head. "Good dog!"

"What are you going to do?"

"I will give him a big treat."

"What about me?"

"You don't deserve a treat."

"Please get me down from here."

"And then?"

"Help me get home."

"Hello, I'm Perdiki, here is your son, Mickey? I don't think so."

"Whatever you want, then."

"*Lipon*, listen, what I want is for you to vanish and never have been here. But that can't happen, so you will have to be my prisoner until I figure out what to do. You can't escape with a broken leg, so you will be dependent on me. If you give me any trouble … well … you've already met my dog."

"Anything," said the desperate young man, calling out in pain between words.

"I'm going to find something to use as a splint. Now, don't run off."

Perdiki rummaged through the ruined village until he found a stick that would serve, and a length of thin rope he could use to tie it on the injured leg. Climbing with great care, he managed to reach Mickey and realized that his face was barely developed and that he was little more than a boy. Amidst a stream of Mickey's howls, Perdiki immobilized the leg, guessing from the feel of it as he tied on the makeshift splint that the bones were all intact, and that if it were truly broken, it was only a simple fracture that would not require setting.

Slowly, he helped the young man rise to his feet and steady himself, ignoring the yowls of pain and focussing on getting Mickey into motion. When the young man was finally settled enough to listen, Perdiki instructed him to "Turn in and face the cliff." With his arm around the boy, he helped him accomplish the maneuver through a series of hops that were accompanied by yelps of pain. Ignoring the noise, Perdiki continued, "You need to use your hands to hang on, not to me, but to the rock. I know you can't put any weight on that leg, so we'll have to do this very slowly. You're basically going to hop on one foot from foothold to foothold. At least you chose well when you picked your right leg to injure because we are going to edge our way off this ledge to our left. Put your arm around my shoulders and lean some of your weight on me as you make each hop. Make sure, though that your hands are doing most of the supporting. That's the key because I'm not sure I'm strong enough to bear all your weight and I don't want to find out. We only need to make it back to the main path and then you can rest for a few minutes where it's a bit wider. The rest of the way down will be a lot easier than this first stretch. We'll take one very slow step at a time."

Mickey wept with the pain of his dangling injured leg, and though he nearly slipped several times and hung far too much of his weight on the musician, they eventually reached the main path. Perdiki was shaking from the exertion and tension. and once he'd found a perch for Mickey, he had to sit for a while on a boulder and try to stop the pounding in his chest. When he could finally breathe freely again, he turned to the boy and said, "You stupid malaka, on top of everything else, I was busy writing when you dropped in on me and destroyed my day."

"I like your music," Mickey said.

"Give me strength," groaned Perdiki, ironically.

"I have all your records hidden in my room."

"Would it be considered euthanasia if I just left you to die?"

"I don't understand you," grimaced the boy as he tried to shift position.

"I'm well aware of that. Why do they call you Mickey? Where did you get that name?"

"We lived in Cleveland, Ohio for ten years. My family, I mean. The kids there couldn't say Mihaeli so they called me Mickey and it stuck. Same thing with my brother. His name is Panteli, so they called him Pete and that stuck too."

"Okay, Mickey from Cleveland with the brother, Pete, it's time we made it the rest of the way down." He rose with his back and muscles stiff from the effort of getting the boy off his precarious perch. The musician reached up an arm to help the little son of a bitch to his feet just as Argos came up to join them. The boy shrank back, lost his balance and fell with a scream. The giant dog watched him with a mild curiosity but not a lot of interest and was untouched by the boy's screams.

Perdiki helped Mickey back up to his feet, and slowly they made their way down to the abandoned village and the cave-house, with Argos leading the way and occasionally glancing back to check their progress. When they were finally inside, Perdiki eased the boy onto the one bunk and brought him a cup of water. Wordlessly, he heated two cans of stew, poured off a little of each for Argos and divided the rest of the food between two bowls, handing one to Mickey and keeping the other for himself.

When they had finished eating, he collected the bowls and washed them under the spigot that ran cold spring water nonstop into the stone sink. He cleaned Argos's dish as well and filled the dog's water bowl.

Finally, he turned to the boy, who was whimpering. "There is nothing more I can do for you until someone comes with supplies and I don't know when that will be. With two of us, the food will have to stretch until then. Your leg may be broken, but if it is, I can't feel anything, which means at least it's still in place. That's good because I would have no idea how to set it."

When the boy didn't respond, Perdiki turned to him. "Can't talk?"

"I'm just thinking how stupid I've been."

"Welcome to the consensus. And add in inconvenient while you're at it because I really don't need you or any of this."

Mickey tried to rise up on his elbow to speak, but sank back from the pain and held up his hand until he could finally speak. "They know about the concert," he said. "The word is around the island about it. That's why no one is looking for you because the police know you'll be coming right to them. And then they will arrest you for murder. They are telling everybody that you killed my brother and the other soldier, even though they're both still alive. My brother told me that they'll be sending him away as soon as he can travel. That way they can arrest you at the concert and nobody can say anything."

"Thank you, Mickey. You have just earned your keep."

"My brother also told me that another soldier killed Maria … I knew her, she was really nice."

"Mickey, you are coming to the concert as my guest."

"I don't think I should do that. I could get in a lot of trouble. Besides," he said, indicating his splinted leg, "how would I get there?"

"You'll get there if Argos and I have to drag you. You're going to be the opening act."

"Why would I do that?"

"Because I saved your life and will continue to do so. And because you know that I didn't kill anyone and somehow there must be a gram of conscience in you. Besides, you like my music. So, you're going to get up on stage and tell everybody the truth."

"Won't I be arrested?"

"The truth is sometimes expensive and somebody has to pay for it. I've paid for years. Now, it's your turn."

"What does that have to do with …"

"The concert?"

"Nothing of consequence will happen to you. I may get myself killed with this concert, but I want everybody to know that it was for my music and not murder. You're going to tell them the truth."

"But then they'll arrest me."

"It's true that's a habit with this government. But you will have the golden pass. They won't touch you because the international press will be there. It might be a good idea, though, to leave Mythos until there's a new bunch in charge because once the press leaves, they may come after you."

"What about you? Can you get away?"

"I'm not your problem, so don't think about it. But you're going to have to leave Mythos, regardless, because if you don't get up at the concert and tell the truth, you won't have a friend on this island because I will make sure everybody knows."

"Then I'm damned if I do and damned if I don't."

"You're only damned if you don't. You'll be praised if you do the right thing. Who knows? I might even write a song about you."

CHAPTER 38

The Old Man and Spiro

The old man revived a bit with the story of Mickey and moved to the cockpit where he was watching for the impending dawn. "Quickly," he said. "Tell me how you finally got here because I need to tell you the rest of my story and I want to get to bed by the time the sun comes up. Tell me the rest about you and your Anastasia and why you left her arms to come to this island and spend the night talking to an old man."

CHAPTER 39

Spiro

The woman in the bakery now knew Anastasia and always gave her two cookies, one for each of us.

Whenever she visited her parents, Anastasia came back with one or two of her paintings. They filled the walls, and the passion and strength of them were nearly overwhelming in the tiny apartment. It was as if I were in the midst of her interior landscape. Her dynamic style reminded me of Athena's and I loved her for it.

What I know about art I learned from Thea Athena. "It's always the eye," she told me the afternoon she showed me a print of Hopper's Nighthawks. "It's obvious that it's great, and yes the style adds immensely to it, but it's the eye that landed on that image that counts. You either have that eye or you don't. You can be a talented painter and not see a damn thing. It's that twist in the universe that everyone else misses that makes art."

Anastasia had that eye and now I really knew who was watching me.

I avoided asking her why she was no longer painting, but assumed it was because of her political involvement. Eventually that resolved itself when Anastasia took off for a demonstration in Thessaloniki and two days later phoned from a hospital. "The police rushed us," she said softly. "And when I fell, this time you weren't there to rescue me. I couldn't get up and the crowd ran over me. Nobody did a damn thing, my Spiro. They all just ran away. Can you come take me home?" She sounded weak and depressed and scared. "It was the police who brought me to the hospital. I've had enough. They can have their useless demonstrations without me."

Two hours later, I was on a flight to Greece's second largest city, and a half hour after that I was sitting beside Anastasia's bed. She was hooked to an IV and looking pale green in the fluorescent light of the hospital. One side of her face was covered in bandages and she had a cast on her left wrist.

We kissed awkwardly because of her bandages, and she held onto my hand when I sat down. "The doctor said I can go home tomorrow."

"I love you, Anastasia."

"Tell me that in bed, my Spiro. Right now, we need to be very practical. My clothes are in my room at the hotel where I've been staying. Can you bring them to me tomorrow? The room is booked for tonight, so I'll just give you the key and you can stay there. Do you think you can get us a flight out of here right away?"

"I'll make reservations as soon as I leave here."

"I want to be back at your little apartment with you." She looked at the cast on her wrist. "I won't be able to play the baglama for a while, but I can think of some things to keep you happy."

"Well, you do have a good singing voice."

Although she was a little shaky the next afternoon when we left for the airport, by the time we were halfway to Athens her strength returned.

We took a taxi to the apartment. Like the night we met, I had to help her up the stairs and into the apartment. Once she was settled on the couch with a light blanket over her legs, I turned to the kitchen to make her a cup of tea. When I turned back, I saw that her jeans were lying on the floor.

"My legs were scraped up, too," she said. "I'll show you." When she drew the blanket back, I saw that like the first time, her panties had shifted over to one side. "This time," she said, drawing my face to her tight, black curls, "you're going to be a different kind of gentleman. The intimate kind."

Late in the evening, after I'd helped Anastasia to bed, we lay together talking about what came next in our lives.

"I want to spend my time painting and being with you. Is that okay?" she asked. "I don't know why I ever made that stupid decision to give up painting to make noise in the street. Now that I've figured out what I want, what are you going to do, Spiro?" she asked. "Sail for big money or write what you want?"

"I don't know what I want."

"Before you met me you were planning to spend time on Mythos after you finished the damn sailing book, right?"

"Yes."

"The book is done."

"But now you're here," I said.

"I'll be here when you get back."

"Come with me."

"No. I think this is something you need to do on your own."

"What will you do?"

"I will be very busy messing up your floors with paint. You need to go to that island where people live so long and strive so little. Go feel who you are. If someone wants to talk to you, listen. I want to be with you but I can't just be with the half that you reveal. You need to have the rest of yourself filled in to replace all that pain and guilt that is clogging your mind. I'm in love with the part of you that I know, but I'm greedy and demanding and I want the other half because it's not enough otherwise. I may not love the other half of you and that I don't know. I won't know until I see him … feel him … know who he is."

CHAPTER 40

The Old Man and Spiro

The old man stared at me, stared right through me. "Just because I'm old and my senses aren't what they were doesn't mean I still don't recognize bullshit. Tell me what really happened and quit writing fiction."

"She kicked me out."

"Is that, then, the truth?"

"I told you the truth, but she was more harsh, more finite."

"Finite? That's one of those writer words."

"Okay, then. It was an ultimatum."

"She stayed with you while you finished the last book and then kicked you out? Maybe you're like Hemingway and you just get one book out of a woman."

The old man laughed while I struggled for a comeback but he spoke again before I was able to think of one.

"I shouldn't have said that," he said, "because I think this Anastasia of yours is a very smart and deep woman. There are some women, I've heard, who can't sit around while you're busy writing. They want a full-time person, not someone who drifts off for hours at a time. But I don't think that's the case here, although I've never met your Anastasia. She's a painter and if she's now working again, she'll be drifting off too."

The old man rummaged through the cabinets and finally looked up, puzzled. "This is one of the things about age. Sometimes I'm not sure what I'm looking for." He looked up at me from under his long, unruly eyebrows, the grey hairs wiry and tangled. "If you live on one side of Mythos you get to see sunrise over an island, and if you live on the other side, you get sunset over a different island. Do you know what that means?"

CHAPTER 41

Perdiki

Perdiki lay on the floor, silently cursing the boy with the broken leg who was sleeping in his bed. At least the boy was asleep, because he seemed to be a bit thick and Perdiki could only take so much of his company. The kid was too young to successfully hide his resentment for his dependence on Perdiki. He regretted his frankness when he'd told Perdiki about the soldiers who had been injured on Samos. It was said in a moment of weakness. But there were no further revelations, and mostly he didn't talk. He seemed to be waiting for someone to rescue him and didn't realize that Perdiki already had.

The air was textured by the dampness caused by the spigot that never stopped running and the sound of its splashing water would soon have him out of bed to relieve himself. It was time. Shafts of morning light penetrated the darkness of the old wood door of the cave-house and reminded him why he never lit the lantern when it was dark outside, lest his light reveal his existence.

He still had no idea what to do about Mickey. The boy needed medical care and for that he had to somehow be transported to one of the villages below, but how to accomplish that without getting himself caught or endangering any of his friends eluded him.

Argos suddenly rose to his feet and snatched Perdiki's attention away from the problem. He'd been with the big dog long enough to recognize that Argos was expressing anticipation rather than a reaction to danger as he stood waiting at the door. When Perdiki swung it open, the dog charged through the deserted village and headed up to the mountain path. Perdiki followed and stopped at the end of the village to wait for Argos to return with whoever was bringing supplies and news.

After a minute or two he heard the voice of Zev, "You look like an Egyptian goat, on that cliff, Pharaoh."

A second voice spoke. "I wish I was part goat. The last time I was up here I swore I wouldn't do this again, and now look at me."

The two men emerged from behind the last of the boulders at the end of town. carrying full packs and looking weary from the difficult traverse. Argos trotted ahead, proud of who he was bringing to visit. Before they could come any closer to the entrance to the cave-house, Perdiki held up his hand.

He quickly explained the situation with Mickey and cautioned about the boy catching sight of them. "So far," said Perdiki, "he doesn't know who is helping me."

"Can he walk?"

"Not so far."

"Maybe we should break his other leg to be sure," Pharaoh suggested with an exaggerated grin.

"That would just make it harder to drag him out of here," countered Zev.

The pair sat on boulders at the far end of the village while Perdiki brought the packs into the cave-house. Mickey awoke while he was unpacking the supplies. "Is someone here?" he asked.

"I have a couple of friends outside. We are trying to figure out how to get medical help for you without exposing anyone. These are my friends, not a political group. Do you understand that?"

"I wouldn't say anything," Mickey quickly responded.

"I don't want to test that. Just stay in bed. It's in your best interests. If you don't get help soon I don't know what will happen with your leg."

The afternoon passed as the three men sat on boulders and talked. A couple of times Perdiki went into the cave-house to make coffee. Because he was set for the near term with ample groceries, he was able to give Argos a full can of sausages and watched his enjoyment of it while he put together a plate of cheese, olives and bread to bring outside along with the coffee.

He sat with the others on boulders at the end of town, discussing whether to bring a doctor to examine Mickey. There was one they knew from the old days who would help them, but that would expose his face to the boy and they couldn't trust Mickey to keep it to himself. A masked doctor, then? Just too absurd to consider, though it might actually have solved the problem.

Finally, they realized that the only practical solution was for Perdiki to help Mickey down to where the lower path was blocked by boulders, leave him there, and then head back to the other side of the island and Pharaoh's house, where no one knew he'd ever stayed. He would be secure there until the concert.

It was a fairly navigable path, even for someone in Mickey's shape and he was sure he could make it. Once he'd left off the boy and was well on his way, someone would anonymously contact the small island hospital and tell them that they should bring a doctor to where they'd seen him. Perdiki would ask Mickey to say that he'd slipped while climbing over the boulders and hurt his leg and not say anything about Perdiki or his whereabouts. He was to say that he'd managed to splint his leg by himself, but had no way to make it over the boulders. It was asking a lot of the boy to make the story believable and Perdiki doubted he would even try.

One of the packs the men had brought contained groceries and the other a change of clothes for Perdiki to wear at the concert. He was not going to carry anything extra to Pharaoh's house, so he asked Zev to hold the clothing for him until the night of the concert.

After Zev and Pharaoh were gone, Perdiki explained to Mickey the part of the plan that involved him. The boy grimaced at the idea of getting down the path, but assured Perdiki that he would do exactly as he was asked and not reveal that he had contact with Perdiki. There was no reason to believe him.

"Mickey," he said, "let me ask you something. What, exactly, do you think I've done wrong that the police should be chasing me?"

"You escaped."

"But why were they holding me at all?"

"I don't know. That's the government's business. They know what they're doing." There was a certainty to the set of his jaw that was disturbing. The challenge was to find a way to unbalance him.

"You think so?" asked Perdiki. "Then, I ask again, why did they arrest me?"

"Because you are a communist or an anarchist." The boy practically sneered. "That's what my brother says. He says you are dangerous."

"Mickey. I am not a communist or an anarchist or any other *ist*. I'm a songwriter and a musician. That's it. And if I were dangerous, I would have left you up there or pushed you the rest of the way off the cliff. Instead, I risked my life to save you and I've asked my friends to do the same."

"I appreciate that."

"Then appreciate this… you will be lied to throughout your life by governments and people, even relatives and friends. Even your own brother because he doesn't know any better. I will never lie to you or anyone. That's why the government wants to get rid of me. You know what they're like because you know they lie. You were the one who told me that they were going to claim that I had killed that soldier they hid away."

"I shouldn't have told you."

"Why not?"

"I shouldn't be helping you."

"*Panagia mu*, mother of god, why not?"

"Don't try to trick me, Perdiki. You already know why."

Out of patience, Perdiki gave up for the day and spent his time outdoors, sitting on a boulder with notebook and pen and trying to blot out the world so that he could have at least one new song for the concert. Every couple of hours he would check on Mickey, give him drinks and food and help him outside to relieve himself. They talked no further that day until just as the sun was setting, Perdiki perched Mickey on a big boulder, as comfortably as possible.

"Look," the boy said, "I appreciate that you're taking care of me and I think I understand what you were trying to say earlier."

"There is something I want you to think about, Mickey. Maybe you owe it to me or maybe to your conscience to do something for me."

"I already told you that I won't reveal to anyone that I was here with you."

"There's more, Mickey." When it was explained to him, the boy shook his head. "I don't know if I can do that," was all he would say.

CHAPTER 42

The Old Man and Spiro

The old man had settled in comfortably, with his feet up on the bunk and his back against a bulkhead.

"I began this by telling you some of the history of Mythos. What I didn't tell you is that the island knew everything. It had long ago sprouted these people and had always been aware of their latest mischief. This time it was a secret concert that everyone knew about, even those who weren't supposed to be in on it. People were readying their best clothes and cutting their hair. Young girls were trading makeup with each other and everywhere the songs of Perdiki were being hummed. Chairs were being brought to the concert site in the back of the vegetable truck that made the rounds through the villages every day. Big secret, neh?

"But even the island was unaware that the international press was coming. That was the real secret and nobody was telling it. Athena had set it all up and only Zev, Pharaoh and Perdiki knew. It was one secret that the island telegraph couldn't broadcast. And even Mythos, itself, was for once ignorant. It was a wonder that it didn't have an earthquake when it found out.

"The concert was to be held in a village square that was on a cliff above the sea. Beside it was an old church whose young priest carefully made his way to the beach each morning down a crumbling path that had started out as a goat path and had progressed little beyond that point. For two full days, to the delight of the Father, three men had worked to better the path. He knew it wasn't a miracle and exactly why it was being done, and of course everyone on the island knew as well and Mythos itself let loose easily of rocks that needed to be moved.

"Not that Mythos was incapable of a little mischief, but it was limited. The first time the people set everything up, the wind came from a direction where it only blew the chairs off the square and not into the sea.

"The villagers went to church frequently to pray for good weather for the concert because they couldn't speak directly to Mythos, but the island heard their prayers. It had conferred with a few friends, Aeolus, Poseidon and even Zeus and had reached an agreement for a mild night, providing the music were soothing enough. With that crew there is always a catch, but this seemed a reasonable one.

"Although Mythos was ashamed of the wine its grapes had produced that year, the villagers were bringing out their precious store of the previous year's vintage in preparation for a hell of a night. Up in one of the mountain villages, Papa Souza was selling his tsipouro as fast as he could bottle it, and trying to avoid having a drink with each customer. There was mass to serve, too!

"The police were preparing their own little surprise, that everyone knew about. It was Mythos. What did they expect? These people had been together for centuries. They were, they are, aboriginals." The old man stopped for a minute to take a sip of water.

"It is like this with some of these islands and their people," he continued. "There is no mystery about it, it's just fact. Not the islands so full of tourists and nightclubs that they have lost their souls, no, the smaller islands like this one, this Mythos, where the people and the soil are one."

The old man took a breath. "And now what about you, Spiro?"

"You already know my story."

"But you still don't know your own story. Yes, I know, your girlfriend kicked you out because you can't solve the mysteries of the universe and you're not welcome back until you do. And you think you're responsible because nature went against you and your last girlfriend died. That's as much as you can tell me about yourself, so now I'll tell you the rest."

CHAPTER 43

Perdiki

Perdiki was thinking about being with Athena in Paris. When he made love with her, bits and pieces of him flew away, parts unrecoverable, the beatings, the days on the run, the politics … all of it. He needed that and he needed to talk with her, to listen to what she said. He was tired and his chest hurt some of the time and he knew he needed to get out from under what had happened to his life.

Getting Mickey to the boulders that blocked the lower path had been more difficult than he'd imagined. The way was steeper and covered with more loose rock than he remembered and presented constant obstacles to their progress. The boy leaned heavily on the musician as he hobbled and hopped between the rocks that were scattered along the path.

There was little fear that they would be discovered. It was early enough in the morning that it was unlikely anyone would be out and surely not on a path that led only to an abandoned village and was blocked by giant boulders.

Theirs were the only human voices and they rarely spoke. Mickey grimaced and Perdiki was immersed in listening to the morning birds. There were fragments of tunes in everything he heard and when a chorus of *zizigas* cicadas began to sing as the sun warmed the scrub pine and woke them from their sleep it became something from which he could draw.

Perdiki had stuffed everything he needed into the pack Zev had left and then closed up the cave-house, pushing the big rocks back in place to conceal the door. He checked that his notebook was in place under his shirt while Argos sniffed around him, wondering where they were off to next. The musician felt a melancholy leaving the cave-house, where he'd stayed longer than anyplace else this time on Mythos and knew he would one day write a song about it. The phrase, "Running water but no stopping water" would be the refrain. Maybe call it "No Stopping Water." After he dropped the kid off at the boulders, he would have a long hike to Pharaoh's place and it would give him time to think and see what he could fit together and when he stopped to rest he could get some of it down in the notebook.

With Mickey's arm slung over his shoulders, they struggled through their first steps together until they found a rhythm that would work. It was a slow shuffle that frustrated Argos, who bounded ahead and then back to them to burn off his energy.

On one steep section, Mickey slipped on a patch of loose gravel and brought Perdiki down to the ground with him. Neither was hurt, but they remained on their backs for a while, gathering the strength to get up and go on. Perdiki's shoulders were aching from bearing Mickey's weight and his chest was sore from the strain of the pack he was wearing on his back. but there was no other way, so he wearily got to his feet and strained his shoulders, further, helping Mickey to his feet.

"Onward, you little son of a bitch."

"I'm bigger than you."

"You're still a little son of a bitch."

"Will you really write a song about me?"

"Yes, it will be called the little son of a bitch gets his other leg broken for being so awkward. Don't fall again! Gravity is not your friend."

The path levelled out and then led through a ravine that had Perdiki half-carrying the damn kid. He needed to hate him thoroughly in order to keep going, to keep pushing until they finally reached the boulders that blocked the path.

"This is where I leave you."

"But you haven't broken my other leg yet."

"I don't have the energy. I'll save it for the next time I see you."

"What happens now?"

"Someone will be bringing a doctor to you an hour or so after I leave."

"Thank you, Perdiki. You saved my life. I will always be grateful. And for the record you're not dangerous at all."

"Will you do as I asked?"

"I swear I won't tell anyone that I've seen you, not even my brother, especially not my brother."

"And the rest?"

"Leave it at that."

"Will you be at the concert?"

"If they have to drag me there."

"Then will you do what I asked? It might save my life."

"I'm not as good as you, Perdiki. Leave it there. You better get going before you're seen with me."

Perdiki spent the rest of the day making his way up through the terraces where he'd once fled with Zev in the lead. Now he had to find his own way. He would have had to hunt for each set of stone steps leading up to the next level, but Argos took the lead once he understood where Perdiki was taking them and led him to each one.

Perdiki did not plan to stop until he reached the cabin beside the vineyard, where he'd stayed for one night what seemed years ago, but he ran out of energy at the very top of the series of terraces and nearly fell to his knees with exhaustion. His chest was still hurting and he lay beneath an old, twisted olive tree until the pain subsided. He would have to stay for the night in the vineyard cabin because he didn't have the energy to go any further.

The musician was barely able to push himself back on his feet and had to put a hand on Argos's broad back to steady himself. Then a bit of dizziness overcame him and he took advantage, again, of Argos's broad back to lean on. Once it passed, he willed his feet to carry him up the final path, stopping every hundred meters or so to catch his breath. Argos stayed beside him wherever the path allowed, providing a steadying point whenever Perdiki needed one.

There were fewer birds than in the earlier part of the day, but the wind came up a bit and whispered against the dry brown and yellow brush alongside the trail. As he climbed, step after tired step, he tried to work the sound of the wind into the music that had been in his head all day, but his weariness overwhelmed all else and he gave into softly singing one of his old songs, step after step, the tempo slowing as his energy ran out.

When the cabin came into sight he hid in the same spot as the first time he'd been there, and watched for a while to be sure it was unoccupied and unwatched. What he saw was a deserted, stone cabin, set just in front of a vineyard that stretched down the slope toward the other side of the island and Pharaoh's house. When he was sure it was empty, he needed to lean heavily on Argos to rise to his feet. With very deliberate steps and walking slightly stooped over he managed to reach the cabin door. When he entered, everything was as he'd left it and he had only to drop the pack on the floor, lower the mattress that was suspended by ropes above the bed, and let himself rest for the first time in many hours.

Music began to range through his head, occupying him completely and carrying him away from the pain he was again feeling in his chest. Time passed musically, with no other measure. At the edge of sleep, images snapped through his mind, faces he'd never known and faces almost familiar, until sleep carried him into dreams of loss and frustration.

He dreamed of a friend telling him that he only ate fish when he was in the sea, and then only the bite-sized ones. It led him underwater to a hotel entrance, where he was to swim to his room, but he could never find it.

When he awoke, hours or minutes later, he didn't know which, his chest was aching and he knew he was in trouble. The dizziness had returned and he was sweating enough that his shirt was soaked. He knew that he should try to sit up to see the seriousness of his condition and it took all his will to make the maneuver. Everything whirled and he could see floating spots on the walls and flashes of light at the edge of his vision.

He had no idea how long he'd lain like that until the evening must have come on and with it a coolness that had the sweat on his shirt turning to ice. He called Argos to his feet and huddled against the furry beast for warmth until he found a little strength returning. The spots and flashes of light diminished enough that he was confident he could light a small fire in the potbelly stove. The last time in the cabin he'd noticed a neat pile of wood beside the stove, but Zev had cautioned him not to light it lest he attract attention to his presence. The flu, or whatever he had, was serious enough that he had to take the chance. And maybe he'd attract the right kind of attention, because he knew he needed help.

There was a blue box of big wooden matches on a shelf above the little stove, a pile of twigs and thin sticks and some sheets of old newspaper. Although it was difficult for him to stand, Perdiki had a fire underway in minutes. He packed it with as much wood as he dared and sank back onto the bed.

Just before he'd left the cave-house he'd filled the empty tsipouro bottle with water from the always-running spigot and stuck it in the pack. Before he lay down, he'd fished it out, along with the tin of aspirin from the little first aid kit Zev had placed in the pack. He took a drink, swallowed two aspirins, and put the bottle on the floor beside the bed. It was good that he had it with him because he could not have made it outside to pump water, or even if he made it he wouldn't have been able to work the pump. He was about to drift away again when he remembered that Argos hadn't had a drink in hours. Carefully, he rose, waiting until he was steady enough on his feet to move the couple of steps across the boat-like cabin. He poured half of the remaining water into the same bowl he'd used the last time he'd stayed at the cabin and bent over to put it on the floor. The bowl landed with a thud, followed by Perdiki thinking that he was falling into the island as he crashed to the floor, unaware of the pain of hitting its rough flagstones. Unaware of anything. Just black. All black.

CHAPTER 44

Athena

Two days before she was scheduled to leave for Greece, Athena began throwing paint at anyone who came to her door and only wished she could do the same when they phoned. There was nothing further to be planned but the media people were like big babies and had to be constantly reassured and coddled and practically breast-fed and she hated every snivelling one of them. Every one she wanted was covering the concert. Now they should shut up and come.

The larger the painting grew, the more it took of her, until she realized that the concert would free her of the obsession of this work for long enough to regain herself enough to reconnect with the world after living only within the painting for months.

There had always been hours when she faded into her work, but never days and months like this. She believed that if the painting were great enough and huge enough and filled with enough truth that Perdiki would survive and be with her. She wanted it to happen quickly; it had to happen quickly because she was being devoured by her own work. It was dining on her being and taking everything she had.

If the concert hadn't come up, she wasn't sure how she could have pulled free from her work so that she could breathe. Art can take as much life and breath as it can give. The daily connection with the press and others had forced her out of her work in short bouts, but stepping away for the next few days was a freedom her entire being lusted over.

Despite the interruptions, she'd continued painting, delicate pieces of work and broad strokes of sadness and longing, greatness and magnificence and music. She was painting a symphony if only the fucking media would leave her alone. But she cherished them too.

They were her ammunition for getting Perdiki out from under what Greece was doing to him. They were all to meet in Athens where she'd chartered a boat to take them to the island of Mythos for the concert.

Athena was growing thin because she spent days at a time not eating, not thinking about food, and when she finally noticed she was hungry, she'd leave the studio for an hour to gorge on whatever the local restaurant had to offer as their special of the day. In Paris, a city of extraordinary cuisine, it was a bad restaurant and their special was often an example of food at its worst, but she ate it anyway, cursing the cook with each bite, knowing she'd feel ill for an hour afterward. Their wine, however was always fairly good and a few glasses of it could mask the taste of soggy pommes frites and overdone steak.

One afternoon, in a moment of frantic anxiety, when her brush kept missing the canvas, she'd packed a suitcase, which now sat beside her bed. Now, she sat beside it, trying to center herself the way she did with clay when she'd used a potter's wheel, pressing her hands to each side of a lump of clay as it whirled around and gently nudging it here or there until it spun true and centered.

Late in the afternoon, she called Stratos, or rather, Emma, because the crippled musician never came to the phone until the American girl told him who was on the line. Even then, he was reluctant to speak because, no, he didn't know yet if he was coming and, yes, he knew there were only two days until he should be leaving.

"I can't play, yet, you know," he said, "so I'm not sure why you want me there. Emma has been telling me about Django Reinhardt."

"The gypsy guitarist?"

"That one. He had only two good fingers on his left hand, because he was burned in a fire and yet he became one of the greatest guitarists in the world. Emma has been holding him up as an example for me, but I just can't do it. Far too much pain and the doctors tell me not to push it because I'm still healing and I might make things worse."

"But you need to come anyway, for Perdiki's sake."

"That's what Emma says and she's far too pregnant for me to argue. She already postponed our move to America so if she insists, I guess I'll have to go. I know that she has already bought us the plane tickets to Athens. I don't care so much about the concert, I'd just love to play with Perdiki again. I keep trying, but so far, I can't do it." His voice dropped as he said the last and he abruptly got off the phone, handing it to his wife.

Athena spoke with Emma, who assured her that the pregnancy was going well and that she would have no trouble travelling if she could get Stratos to agree. There was nothing more to say except that she hoped to see Athena at the port of Piraeus to travel to Mythos with her and the press.

When she'd hung up the phone, Athena looked at the massive painting and couldn't push herself to work any more. Enough! She would spend the next two days eating at a better restaurant, walking and even talking to people to help re-acclimate herself to society. She would also bathe and rest and try to restore her physical balance.

Standing before the massive work, she noticed that there was something wrong in the background of one part, just a stroke or two that wasn't quite right and interrupted the flow. It was one of those things she knew she'd better fix right away while her mind and eye were focussed on it.

Late that night she finally dropped her brush to the floor and collapsed on the bed. In the morning, she would finish that last bit.

CHAPTER 45

Perdiki

Perdiki was confused. He could hear voices but everything was still swirling behind his closed eyes and he was frightened to open them. He knew he was in the cabin beside the vineyard and should have been alone. Falling, just as he placed Argos's water bowl on the floor, was the last thing he remembered and he supposed he'd fainted. The pain in his chest seemed to have settled down, now, to a dull throb and for some reason his arm felt strangely encumbered. There was also something in his nostrils and that made no sense. He realized that he was lying on the bed, but had no idea how he got there from the floor where he fell.

Finally, he opened his eyes to see a small, dark man smiling down at him. "I am Aladdin," the man's voice said.

"You're a genie?" Perdiki managed to croak out.

"No, you haven't rubbed a magic lamp, I was born in Syria and that's just my name," the man said with a smile. "I'm a doctor and you have had a heart attack."

"But … how did you …"

Another voice, that of Pharaoh, spoke up. "Zev and I were on the trail on the way to meet up with you. We'd planned to accompany you the rest of the way to my house. When we saw the smoke from the chimney we figured either someone else was in the cabin, or you were in trouble because otherwise you knew well enough not to light a fire. We ran the rest of the way and found you here on the floor."

"And the doctor?"

"Zev went to fetch him as soon as we found you lying on the floor. He told Dr. Aladdin the state you were in and he grabbed his bag and a small oxygen cannister. Zev carried the oxygen and the two of them rushed here. There's a drip in your arm full of, I guess,

171

medicine for the heart. Anyway, the doctor says you will be all right."

"Is Zev here?"

"No. He went to find a donkey so that we can bring you down to the road and from there an ambulance will take you to the hospital."

"I thought you said I'm okay."

"So far," Aladdin said, "you are a very lucky man. You survived. But now I need to run some tests and give you some medication."

"I felt sick and there was a heavy pain in my chest, so I took a couple of aspirins."

"Then you probably saved your own life when you took the aspirins. But you'll need rest for a few days and when you leave the hospital, I'll give you pills to take to keep your blood flowing freely and to keep your blood pressure down."

"So how am I now?"

"As far as I can tell, your heart is working normally now, but I need to run some tests to see what caused the problem. The first thing I need is an electrocardiogram and an echocardiogram and that will tell me a lot." He gazed at his patient and asked, "Are you under a lot of stress?"

At that, Pharaoh began to laugh. "Did you forget who this is?" he asked the doctor. Even Perdiki attempted a chuckle.

"I wasn't thinking," said the doctor, laughing at himself. "It's just an automatic question I always ask heart patients. Of course, I know who you are, Perdiki. I was planning to come to the concert. Now, I guess it will be called off. We can talk about that later because right now we have a more immediate problem with the hospital staff. I don't know if I can trust them to keep quiet about your presence."

"Can you just run the tests at the hospital and let him recuperate at my house? It's very close to the hospital."

"I suppose so."

"What if we slip him in late at night for the tests? Can you do them yourself?"

"Yes, but there is still the night staff. They will see us and I don't know who is on duty tonight. It might be people I can trust, but it might not."

"We'll have to take that chance."

"I suppose so."

Dr. Aladdin turned to Perdiki. "Let's see how you are now. How do you feel?"

"A little weird, but much better. I'm not dizzy any more and nothing seems to hurt, though I still have a bit of a breathless feeling."

The doctor put his hand on Perdiki's pulse, staring at his watch as he checked the musician's heartrate and then carefully examined Perdiki with the stethoscope, pausing a long time at several spots. "Everything sounds right," he said. "Because we have so little time before we need to move you, let's try sitting up. Careful of the needle in your arm."

Until then, Perdiki had been unaware that he was attached to a drip and that a needle was taped to his arm. With help from Aladdin and Pharaoh, he sat up in bed. They held onto him until he seemed steady and then stepped back.

"How does that feel?" the doctor asked.

"I think I'm okay," said the musician. "I'm not hurting and the dizziness has passed. That's a good sign, right?"

"Better than the alternative. As I said, you're a very lucky man. Sit there while I take out the needle. You can't ride a donkey with that in you."

"Can I really ride on a donkey?"

"Yes, and you'll be riding in the company of the oxygen. If you feel faint you can take a whiff. We'll move very slowly and it will be a lot easier than walking. I can't leave you here in this cabin so it had better be okay."

Suddenly, Perdiki looked around. "Where is Argos?"

Aladdin responded, "If you mean that furry monster friend of yours, we let him out for a walk. He'd been in here alone with you for a long time and wouldn't leave your side. Pharaoh needed to go out with him to let him know that you were okay."

"Can I lie back down and rest for a while until Zev gets here with the donkey?"

"Sure. I think I'll leave the drip in you until it's time to go. Let more of that medicine work through you."

The musician lay back on the bed trying not to think. He stared at the wood ceiling of the cabin and watched a huge spider add to the complexity of its giant cobweb until he fell back to sleep. He dreamed that he was running from the first huge wave of a tsunami, running toward a mountain filled with soldiers, calling his name. He didn't respond until they called several times and opened his eyes to find Zev standing over him.

"Perdiki," Zev said, "your ride is here."

Becky was a sweet, old donkey, reliable, sure-footed and in no hurry. Perdiki rode side-saddle, with one leg in a stirrup and the other dangling until Argos pushed his way under the musician's free leg so that he could rest it on his furry, broad back.

Pharaoh had gone on ahead to have a car ready as soon as they reached the road. Aladdin was on Perdiki's left, with an arm around the musician's waist to steady him. Zev held the donkey's lead rope, but it was Becky who found the way and the best places to step.

Every few minutes they would stop while the doctor checked Perdiki's signs and when he was satisfied they would begin moving again. After an hour, Aladdin insisted that they stop for a rest. Perdiki slid down from Becky's back and stood, feeling much more solidly planted on the earth again than he'd expected. To prove it to himself he walked down the path a bit before Aladdin called to him, "Where are you going, my friend?"

"I'm feeling well, again," the musician called back to him.

"You just had a real heart attack," Aladdin called to him, hurrying down the path with his stethoscope flapping against his chest. "We don't even know why it happened yet or what kind of damage it's left." As he reached Perdiki the doctor took a few breaths to slow his own breathing and then checked Perdiki with the stethoscope before saying, "It's a good sign that you're feeling well so quickly, but let's do everything slowly until we know more."

"Can I walk for a while? My butt is sore from that donkey."

"Slowly, and just for a little while. It's going to be a long day."

After ten minutes, Perdiki was ready to be helped back aboard the donkey and fifteen minutes after that, they reached the end of the path where it met the road. They ducked into an old, open warehouse to keep out of sight while they waited for the car that was to take Perdiki to Pharaoh's house. He would wait there until the late evening shift came on at the hospital.

Perdiki had expected to feel exhausted, but felt exhilarated instead. The cicadas were buzzing in harmony and somewhere in the distance a cat was howling out its lust in the late afternoon. The sun was low on the horizon and ready to duck somewhere beyond the hills into the sea. Beside the old warehouse where they waited, there was a new vineyard, with wire between posts to support the young vines. Across the road, two brown-faced sheep grazed at the scrub. Behind them were hills that led to the harbor where he had left the island with Maria.

When he thought of Maria, the pain returned. The guilt never faded. He just repressed his feelings so that he could navigate the world. The image of her body on the deck of the boat beside Argos as they roared away from Samos never left his consciousness for long.

At the same time, although he felt awake and strangely confident, he also felt that he was in the last part of his life, though he didn't know how long that would be. The heart attack had left him with the sudden awareness that mortality didn't just apply to other people.

The arrival of a dented old Fiat taxi caught his attention. It was driven by a plain-looking, middle-aged woman Perdiki had never met. She stared grimly ahead as if she were scared to look at the famous musician. "Katina," Zev said, catching her attention, "meet Perdiki."

She swivelled her head quickly in his direction, wet her lips, and stammered, "Pleased to meet you. I love your music, but I never thought I'd actually meet you."

"Katina drives a taxi and runs a café in one of the villages," Zev said. "She is a friend who has helped me and my friends many times."

"Then I'm honored to meet you," said Perdiki.

Argos filled the back seat of the small taxi leaving only room for Perdiki in the front and a very cramped Aladdin in the back. They drove directly to the house with a huge boulder for a roof where Pharaoh lived. The door was unlocked and as soon as they entered Aladdin insisted that Perdiki lie on the bed while he checked him with the stethoscope and felt his pulse.

"You are better than you should be but that just means that you've survived the journey. Now I'm going to hook you up to a drip for a while and pump some drugs into you while you lie there and sleep if you can. I'll stay here and keep an eye on you until Zev and Pharaoh get back. I have to be at the hospital after that and I'll see you there later tonight."

Perdiki drifted in and out of sleep, vaguely aware when Pharaoh and Zev returned and Aladdin left, and then he was gone again in a whirl of dreams that were filled with flashes of light and meaningless images. When he awoke the first time it was as if he were exiting a storm into sudden clarity and the certainty that he was going to perform at the concert. With that somehow settled, he slid into a dreamless sleep and woke with Zev shaking him and saying that it was time to leave for the hospital.

Pharaoh stayed at the house with Argos, and Zev came with Perdiki. It was only a ten-minute drive and when they reached the hospital Aladdin was waiting with a gurney.

CHAPTER 46

Athena

With the cabin still empty ten minutes after she'd boarded the Olympic flight from Charles de Gaulle to Venizelos airport, Athena had hopes that she would have business class to herself. They had already brought her a second glass of champagne and three little bowls of smoked almonds and she was looking forward to takeoff and a prettied-up business class lunch. She hoped there'd be enough food. When she'd awakened that morning and knew she was out of the grip of the massive painting, she realized that she'd barely eaten in the last couple of days and was now ravenously hungry.

To divert herself she began to draw with a charcoal pencil on the sketchpad she'd laid on her tray table. Her hand automatically moved to draw one of the strange, bloated characters she'd invented in her childhood. She'd always placed them in very green Victorian gardens and she found that if she thought green as she sketched with the light black charcoal somehow a green light emerged. She loved doing this, having colors emerge from strokes of charcoal. It had been remarked on by every critic the few times she'd shown her early sketches. Because she didn't want to be known for doing a trick, she preferred to work in oils. In her current painting, the massive one, she could feel music emanating from it just as she did color with her charcoals. It made her wonder whether she could do scents?

Entertained by her own thoughts, watching her hand sketching, she didn't notice when, just before they were ready to close the doors, a couple came panting down the ramp, the woman in the lead and nearly dragging the man.

"Wait!" called the woman in English and then "Arrêtez!" in French and finally "Stamata!" in Greek.

The flight attendant waved his hand gently downward to indicate they should slow down, that they weren't to late to aboard. When they breathlessly entered the plane, the flight attendant realized that the woman was pregnant and immediately became very solicitous.

He took her by the elbow and said, "Where would you like to sit? There is only one other passenger in business class, so you have your choice of seats."

They chose the first row and settled in while the flight attendant put their two bags and two, small, oddly-shaped cases in the overhead for them and brought flutes of champagne and little bowls of smoked almonds. The attendant noticed that the man had a bit of trouble with his seatbelt and had to be helped by the woman.

The heavy doors swung shut and the usual pre-flight instructions were announced. She took another sip of champagne before the flight attendant swept it away prior to the engines starting up and the plane disconnecting from the gate. They made her put up her tray table and place her sketchpad on the empty seat beside her. After an interminable time taxiing, the plane suddenly halted, got ready, got set and vaulted off into the air.

Stirred out of her reverie, Athena heard a familiar voice coming from the seat in front of her. "There's a menu, Stratos. What would you like?"

"Just food. I don't care. Order me something. You choose it."

Athena rose from her seat, ignoring the seatbelt sign and greeted the pair. "I didn't think you were coming."

Stratos answered. "Neither did I until Emma had me in the taxi and we almost left with my leg still hanging out."

Emma answered matter-of-factly, "We only had forty minutes to make it to the airport and we barely made it at that. Stratos wanted to finish his coffee and pan chocolat before we left. Can you imagine?"

"You can't get good pan chocolat in Greece."

Emma didn't bother responding. When a young flight attendant came rushing over to ask Athena to please sit down until the seatbelt sign was off, she sat across the aisle from Emma and Stratos so that they could continue their conversation.

"We have no idea where Perdiki is right now," Athena said. "We can just hope he's all right and can make it to the concert." She stopped. "Really, I just hope he's all right, concert or no concert."

"What is the plan to get him out of Greece after the concert?" Stratos asked.

Athena realized that Stratos was far more awake and alive than the last time she'd seen him, but decided not to comment on it lest she break the spell. "There's a path down to the sea below the churchyard where the concert is being held. We're set to get him off the island in a boat that's too fast for anything the police have to catch up. He'll go to the Turkish coast where there will be friends who will help him get to Paris. The Turkish government would never send him back to Greece so there should be no problems as long as we can get him there."

The food came and Athena was too busy eating to talk any more, and after that, too busy hustling the flight attendant for a second dinner.

CHAPTER 47

The Old Man and Spiro

The old man stared at me out of eyes exhausted from the long night. "So, the three wise men brought Perdiki out of the vineyard on the back of a donkey. There's something positively biblical about it." He raised his wiry eyebrows, chuckled, gave a deep cough, stood up, and went out on deck. Standing with his back to me, he began to hum one of Perdiki's songs. "You know that one?" he asked.

"I've heard the live recording," I told him. "The one where my father has a long solo and the audience is cheering so loudly by the time it was over that they had to stop playing until the applause subsided before they could finish the song."

The old man's eyes teared up. "I was there that night. You probably heard me cheering."

"Who *are* you?" I asked.

"I'm from Mythos. I told you that when we first met. Perdiki was not from this island, but the closer he came to that concert the more it enfolded him and made him one of us. That's all you need to know. That and the rest of the story, because, Spiro Glaros, the son of my old friend, you, too, are part of this island."

He hadn't answered my question again.

CHAPTER 48

Perdiki

The hospital was small and old, but filled with all the necessary equipment. It served half the island and at peak times of the day there were as many as eight or nine doctors in and out its doors. The exterior of the hospital was in need of a paint job, but inside everything was crisp and neat and clearly well-organized, if a bit old. There were two buildings, separated by a wide driveway. One was filled with rooms for patients and doctors' offices. The emergency room was in the second building, along with a surgical suite, x-rays and a lab.

Perdiki was in an alcove in the emergency room with electrodes pasted to his chest, their wires leading to an electrocardiograph with a paper tape rolling off of it. When the machine was finished, Aladdin reviewed the tape, running it through his fingers, frowning in couple of places. "You have some arrythmia," he said. "How are you feeling?"

"Normal. I feel like myself, though I could still use more sleep."

"Before you can rest, I want to do an EKG and take some blood. There are proteins emitted after a heart attack that can give me a lot of information. The lab is closed, so the bloodwork will be done in the morning."

Once the EKG was done and they were about to leave the hospital, Aladdin told Perdiki that he should rest easy, and he would see him in the morning with the results of the tests.

Faithful Katina with the plain face and the slightly hunched back was waiting in the driveway between the two hospital buildings in her old Fiat taxi. As she drove to Pharaoh's house, she kept sneaking glances at Perdiki, who was sitting beside her. She was still amazed that he was actually there in her car. When they reached Pharaoh's house, the musician thanked her and kissed Katina on the cheek. She drove off with her hand to her cheek where the famous musician had kissed her.

The musician slept through the rest of the night and woke as light began to find its way through the cracks in the door. Pharaoh and Zev were already sitting at the table, drinking coffee and quietly immersed in an intense discussion. Argos was seated with them with his massive head at table height and looking as if he were involved in the conversation. The men's faces looked tired and lined in the demi-light of morning and their shoulders were hunched over with fatigue. He wondered if they'd slept at all.

"You seem very serious," Perdiki called out as he sat up.

"There are a lot of people to contact to cancel the concert. First, of course, we need to call Athena. She'll be disappointed, but she'll also be glad to know you're alive."

"I'm alive enough to do a concert."

"I don't think so," said Zev calmly. "You had a heart attack, Perdiki! You need to rest and recuperate and maybe you'll need surgery. Aladdin says he doesn't know yet."

"It's my decision to make. I have this one life only and ultimately that's all I own that is completely mine. I'll do the concert."

"And then what?"

"I'll go for a boat ride and then I can rest. When I get to Turkey, I can see a doctor, even go to a hospital. Here, what can I do? We were lucky the only nurse in emergency was a friend, but you know I can't go back there or to the other hospital on Mythos. The police would have me in a minute. That is what would be the worst for my health."

"Then cancel the damn concert and we'll just get you to Turkey."

Perdiki wasn't going to say anything more about it until Aladdin arrived with the test results. The musician wanted at least a cup of coffee and something to eat before defending himself any further. How could a man argue anything without at least a cup of coffee? He would listen to what Aladdin said, but, ultimately, he knew he wasn't going to change his mind. It was the only direction left in his life. After that it would be all retreat. His own country would no longer be beneath his feet nor would this island, this Mythos, that had hidden and protected him in the cave-house and in its contours as he ran. If he survived, if Greece survived, he would to return to Mythos to live. How Athena would fit into his plans was as unknown as anything else. With so much fog in the future he needed this concert as an anchorage. He could not really see anything past the concert, as if it were at the very end of his life. He couldn't even envision the boat to Turkey and beyond.

CHAPTER 49

Spiro

It would have taken only an hour by plane to reach Mythos, but after Anastasia kicked me out of my own apartment, I needed eight hours on a ferry to recover. I stopped at the bakery to buy a loaf of bread for the trip with my suitcase dragging behind me and a small rucksack perched on top of it. No sense wearing it until I needed to.

"Back soon?" the woman behind the counter asked.

"Don't know."

Along with my bread, she handed me five cookies and wished me good luck. "Girl still here?" she asked.

"Yes," I said.

"Then you'll be back," she laughed.

It was Saturday morning in Exarchia and Kalidromiou was blocked off for the weekly farmer's market. The street was filled with vendors of olives, flowers, fresh fruits and vegetables including zucchini so fresh the blossoms were still on the ends. The crowds were overflowing the sidewalks and blocking the intersection where the road met Harilau Trikoupi. Rather than push my way through, I walked two blocks up the hill to Ipoucratou to flag down a taxi.

After so many months in the quaint, narrow streets of Exarchia, I found myself propelled through a very different part of Athens as if I were entering a different world. There were big buildings, fancy banks, huge historical buildings, and then a broad avenue lined with low shops and the occasional office building. After twenty minutes, we entered the funky streets of Piraeus, the hub of ferry traffic for all the islands. There were shops with old nautical gear, used furniture stores, souvlaki stands and one travel agency after another. I had the driver drop me at the Blue Star ticket office at dock E9, where the boat to Mythos berthed. It was a large car ferry, more like a ship, with several classes of travel. I bought a first-class ticket because it was only a few Euros more and I knew it would be considerably more comfortable, Beside the boarding ramp, there were carts selling sesame sticks, koulouria, small packets of pistachio nuts and bottles of cold water. I bought a packet of pistachios, stuck it in my jacket pocket and boarded the ship. I dropped my suitcase in the big iron cage marked Mythos and followed the crowd up an escalator to the passenger deck.

The first-class lounge was at the bow, at the far end of the ship, past the sign for the stairway for deck class and the rows of seats for tourist class. When I reached the glass doors with the sign that read "first class" in several languages, my ticket was checked by a steward before I was allowed in.

There was a semi-circular coffee bar in the center of the room and surrounding it, trios of plush chairs grouped around low tables. I found a table in a corner with all three of its chairs empty. I threw the pack on one, my jacket on the second and sat on the third. Secure of my solitude, I got up long enough to buy a Greek coffee at the bar and then sat back eating the cookies they'd given me in the bakery and wondered what the hell I was going to do.

At least I knew where I'd be staying. My cousin had given me the keys to the old family home on Mythos the last day I worked in his restaurant. "You may not have a lot of money," he said, "but at least you'll have a pied-a-terre in the city and a country home. When you get to the island, you won't have to worry about finding the house. Get in a taxi and mention your father's name. Any driver will know where it is."

In my pack, along with my laptop, I had a small bag of Greek coffee, another of sugar, a chunk of feta and the loaf of bread I'd bought in Athens. My cousin had told me that the house would have everything I needed except food because he used it sometimes and had taken care of the maintenance over the years. There were even fresh linens that he'd bought a year ago.

With no travel details to concern me I booted up the laptop and tried to divert myself by writing, but it didn't work. The world had been thrown off its axis and I couldn't ignore it. The night Anastasia went crashing out of a demonstration onto the sidewalk in front of me had changed the trajectory of my life. But whether we would stay in orbit together was yet an unknown. I loved her … right now …

and she had told me she felt the same. But right now was bounded by something she found missing in me, and I knew it wasn't my indecision about what to write. I felt a lack in myself too, but I didn't know whether it was an existential one or something I could find, something other, just as finding Anastasia was finding somebody other, a gift, an extraordinary gift of the universe. Now, I owed something for it.

Trying to escape my thoughts, I went out on deck to watch as the ship slowly navigated through the busy port. We slipped past several small ferries scurrying around and a huge one running a parallel course with ours on the way out into the Aegean and the islands beyond. The intense morning sun was dead in front of us and the glare so terrific that I ducked back inside and returned to my table like an animal returning to its perch.

For the next couple of hours, I dozed, waking finally when the boat hit heavy weather and began rocking. It was a big ship, and there was really very little motion from the storm, but it was enough to have cleared out the dining room and I had my choice of tables. Sitting through dinner I realized that eating alone now felt strange and I slowly began to slip back into the fog that had enveloped me before I met Anastasia.

But, when I looked around, I realized that I didn't feel disconnected as I had before. As much as my world with Anastasia had been circumscribed as it is with new lovers, I felt part of the people gabbing at the tables around me even though I didn't feel like listening to their chatter right now. I was one of them. I wasn't slipping anywhere. What was wrong was that I missed Anastasia.

It felt as if she'd sent me out on a quest, but I didn't know what it was that I sought. Anastasia had said, "Don't come back with only half of you. I don't care what you decide to write as long as it's all of you doing it."

Maybe I would find it on Mythos. There might still be someone who remembered my father and while I was there at least I might learn something about him. I didn't know how that would help me but it was a start.

CHAPTER 50

Perdiki

Argos insisted on riding in the car with Perdiki, and by the time he fitted his big, furry body into the back seat there was no room for anyone else. So, it was only Perdiki in the passenger seat up front, and Aladdin at the wheel. The doctor wasn't happy about Perdiki travelling, let alone performing, and had argued about it but the musician was unmovable. He was going to perform at the concert.

Zev and Pharaoh rode with Katina, who was put out that she wouldn't be driving Perdiki until Pharaoh patiently explained that Aladdin needed to be able to keep an eye on his patient. She was content with that and returned to her usual taciturn self, perfectly in control of the car, a damn good driver.

The normally quiet road was filled with traffic of all kinds except police cars. They knew about the concert everywhere on Mythos in the small, quiet villages above the sea and the mountain clusters of houses. It was a tingle that ran from spine to spine, a subtle electricity that they dare not allow to grow. You couldn't trust the ones who mingled with the tourists and the police in the two big port towns, but in the villages, you know who was who. You knew their brothers and chased their sisters through the hills. Their parents fed you and everyone's uncle knew your name, so you could talk. But quietly lest the wind carry it to the ears of strangers.

The two cars sped through nearly-deserted villages, which puzzled them until they realized that everyone must going to the concert. Both cars merged with the traffic as it headed toward the seaside village where the concert would be held. When they approached the village of Mavrato, traffic suddenly slowed and Katina, with a wave of her arm to follow, swung her car across traffic and onto a small dirt road, with Aladdin barely avoiding an accident as he shot between a farm truck and two motorcycles travelling side by side.

The dirt road wandered up into the mountains and away from the sea, with both sides of the road filled with olive trees, grapevines and the occasional old, faded white stone house. Several times they had to swerve to avoid goats crossing the road and once a ram stood his ground as Katina slowly inched forward until the car was almost touching the animal and then she suddenly honked her horn and revved the engine. The ram wheeled around and took off but not before Katina caught sight of a trail of dust in the rearview mirror.

Half a kilometer further down the road, she swung a quick right onto what was little more than a muddy tractor path through a series of commercial vegetable gardens that had obviously just been watered. It was slick and difficult to drive, but there was no dust cloud left by the two cars as they bounced through the ruts and they thought they'd eluded their pursuers until they came to an insurmountable stone wall. Slamming on the brakes, Katina was able to avoid crashing into it, but Aladdin hit his a few seconds too late and plowed into Katina. No one was hurt and there wasn't much damage but as they walked around the cars to inspect them, a police car came roaring up with its lights blazing.

Argos began to growl as the doors opened on the official car and its sole occupant, got out. He was an older man with an expressionless face, dressed in a dusty black suit with an open-necked white shirt. In his hand, he held a pistol. If the window had been open in the car Aladdin was driving, Argos would have gotten his bulk through it, but he was stuck inside pushing and groaning as he tried to force his way out.

When the expressionless man pulled at the handle and found the doors were locked, he demanded that Perdiki open his window. "You remember me?" he shouted through the glass.

"Did you bring your bell?"

"So you do remember me."

"Yes, Xenos, you remain in my mind like a near-fatal disease."

The expressionless man held his gun up to the window. "Open it, or I will shoot."

Aladdin called out, "Perdiki is a very sick man. Let him alone. He has had a heart attack and we are getting him to the hospital."

"Doctor Aladdin, do you think I don't know that you already had him in a hospital? Are you out for a nice Sunday drive with your patient on this goat path? I'll deal with you later."

"There is a cardiology wing in the Agios Pandelemonos hospital. Perdiki may need surgery and that's where it will be done. If you're worried about him singing at a concert forget it. He's going to a hospital. You are delaying us."

"Then, Doctor Aladdin, you tell Perdiki it will be bad for his health if he doesn't open his window because otherwise I will shoot it open." He held the pistol up to the window. "Open it now!"

All of Xenos's attention was focussed on Perdiki and he failed to be aware that Pharaoh had slipped silently out of Katina's car and was standing directly behind him with a knife in his hand. Xenos had learned his skills in the Greek Civil War and the life of a fisherman had kept him as strong as ever. Sharper than an old torture-master in a dusty suit. The son of a bitch! Pharaoh drove the knife partway into the man's back, causing him to scream and drop the gun. He'd done his work. Now sepsis would do the rest unless Xenos had medical help.

The old torture master lay on the ground writhing in pain and overcome with fear. There was a look of terror, that manifested itself as deep lines and complex wrinkles on his usually- emotionless face. "Don't let me die," he shricked.

Pharaoh looked down at him with his face frightening in the anger it held. He glared at Xenos and said, "Got you in the kidney, did I? Do you know what happens when the kidney is stabbed? If I pull the knife out now, you will bleed out in twenty minutes. If it's left in, maybe we can get you to a hospital in time. Lucky for you we have a doctor with us, the one we forced to come along to take care of Perdiki. Unlucky for you, we might not let him help you. Do you know who I am. You remember me, don't you? It's because of you that I limp. Remember? Does my face ring a bell? Oh wait … you were the one who rang the bell, right? You had them twist my leg until it was broken and even after and every time they twisted it you rang that bell. Well, now the bell tolls for you. If it were up to me we would pull out the knife and leave you here."

Aladdin came out of the car with his medical bag and pushed Pharaoh aside. "Let me see him," he said.

As he bent down to examine Xenos, Aladdin looked up at Pharaoh. "I know this awful man because I've had to clean up his work, but I'm still obligated to help him." With that, he focused on the patient. After a few minutes, he took Pharaoh aside and told him that the knife hadn't gone in very far and had missed the kidney. Xenos wasn't in any danger as long as he made it to a hospital.

"I never miss," Pharaoh softly to the doctor. "Unless it's on purpose. I didn't want to kill him, just get the bastard under our control. As long as he believes he's in imminent danger, he'll do whatever the hell we tell him."

"Which is what?"

"I am going to drive his official car with him beside me. We will drive in a convoy with Katerina and Zev in one car and you, Perdiki and that enormous beast in the third. We will be able to get through any roadblock because I can threaten Xenos to pull out the knife."

"Would you do that?"

"Ask me when the time comes. Can you help me get this animal into the passenger seat of his car. Then you can go back to your patient and we can get going. We've got concert tickets and we don't want to be late."

"What about the hospital for Xenos?"

"We'll stop there and drop him off."

"If you give me five minutes to get Xenos into emergency, I'll go with you and stay with Perdiki until the concert is over."

"You just want the free seat."

Katina led the way because as one of the island's only cab drivers she knew every back road on the island. With Katina in the lead, once they were out of the tractor path through the vegetable gardens, they turned back onto the dirt road and continued for a few kilometers before making a left down a very steep lane that eventually brought them back to the main road. At that point, Pharaoh in the official car with Xenos took the lead. Traffic was heavier than before, but they were waved past the waiting lines of cars and trucks at every roadblock.

At the hospital, Xenos was put on a gurney at the emergency entrance, Doctor Aladdin spoke with someone at the desk and then turned Xenos over to the on-duty doctor. Xenos was very agitated and frightened, so they gave him a strong sedative, which would give the doctor and the entourage travelling with Perdiki a good head start.

Back on the road they kept careful watch for barricades because now that they no longer had Xenos with them they had no way to get through them. But they were lucky and the rest of the short drive to Agios Pendeleminos was clear of official cars.

As they neared the site of the concert, a churchyard big enough for holding a huge, yearly panigiri, a village party that drew nearly two thousand people to the normally sleepy little church tacked onto a cliff just above the sea. There were at least double that 2000 already gathered for the concert, with more streaming in. The crowd had overflowed the platea and now filled the fields of stubble on either side.

The loudspeakers that were normally set up for the band and singers at the panigiria had been beefed up for the concert, with the addition of further equipment brought from other villages that held their own panigiria.

The old church was situated on one side of the platea and beside it was a long low stone building where food was prepared and sold for the yearly village parties. Behind the building were a dozen barbecues set up for roasting goat and lamb on slowly-rotating, motor-driven spits. There were also rows of deep fryers to produce the hundreds of pounds of fried potatoes the vast crowd would consume. All of this was dispensed out of the long, open counter of the low stone building, along with beer, retsina and red wine as well as soft drinks and bottles of water.

Trucks filled with supplies for the cooks arrived continually, using a service road that skirted the crowds.

The concert had become a celebration and the tension of living under the junta had temporarily been suspended to make room for what naturally lay within the people. These were people who were connected to each other. Thousands greeted each other with kisses on both cheeks, huge smiles and joy at their reunions. This was repeated over and over as they connected with each other, meeting sometimes after only a day and sometimes after years.

It had become a huge organism. The whole crowd was connected and there was a flow of electricity that ran through everyone, united everyone, a magnetic field that turned it into one being with thousands of roots. It was the opposite of a mob.

One of the only attendees who felt isolated was Mickey. He sat on the ground directly in front of the stage, with a pair of wooden crutches beside him and an Ace bandage around his leg. A doctor and two ambulance attendants had arrived two hours after Perdiki left him beside the boulders that blocked the path to the cave-house. They'd brought him to the hospital where an x-ray revealed that there was no break in his leg. The doctor put an elastic bandage on it and handed him a pair of wooden crutches with the advice that he should take it easy for a few days.

Once the doctors were done with him, the police took over and their examination was far less gentle than that of the medical people. Three of them took turns asking him the same questions until he wanted to throw something at them, but he stuck to his story that he'd never seen Perdiki. He felt he owed him that much for the care the musician had given him and besides, he knew his life would be a lot easier than if he'd told the truth.

In their focus on him, the police had overlooked the fact that Mickey's brother, Pete, was one of the two injured soldiers Perdiki was accused of murdering and that he was still in the same hospital in which they were now grilling Mickey. Once they were finished with Mickey, they left abruptly, having no further interest in him. As soon as they'd left the building, the boy hobbled to the elevator, punched the button for two, and freely walked its corridor, unmolested, until he reached his brother's room.

Mickey talked with Pete for an hour before he hobbled down the corridor, took the elevator to the ground floor and checked himself out. One of the nurses who was going off duty gave him a ride and dropped him off at his insistence at the platea where the concert was to be held, even though it was hours early. He'd slowly made his way to the long low stone building where they sold food and bought the first of the roast goat that came off the spit, and a plate each of salad and fries as well as two bottles of water. One of the servers carried it for him to the front of the stage and helped him get seated on the ground on a blanket he'd lifted from the hospital.

He sat stone-faced, stoically watching a stage that would be empty for hours. He was still grappling with the favor Perdiki had asked of him back at the cave-house. Mickey knew that part of him was going to be lost no matter what he chose.

There was a driveway that ran directly to the church and the long low stone building so that during panigiria they could circumvent the crowds and get supplies and people brought in. It was directly to this supply road that Katina led the little convoy. They drove through the first fifty meters, unmolested and unnoticed. Along one side of the road was a wire mesh fence, and pressed up against it were the crowds, but no one as yet had noticed them.

Newly-erected across the supply road was a swing-up gate and controlling it were four uniformed, armed policemen. When the little convoy stopped in front of the officers stepped forward and demanded that everyone exit their vehicles. He had several stripes on his shoulder and the bearing of someone very senior.

"All of you out of the car," he commanded when Zev rolled down his window.

"Only me," called Zev, in a voice loud enough to be heard by everyone in their little convoy. Several people in the crowd turned and watched with curiosity what was enfolding in front of them.

"We would like Mister Perdiki to step out. He is under arrest. In fact, all of you are under arrest."

"My hearing is not very good because I was tortured by you people years ago and you need to speak louder," called out Pharaoh, getting out of the car.

The officer's face turned red as he raised his voice to a shout. "I said, Mister Perdiki is under arrest for the murder of two soldiers and the rest of you are accessories."

From the crowd pressed against the fence, there was a shout. "Hey, they're trying to arrest Perdiki. He's there in the car ... the blue one."

More people turned from what they were doing and pressed against the fence. One of them shouted, "You can't take him. He doesn't belong to you!"

Someone else called out, "He is not yours!" and it was soon taken up as a chant that echoed through the vast crowd, far beyond those who knew what was happening.

"He is not yours!" shouted thousands of people. With the chant, the fact that they were trying to arrest him spread through the crowd and it began to surge forward, compressing itself, becoming an ever-tighter mass as it pressed forward until a large section of the fence collapsed, letting the crowd pour through.

The four police officers backed away from the crowd and retreated to their car. As the crowd continued to chant, "He is not yours!" the police turned their car around and headed up the supply road, away from the concert site.

Carefully, the musician opened his door and straightened up beside the car. There was sweat on his forehead and he felt weak and dizzy. Aladdin stepped out and opened the back door of the car to allow Argos to jump out and push himself beside Perdiki so that the musician could rest a hand on him.

Perdiki steadied himself, took a slow breath and raised his arms to the crowd. A cheer rose from those who could see him and the ones, further back, who were only aware that he was there. After a couple of minutes, Perdiki lowered his arms, palms down, to indicate that he would like the crowd to calm down so that he could speak. It took a full minute for the message to find its way all the way back through the thousands of people, but eventually there was only silence.

"I am your friend, Perdiki," he called out, and the crowd again began chanting, "Perdiki, Perdiki, Perdiki!" When he managed to silence them, he spoke again, patting the big dog's head, "And this is my friend Argos!"

"Argos, Argos, Argos," cheered the crowd.

When they were finally settled down, Perdiki raised his hands to keep them quiet enough to hear him and he called out, "Will you help us get to the church? Argos and I need to rest before the concert." His words were repeated back through the crowd, from cousin to cousin, friend to friend, and child to child. Perdiki, Argos and Zev returned to their cars, with the crowd breaking itself up so that one group led the way, while other clumps of people surrounded the cars and guarded their rear. The police officers had vanished.

CHAPTER 51

The Old Man and Spiro

"We are reaching the end of this night," the old man said, with his very being drooping as he sat back against a bulkhead. But his eyes were still alight and he kept talking.

"Before I finish telling you the rest," he importuned, "promise me that one day you will go to the church of Pandelemonos and take a look around the platea where the concert was held. You should get a feel for it, like a detective at the scene of the crime. I'm sure you'll find all kinds of evidence."

I could envision the platea, having seen a number of those oversized churchyards on my walks around the island. Why the one where the concert had been held would be any different was beyond me, but the old man was adamant and I was well aware of what he'd been giving me that night and I would honor whatever he asked.

"Let me get back to this," the old man said. "Athena herded her band of press vultures onto the boat she'd chartered with money a wealthy friend coughed up as soon as he was asked." He glanced up at the cabin roof. "Nobody could ever refuse that woman anything." He searched around for a drink, looked with distaste and fear at the bottle of lethal tsipouro, and finally settled on a glass of water before he continued. "Stratos and the American woman, Emma, who was pregnant with you at the time, arrived late as usual. He was wearing sunglasses and a hat that drooped down over his face in case anyone in the press might otherwise recognize him. They were hustled by the boat's crew into the master cabin and didn't emerge for the duration of the voyage. I don't want to go into the details of what happens when you put a bunch of reporters after the same story in a confined space, but they eventually got to Mythos in time for the concert without actual bloodshed."

The old man looked up at the cabin roof, searching his memory. "Your parents and almost you were brought to the concert by the service road so that they could avoid the crowds. They were driven past the now-abandoned gate and taken right to the church where Perdiki and his friends were waiting."

CHAPTER 52

Perdiki
The Concert

Athena ran from the car to Perdiki, crying and pushing people out of the way until she had her arms around him and then her hands were in his hair and running down his sides as if she were examining a sculpture.

He looked at her and smiled. "You have paint in your hair," he teased.

"You haven't changed, either," she said, but it wasn't true. Perdiki was drawn and looked as weak as he felt. His cheeks were sunken and he was pale, not the kind of tone from just staying out of the sun, but a sick pale, tinged with green and yellow. Athena saw all of it, the colors, the pastel softness of his tired features and even the slight droop his nose had developed.

The sound of Athena's voice lifted him beyond everything. The past weeks dropped off, with their constant fear-driven motion, panic and death. Although there was a babble of voices in the air, he filtered out everything and could hear only Athena.

Before they even kissed, he asked, "Can I come with you to Paris? I need to be with you."

"And you need to be out of Greece."

"That too."

"Will you sing to me when we're alone?"

"Yes very private songs."

"Can you live with paint?"

"Can you live with music?"

They finally kissed deeply but were interrupted by Pharaoh who was carrying two folding chairs and a small table that he set up for them.

"Make him rest," he said to Athena. "He's had a heart attack and shouldn't even be here. You need to know about it."

"Who are you?" asked Athena, staring at the shape of the face that had brought him his name. When he told her, she stared at him for a minute as intently as if she were sketching, which is exactly what she was doing.

Her focus quickly shifted back to Perdiki. "A heart attack?" she said. "When?" When he told her, she said, "My god, why are you walking around?"

Quietly, he told her everything that had happened. When he reached the part about the heart attack, she stopped him. "What did the doctor say?"

Perdiki waved to Aladdin to join them. "I'm a doctor," he said when he was introduced to Athena. He quickly explained the situation and added that he had implored Perdiki to cancel or postpone the concert but he refused to listen. Athena glanced sharply at Perdiki, who simply nodded.

"Can he survive this concert?"

"Maybe. Probably. But he should be in a hospital. He needs an angiogram before we really know what's going on and what caused the attack. He might need a stent or surgery. I'm travelling blind here." He glanced at Perdiki and then back to Athena. "And I don't want to lose him," he continued.

Athena sighed, "But …"

"But he is going to do this concert and I can only stay backstage in case of anything."

"What about the boat ride to Turkey?"

"Is that where he's going? No one told me. But I would have sent him by helicopter to the Hippokration cardiology hospital in Athens for an angiogram and whatever procedures or surgery they found necessary. So, yes, he should be all right on a boat for a couple of hours. In both Istanbul and Izmir there are excellent cardiology hospitals. He should get into one right away. Will you be travelling with him? I can't be away that long because I have other patients and responsibilities here on Mythos."

She stared at the doctor, her eyes focussing on all his features at once. A snapshot for later. "No. Of course I don't expect you to abandon everything," she said with a warm smile. "You have already been wonderful in taking care of him." A sudden thought changed her expression. "Are you in trouble for helping Perdiki?"

"I'm the only cardiologist on Mythos. The mayor of this island is my patient and so is the chief of police. What can they do?"

"What about Zev and the one who looks like something from an Egyptian wall painting?"

"I don't know, but I think they're in a lot of trouble. The police are accusing Perdiki of two murders and they will be accessories."

"Murders?" she shouted, stopping all other conversation in the room. "When will this version of Greece end?"

Zev came quickly across the room to divert her attention. Before she could go on with her emotional outbreak, he put his hand on her shoulder. "I'm Zev. Now, I finally get to meet you face to face. You look much better than on the telephone."

"It's always a bad connection to this island," she joked.

Zev looked at the crowd, gathered in the room. "Who are all these people? They're not from here."

"Most of them are press people."

"So, you really did it!"

"I guess so. And thank you Zev for taking care of Perdiki for me."

"I took care of him for all of us," he replied. "And it wasn't just me. It was Pharaoh and Katina, the driver." He looked across the room. "Have you met Argos? He's been helping Perdiki longer than any of us." At the mention of his name, the big dog, who had been chewing through a huge bowl filled with chunks of lamb and goat, raised his head, took a wistful glance at the bowl, and then pushed through the crowd to the table where Perdiki, Athena, Zev and Aladdin were gathered.

"This is my friend Argos," said the musician, rubbing the huge dog behind his ears. Argos let out a soft groan and leaned in to the scratching.

Athena stared for a long time at Argos until tears ran down her cheeks. "He is the most beautiful creature I've ever seen." Argos moved away from Perdiki and pushed up against Athena until she hugged his massive head.

After a minute she pulled away. "Come with me," she said to Perdiki. "There's someone you need to see."

Standing as far away as possible from the gibbering press people was a man in sunglasses and a floppy hat, with a pregnant woman who was holding tightly onto an oddly shaped musical instrument case. When they saw Perdiki on Athena's arm and walking slowly in their direction, they moved toward him until Perdiki was close enough to sweep off Stratos's ridiculous floppy hat and remove his sunglasses.

"How are you?" he asked.

Stratos held up his crippled hand, "Oh good, and you?"

"Well, I'm going to be arrested for murder and I had a heart attack."

"Life has always treated musicians well."

"Can you play?"

"Maybe. I don't know. Emma keeps talking about Django Reinhardt, you know, the gypsy guitarist? He lost two of his fingers in a fire before he became famous and had to invent his own way of playing, but he did it. I've been trying but the pain is too intense still and the doctors say I may do permanent damage if I attempt too much, too soon."

Perdiki simply nodded and put his arm on his friend's shoulder. "If I get out of this, we can still write together. That doesn't stop. You don't need to be a virtuoso to write music."

Stratos's gigantic eyes focussed on his old compatriot with their full intensity. With the ridiculous hat off, Perdiki could see the halo of hair that surrounded the otherwise bald head. He looked exactly as he always had, except diminished.

"Write music with you?" asked Stratos. "A murderer? Now, that's a sign of distinction. The best you ever achieved before was enemy of the state. Are the hours better in your new position?"

"No. They're worse and there's far too much travel."

Emma and Athena watched Stratos emerge from the depression that had ensnared him, livelier in his talk with Perdiki than either had seen him since his torture. As they watched the men banter, the two women wore nearly the same near-maternal expression on their faces. They were both wondering whether the men would perform together, but it was best to say nothing, yet. This alone was worth it.

The sound and video technicians who'd arrived with the news crews had given up trying to work with the local crew setting up the sound system because of the language barrier. It didn't matter because their setup was complete enough to record a whole concert. In their one piece of cooperation with the locals, they called for a sound check together, sending one of their own onstage to repeat "testing," each group testing their audio equipment separately.

The stage was a platform raised three meters in the air so that everyone in the crowd would have a view. Below the stage were two roped-off areas, one for the press and the other for those close to Perdiki or directly associated with the concert. The young Father, whose churchyard the concert had expropriated, had an honored spot within the enclosure. When they began to set up the ropes, at the front of the area there was a boy seated on a blanket with a pair of wooden crutches laid out beside him. No one wanted to ask him to move, and the young Father indicated that he should not be disturbed, so they left him in place.

The afternoon piled up until it was nearly dusk and time for the concert. Perdiki sat on a piano bench with Athena, holding her hand to steady himself as he realized that he hadn't thought about what he would perform. There was one new song that had been floating in his head on the way from the hospital to the concert. It was what had sustained him as they bounced across the island, with its words and chords filling his head. But whether he could perform it depended on how he felt at the concert. Right now, he wasn't even sure he could play.

A curtain had been erected around the stage to give Perdiki a chance to rehearse in private, and behind it was an acoustic guitar on a stand and the grand piano he would be playing. He'd picked up the guitar long enough to tune it and play a few runs. But so far, he had only sat at the piano staring at its keys and seeking support from Athena. Argos lay at his feet, lightly snoring. Perdiki was tired, his will was tired and his fingers felt too heavy to play. His chest felt heavy and he wondered if it were the start of another heart attack.

From outside, he heard someone stumble onto the stage. Argos jumped up and rushed to the curtains where the person was pushing against the curtains in various places until he finally lifted it and came underneath. The giant dog only relaxed when he sniffed who it was.

"Who the hell puts a curtain around a concert stage without an opening?" shouted Stratos. "What are they going to do, rip this thing down when it's time to go on? Curtain time, all right."

Without a breath, Stratos leaned on the piano and asked, "What are you going to play?"

It was a ritual they'd always followed when they performed together and it broke through Perdiki's miasma. His fingers began to move on the keyboard, playing the melody of his latest song for the first time and embellishing its simple tune with what he called piano tricks to fill in where normally Stratos would be playing.

Perdiki looked up at his friend, "Can you do it?" he asked.

The morose Stratos reappeared and his shoulders suddenly drooped. "I don't know." He looked down at his hands, trying to flex his remaining fingers. "Let's not find out right now. Just keep playing."

Athena quietly left the stage, easily finding the opening in the curtains. She returned to the Church, to wait with the others while the men rehearsed. A number of the press people approached her about an interview with Perdiki, but she held them off until after the concert.

Perdiki continued playing his new song on the piano. He looked up from the keys at Stratos and asked, "Even if you don't play, will you at least sing harmony with me at the concert?"

"I can do that," Stratos brightened. "That much, yes. I know all the old stuff, but what were you just playing? I know it's new and I've never heard anything like it. Are there words yet?"

"I've only just now thought of the refrain and the rest is done. Let me run it through for you. And me. It's all been in my head until now. This is the first time I've played it."

The men sang softly to avoid being overheard by anyone near the stage, though the boy with the crutches thought he could hear something. In the quiet of the late afternoon he'd been snoozing on the blanket and it was like a soft song in a dream.

The closer the time came for the concert to begin, the quieter the crowd became. Nothing they had to say was more important and everybody wanted to hear what was going on. They sat quietly in groups, having family picnics in relaxed anticipation. Even the children played only quiet games and many were napping as they waited for what they'd been told would be a great event. Not many great events happened on this side of Mythos, so they wanted to be well-rested for it.

In the lines at the food counter, people waited quietly, nearly whispering in their muted conversations with their neighbors, relatives and old friends. When a dozen uniformed police officers pushed their way toward the stage, a murmur began to break out in the crowd. But they held their silence anticipating trouble and wanting to hear whatever was said.

One of the press people who happened to be looking away from the stage and at the crowd, saw the determined approach of the uniformed men and shouted out to the technicians who were dozing in folding chairs, waiting for the concert to begin. "Get the audio on, I think we've got a situation. The police are headed this way."

Units were powered up, squeals were heard from microphones as they were adjusted and cameras began to track the progress of the police through the crowd. Someone shouted, "Perdiki, the police are coming!" Onstage, the curtains began to move as the men behind them sought to pull them apart.

With everyone turned away and watching the police, the boy with the crutches worked his way up to his feet and managed to slip onstage without being noticed. He hid behind the curtains at the rear of the stage.

By the time the police reached the platform and climbed its stairs, the sound system was humming. Perdiki and Stratos had taken up positions beside a microphone on a stand in center stage. As the police gathered below, with half a dozen cameras following them, Perdiki spoke into the microphone, gesturing at the approaching police. "Let me introduce the chorus."

The crowd roared with laughter, but the police captain leading the group, puffed up in his stripes and filigreed hat, just steamed, apparently powerless to do anything.

But as Perdiki was about to begin singing, there was a fracas in the area where the police were standing as a furious official dressed in a black suit with a white shirt and no tie, pushed his way through the crowd, demanding that the concert be stopped.

"You are under arrest, Perdiki," shouted Xenos from below the stage. "For the murders of Panteli, known as Pete Spanos, and Dimitri Pappas. You are ours." He turned to the officers standing behind him and commanded, "Put them in handcuffs." Xenos paused to stare out at the crowd. "This concert is cancelled. Perdiki is under arrest. He is ours, now."

From backstage, Mickey heard this and tried to push his way through the curtain. Finally, he made his appearance onstage, crawling under the curtain, dragging a pair of wooden crutches. With difficulty, he pulled himself to his feet, steadied himself on the crutches and hobbled up to the microphone, standing between the two musicians. One of the policemen, who had made it up to the stage, grabbed the boy's sleeve but he managed to pull away.

Leaning into the microphone, Mickey said, "The police are lying to you. My brother is Pete Spanos and he's here in the audience. Pete stand up and wave your arms."

He waited, then repeated his message, and a young man with a bandage on his head, only slightly older than Mickey, waved his arms over his head.

"Does he look dead to you?" he shouted out to the audience. "That's him. That's my brother. And the other one, Dimitri Pappas, is hidden away in Thessaloniki. Perdiki didn't murder anyone. They just want to take him away from you… from us." He turned and pointed at the police, "But he is not yours."

The crowd cheered and someone shouted, "Let the concert start."

Perdiki put an arm around Mickey and spoke into the microphone.

"Before we begin, I want to introduce you to the bravest man I know," he said. "He is my friend, Mickey. Don't let anybody ever hurt him for being honest. And please, get them to quit trying to make me stop singing. My songs couldn't be that bad."

The crowd roared as he took his seat at the piano, with Argos sitting beside him, his chin on a level with the keyboard. Resting on the piano, above the keyboard, was the black, speckled notebook he'd carried through everything. It now had spots on the cover, where water had seeped through the plastic envelope in which he'd carried it. The edges of many pages were water-stained and the binding was beginning to come loose. He looked through a few pages for the words of the songs he'd written along the way.

Stratos pulled the microphone away from center stage and set it in front of a low stool that had been placed beside the piano. As they were about to begin, Emma rushed onstage and handed Stratos his lyra.

"Think of Django," she whispered.

"Fuck you," he said.

"Later," she whispered. "For now, think of Django."

Stratos sat on the low stool, glaring at the instrument before he finally began to flex what remained of his fingers and run them along the neck of the tiny, violin-like instrument that perched on his knee like a miniature bass. He pushed his fingers along the neck where the notes would be when he bowed the strings and listened to the sound in his mind. It would be easy if he could play with his mind and not be bound to the crippled instrument of his hands. But this was what he had and it was something, something to be beside Perdiki on this night, even if he didn't manage to play.

To get the attention of the audience, Perdiki played for a minute on the piano. Then he moved the microphone so that he could look out at the audience as he began speaking.

"This concert is dedicated to the memory of Maria Pannas, who brought me food and was killed for it. We're a small island. You knew her, or your friends knew her. You might even be related," he added, looking down at Zev who was standing in front of the stage. "She was shot by a soldier on the island of Samos in front of my eyes. I will not forget her and you will not forget her and we will continue to nourish each other as she would have." He paused, breathing softly for a minute to gather his strength.

"Sometimes life seems as though it has arthritis. So much pain. But there are warm springs that can ease the aches. Let's make tonight one of those healing springs." Perdiki looked pointedly at the waiting police, now gathered beside the stage. "These springs are not political. We're talking about the aching spirit."

"For a while I stayed in a house that was really a cave and in it there was a spout that came straight out of the rock and I always had running water. But there was no turning it off, no stopping water. It makes me think of all of you. There's no stopping water here, either."

"I am going to sing for you," Perdiki said softly into the microphone, so softly that no one heard and he had to hold up a hand to ask for quiet. "I am going to sing for you because that's what I do. It has caused the deaths of friends and even people I never met and it was all just songs. You are taking your chances listening, taking your lives in hand because others have died for just knowing me, listening to me, knowing my music. So beware. This concert may be your death." Under his breath he mumbled, "It will probably be mine."

Stratos forced a tender note out of the lyra.

Perdiki continued, beginning to play one of his well-known tunes. "We live in the myth that holds us together, a fable, with ancient pillars and writing so deep we have yet to fully understand it. Our shared fear is that it will vanish, that we will no longer sit in the cafes and drink coffee with our ancestors. And so, we sing to each other."

Perdiki was an old man that night in the square on the small stage in the middle of the Aegean in what was eternally Greece, with his heart as untamed as his hands which roved on their own over the keys. His voice had been weak since the heart attack and he wasn't sure whether he could sing or would only be able to talk his songs. It felt as if he were close to being harvested, after blooming season after season for all these years.

Stratos sat on the low stool, glaring at the lyra before he finally began to push his fingers along the neck where the notes would be when he bowed the strings and listened to the sound in his mind. It would be easy if he could play with his mind and not be bound to the crippled instrument of his hands. But this was what he had and it was something, something to be beside Perdiki on this night.

As the music began and lifted the audience, Stratos forced his fingers to move through their positions and began bowing without yet touching the strings. Pain radiated up his arms, but his fingers felt somehow immune and he knew he could play. He settled in quietly behind Perdiki, at first, softly accompanying his songs and taking easy breaks as he found his ground and evolved as he played.

The music enveloped the audience, and they became part of it, swaying, humming, smiling at each other at the personal significance of some of Perdiki's well-known love songs, or just holding hands, sometimes as many as a dozen at a time.

At the very joy of it, Stratos, who had always been a shy figure onstage, leapt into dance while Perdiki pounded on the piano and roared.

At the close of the concert, Perdiki began his favorite song, the first one he'd written with Stratos. It was on Mythos the first time Perdiki was exiled to the island. They'd been playing together at a friend's house and stepped outside for a breath, still holding their instruments. The sky was filled with a meteor shower that had them throwing musical riffs as the shooting stars zoomed across the sky and what they were playing evolved into a song with a melody that sounded eternal and seemed to contain the entire night.

The audience could feel it in their own night as it descended on the concert in the platea next to the church of Agios Pendeleminos, under the eternal Greek sky and stars that were the playgrounds of her gods who were always with them.

In the midst of it, Stratos gave a nod to Perdiki and played a solo that used everything, all the pain, the debility of it all, the sadness and the loss he'd felt, the love with which Emma had cared for him, the baby that was coming and the story of brave Maria and put it all into one long riff on his ancient instrument, the only one he could still play with his broken fingers, and it felt as if the sky had cracked open and something new was revealed. It came out of the lyra with fingers that didn't know where they were and pain so intense that it disappeared into the music.

CHAPTER 53

The Old Man and Spiro

The old man had tears running down the deep lines of his face. "That concert," he said, "gave me a sense of beauty that I never knew existed. People in the audience were weeping and we were all holding onto each other. I don't think anyone left that concert unchanged. Your father knew what was happening and he stared out at us as if he'd descended from some otherworldly place to bring us the enlightenment of his music. And then, when your father threw in that last, extraordinary solo on the lyra from somewhere far up in heaven, that's when the audience all knew that in one moment music had climbed to a new level and they were present for it.

"At the end of the concert, Stratos and Perdiki threw their arms around each other and wept along with rest of us."

CHAPTER 54

Perdiki

The concert was over and it had been extraordinary, but afterward, the stars were still in their same positions in the night sky. Onstage, with the curtains drawn again, Stratos groaned in agony at the pain from his bleeding fingers and twisted-up hand. He was back sitting on the stool where he'd sat to perform. Emma had her arms around him from behind and the lyra was on the floor beside them.

Aladdin was trying to examine his fingers, but Stratos kept pulling away until Emma explained that the short, dark man was a doctor. Gently, he tried to move Stratos's twisted-up hand, but stopped when Stratos screamed.

"My friend," he said, quietly, to Stratos. "I wish I could do more. Your music has moved me beyond what I can express. But all I can do is stabilize you. You need the best hospital possible and you need it right away. As soon as it's light, I can get a helicopter for you to a hospital in Athens. For now, let's take you to our little hospital, here, and make you as comfortable as possible."

At the piano, Perdiki tried to release the tension of the concert that had built in his chest. He was perspiring from the physicality of it and his head was aching. Athena, who was sitting beside him felt the wetness of his arm and pulled back to have a good look at him.

"How do you feel?"

"Well. I guess the concert drained me. I know it was a great one, but now, I'm not feeling so well."

Athena held the back of her hand to his forehead and shouted across the stage for Aladdin. He rushed over at the sound of panic in her voice. Quickly, he held his hand on Perdiki's pulse, checked his heart with a stethoscope and put a cuff on his arm to check his blood pressure. He grabbed a syringe from his bag, filled it from a vial and shot it into Perdiki's arm. Then he pulled a small bottle of oxygen out of his bag and put a clear plastic mask on Perdiki's mouth and nose.

He turned to Athena. "He's having another heart attack. Get somebody to call an ambulance right away."

Aladdin worked over the musician for the next few minutes until an expressionless man in a black suit pushed his way past everyone on stage to get at him. His shaking hands were the only sign of his emotions, as he elbowed Athena aside and thrust a sheaf of papers in Perdiki's face. "I will deal with you later, Doctor Aladdin. I have papers to arrest Perdiki for treason. He is mine, now."

"He is not yours," said the doctor, breaking from his usual calm demeanor, his dark eyes filled with fury and sadness. "He will never be yours. The spirit of Greece has left this life. And you, you piece of excrement, who has never brought anything to the world except pain that I've had to clean up, sew up, and bury, you wave papers? You cannot have him! You cannot have Greece! We are not yours!"

And Argos, sweet Argos, who rarely made a sound beyond his snoring and occasional groan, lifted up his massive head to the stars that still shone in the Greek night, and howled.

CHAPTER 55

The Old Man and Spiro

It was growing light and the old man was done. I wondered how he'd managed to keep going for so long and had the thought that what he'd said earlier about the old men in the early morning café being past the age of needing sleep might be describing him, as well.

His voice was worn and raspy, but he still had a little more to say and wasn't going to stop until it was all out.

"At the beginning of this long night I promised I'd tell you everything," he croaked. "And I've told you most of it. Enough, anyway. In the end, though, what does it all mean? Does the world now turn counter-clockwise and flip end to end?"

"Is that it?" I asked.

"You want a remedy for life?" He grabbed onto my arm and hoisted himself up from his seat, groaning as his back unkinked. "*Lipon*. Listen, Spiro, son of Stratos. I've told you everything there is. Drag it all back to Athens and see if it's enough for that woman of yours. Maybe you'll get another book out of her." He shook my arm and laughed and laughed, until I was finally laughing with him.

"I'm going home to sleep," the old man said. "Help me off this boat. You go first and I'll turn off the lantern, then give me a hand up the ladder. I'm getting old tonight. You can walk with me to my house, but I will only talk pleasantries and complain about my back. Tomorrow, the rest of the story."

I came up on deck into the beginning of dawn The last of the stars were being squeezed out of the sky and a rosy line was just beginning to appear on the horizon, outlining the islands across the way and the entrance to the rest of the world.

The light inside the cabin was suddenly gone, but no hand reached up to grasp mine. There was a thud and a slight rocking of the boat and then that too stopped. It was quiet in the little harbor and I waited for a sound. I feared there would be none.

"Are you okay?" I called out, hesitantly, to the old man.

His voice came up from the cabin, "Unlike in Hamlet, everyone doesn't die at the end. I'm still here."

We walked up the dock and through the town until we reached the last stretch before his house. "I'll go on from here," he said. "You have a long walk back to your house."

I turned to leave as he said, "Kalinichta, Spiro."

"Kalinichta, Zev," I replied.

The old man looked back at me and chuckled and winked, then continued up the hill toward home. In Mythos. In Greece. In the world. From our end of the telescope.

EPILOGUE

Spiro

It's still dark when I light the stove. Some paper, kindling from a bag in the shed, a few small pieces of very dry wood and one match. When it is burning, I add some larger sticks, then close up the stove and fill the briki with Greek coffee, water and a spoonful of sugar. In North America we say that a watched pot never boils, but in Greece we know that an unwatched briki boils over. When the pot fills with foam and the foam rises, I grab it off the stove and let it sit on a pad on the table until the grounds settle. I divide the coffee between two small cups, with foam at the top of each.

Light is beginning to come in the window beside the stove as I add a few more sticks of wood before heading upstairs. I am in the house where my father, Stratos, was born and lived as much of his life as possible. Anastasia has turned one of the bedrooms into a temporary studio until the one we're building a few feet from the house is ready.

I left Mythos a day after that long night with Zev, but this time I caught one of the two flights a day out of the island's tiny airport. I didn't need any time for thinking. I'd done enough of that.

When I reached the apartment, she opened the door with paint spattered on her cheek and for an instant she reminded me of Thea Athena. But her kiss chased away any thoughts of anyone else. I told her everything I'd learned and she said it was enough.

"Enough for twenty Spiros!" she said, pulling me into bed on sheets colored burnt umber and sienna and drips the color of the Greek sky on a misty morning in October like the one on which we caught a ferry, paid for a cabin and travelled the long way to Mythos.

And while I write the book, in order to understand it better, we go out at night to play in tiny village cafes where they keep the flame of rembetika alive. And sometimes I get up and dance the zembeikiko like my father, Stratos, with the broken fingers who never played for me until he winked out of his own existence and came to life as part of mine.

Shortly after we arrived on Mythos, I kept a promise to Zev and visited the platea beside the church of Agios Pantelemonos where the concert was held. At first, I didn't know why Zev insisted I go there, until I noticed a statue in the far corner of the platea. It was facing out, away from the church, I suppose to avoid any irony.

It was a statue of a huge dog with its face up toward the sky standing next to three men. It was signed, "Athena." On the pedestal that held the statue was written, "We are not yours."

The End

ABOUT THE AUTHOR

Alex Morton divides his time between Vancouver and the Greek island of Ikaria. In addition to *We Are Not Yours*, he is the author of *Somewhere Else, A Little Larceny, Legal Enough, Sex drugs and Unix,* and *The Genius Card.*

www.ingramcontent.com/pod-product-compliance
Lightning Source LLC
Chambersburg PA
CBHW031159010826
48971CB00012B/908